Praise for
Kimberla Lawson Roby

"Roby's fiction . . .
[addresses] issues that are important to women today."
—*Commercial Appeal* (Tennessee)

"Roby pulls you in until you're hooked."
—*Indianapolis Recorder*

"Kimberla Lawson Roby
has reached a pinnacle most writers only dream of."
—*Rockford Register Star* (Illinois)

"Women everywhere will relate. . . .
Roby dishes up enough drama, heartbreak,
violence, and redemption to keep the pages turning."
—*Washington Post*

"Roby [deals] with real issues in her novels."
—*Sun Sentinel* (Florida)

"Kimberla Lawson Roby weaves truth into fiction."
—*Indianapolis Star*

The Best of Everything

Kimberla Lawson Roby

AVON

An Imprint of HarperCollins*Publishers*

A hardcover edition of this book was published in 2009 by William Morrow, an imprint of HarperCollins Publishers.

FIRST AVON PAPERBACK EDITION PUBLISHED 2010.

The Library of Congress has catalogued the hardcover edition as follows:

Roby, Kimberla Lawson.
   The best of everything / Kimberla Lawson Roby. — 1st ed.
     p. cm.
   ISBN 978-0-06-144306-0
   1. African American women—Fiction. 2. Children of clergy—Fiction. 3. Spouses of clergy—Fiction. 4. Compulsive shopping—Fiction. 5. Marital conflict—Fiction. I. Title.

PS3568.O3189B474 2008
813'.54—dc22   2008019194

ISBN 978-0-06-144307-7 (pbk.)

10 11 12 13 14   OV/RRD   10 9 8 7 6 5 4 3 2 1

For my family, friends, and loyal readers.
I love you with all my heart.

Acknowledgments

To God—for everything.

To my loving husband, the rest of my wonderful family members, my devoted friends, my amazing assistant, my incredible agent, my fabulous readers, and everyone at HarperCollins/ William Morrow/Avon (my remarkable publisher) for all your love and support. I would never have been able to accomplish any of this without you, and I am forever grateful.

Much love and God bless you always,
Kimberla Lawson Roby

The Best of Everything

Prologue

Six Months Earlier

Alicia closed her eyes and wondered if she was making the biggest mistake of her life. She was only twenty-two and had just graduated from college three months ago, yet here she was standing next to her father, preparing to walk down the center aisle of the church. As a matter of fact, this was the same church she'd grown up in, the one her father had once presided over, and the first of two churches he'd been thrown out of for one reason or another.

Today, however, her father's past transgressions were the very least of her worries because what she needed to focus on now was the man she was about to marry. Phillip Sullivan. The man her parents, stepparents, and everyone else seemed to adore so completely. The man her father liked so much he'd hired him as assistant pastor of his own church—which, in all honesty, was one of the main reasons Alicia wasn't so sure Phillip was right for her. She did love him, that part she was sure of, but she couldn't help thinking back to all the pain and humiliation her father had previously burdened her mother with. She loved her father and had forgiven him a long time ago, but no matter how hard she tried, she would never forget all the women he'd slept around with whenever he'd felt like it. She would never forget the horrible way he'd treated his second wife, Mariah, or the fact that he'd gone and gotten another woman pregnant, all while married to his current wife, Charlotte. It was true that Charlotte had done her dirt, too, a great deal of it for that matter, but Alicia still wasn't happy about the life her father had once led. She knew he was human and that everyone made mistakes, but it was because of all of his sinful acts that she'd promised herself she would never, not under any circumstances, take any minister's hand in marriage. She'd made a pact with herself a very long time ago, well before she'd become a teenager, and her feelings hadn't changed.

At least, not until six months ago, when she'd driven to her father's house for a weekend visit, gone to church that Sunday morning, and seen Phillip standing in the pulpit. Her father had talked about him often, ever since hiring him three months before, but it wasn't until that weekend that Alicia had actually seen Phillip in person and realized there was noticeably strong chemistry between them. She'd tried to deny her feelings for him, especially with him being ten years her senior, but she hadn't been able to do so. And how could she when her attraction for him had been so intense? How could she when Phillip had made it clear, from the very beginning, that she was going to be his wife?

He'd been adamant about the whole idea of it; right after their first meeting, he had visited her at her college campus once or twice every week, and she'd come home every single weekend to be with him. They'd fallen in love immediately, spent all of their time together, and had quickly decided they didn't want to live without each other. Then, to Alicia's total surprise, her father hadn't objected to her seeing Phillip, and neither had her mother, Tanya. Which was strange, specifically when it came to her father, because he'd always been so overly protective of her when she dated. Partly because he didn't want to accept that she was a full-grown woman and partly because he didn't believe any man was good enough for his daughter.

But that was then and this was now, because today, her father was standing proudly in an Armani tuxedo, smiling ear to ear.

"So, are you ready, baby girl? Ready to make a lifelong commitment before God and everyone else who loves you?"

"I guess so."

"You guess? Don't you know?"

Alicia sighed. "I guess I'm just a little scared is all."

"That's understandable. But as long as you love him, you'll be fine. You do love him, right?"

"I do, Daddy. I love him with all my soul."

"And he definitely loves you. No doubt about it. I knew it the first time I saw the two of you together."

Alicia smiled and her father kissed her on the cheek.

"And I love you, too. You're getting married today, but you'll always be my baby girl and I'll always be here for you. You remember that, okay?"

"I will, and I love you, too, Daddy. I'll always love you no matter what."

Tears filled her father's eyes, and just then the double doors slowly swung open.

It was time.

The harpist and flutist played their instruments softly and beautifully, and Alicia saw Phillip standing at the altar, waiting patiently. She could tell how at peace he was, and she wished she could feel the same way. She wished she could be sure that they really were going to live happily ever after.

So she stood there, unable to move her feet. She stood in place for as long as she could, but when her father nudged her arm, she finally stepped forward.

The church was absolutely gorgeous and based on everyone's facial expressions, so was her pure-white, sleeveless Reem Acra wedding gown made in silk satin at the top and tulle at the bottom. The top was covered with a finely beaded overlay, and the multifoot chapel train trailed gracefully behind her. Her mother had begged to differ, but this dress had been a steal at five thousand dollars, and Alicia was glad she'd chosen it. She was glad she had a father who thought she deserved the world—a father who had generously given her a one-hundred-thousand-dollar spending budget to cover her wedding and reception expenses. He'd talked a lot about how she was his firstborn and how he wanted her big day to be something she could cherish for the rest of her life, and she was happy to say the setting couldn't be more flawless.

But as she walked farther down the aisle, passing all the exquisitely arranged white floral designs attached to each pew, a feeling of sadness overtook her and now she knew the real reason she was so uneasy. She didn't want to feel this way, but she couldn't help who she was and what she'd been used to her entire life: the best of everything, regardless of what it cost.

What she wished was that love could simply be enough for her and that designer clothing and other luxuries didn't matter in the least. But they did matter. And she knew Phillip couldn't give her any of those things—not on his salary. Maybe in a few years he might be able to, especially once he wised up and came to the realization that heading up a megachurch was the real goal he should be working toward. But for now, he'd made it perfectly clear that he was happy right where he was—happy and dead set on learning as much as he could from his future father-in-law, well before branching out on his own.

Now, Alicia wished she'd thought this whole thing through just a bit more thoroughly, but it was too late. Too late for any turning back or changing her mind.

Too late for anything except taking their vows and saying, "I do."

Chapter 1

*P*hillip drank the last of his coffee, set down the local section of the *Chicago Sun-Times,* and gazed across the table at Alicia. She looked back at him and could already tell he was about to start nagging her all over again. Last night, they'd had another major blowup, and for the first time in the six months they'd been married, they'd gone to bed not speaking. They'd turned their backs to each other and hadn't said one word ever since then and as far as Alicia was concerned, the silence between them could continue. She was fine with it, and even more so if he was planning to complain about her spending habits.

"Look," Phillip finally said. "All I'm trying to get you to see is that there's no way we can afford for you to keep spending money the way you have been. I mean, I know you've always gotten pretty much whatever you want, but, baby, things are different now."

Alicia leaned back in her chair and tossed him a disapproving look. "Different how?"

"Different because you're no longer in college and being supported by your father. Different because you're now a grown woman and you're now married to me."

"So, what are you trying to say? That because I'm married to you, I'm supposed to lower my standards?"

"No, that's not what I'm saying at all. What I am saying, though, is that it's time you started being a lot more responsible than you have been and time you realize that we can't always have everything we want when we want it."

"I'm not trying to have *everything*. But at the same time, I'm not about to start living like some pauper just because you don't earn enough money."

Phillip shook his head. "Alicia, your father pays me seven thousand dollars a month and that's a pretty decent salary by anyone's definition."

"That may be. But if you'd do what I keep suggesting, you could be making so much more than that. When my dad was your age, he was earning three thousand dollars a week and that was nearly twenty years ago. So, imagine what you could be earning today."

"It doesn't matter, because I'm happy right where I am, working at Deliverance Outreach. I'm happy working for your father, and for the life of me, I don't understand why you have such a huge problem with that."

"I only have a problem with it because you could be doing so much better. I mean, Phillip, just think about it. You've got a degree in business and also one in theology, so you could easily apply for senior pastor positions at much larger churches. Actually, you should be doing it on a regular basis because if you did, you'd definitely get hired at one of them. Not to mention the fact that once any of those churches see who your father-in-law is and that he highly recommends you, it'll be a done deal, anyway."

"But that's just it. I don't want to be hired because of who I'm now related to. I want to be hired because I've learned a lot about ministry and because I'm truly knowledgeable enough and ready to lead a megasize congregation."

Alicia scooted her chair back and stood up. "Well, you do what you want, but don't expect me to be okay with it. Don't expect me to live with a lot less than what I've always been accustomed to."

Phillip pushed away from the granite-topped island as well. "You're wrong. You're as wrong as can be, and all I can do is pray that you eventually start to see it."

"Whatever," she said and walked over to the kitchen sink and set her glass and plate inside it. "Because it's not like I've been spending your money, anyway."

"No, that's true, but it's only a matter of time before that money your father gave you is gone, and that's why I'm trying to get you to see that you have a problem."

Alicia jerked her head toward Phillip and raised her eyebrows. "Excuse me?"

"I'm serious, Alicia. Because how much do you actually have left in your account?"

Alicia loved her husband, but right now she didn't like him very much. As a matter of fact, at this particular moment, she couldn't stand him. She knew he was referring to the twenty thousand dollars she'd had left over from her wedding budget but that was *her* money and how dare he inquire about it.

"How much?" he repeated.

"Why?"

"Because I wanna know."

"But why do you wanna know?"

"Because I'm trying to make a point."

"Phillip, I'm really getting tired of this, so why don't we just agree to disagree."

Phillip folded his arms. "You've spent every penny, haven't you?"

"No. For your information, I've still got ten thousand of it," she lied.

"Yeah, right."

"Oh, so now you're calling me a liar?"

Phillip slipped on his suit jacket. "I have to get to work."

"Fine. Do whatever you want," she said and headed up the staircase. A few minutes later, she heard him back out of the driveway, and she was glad he was gone. She hated lying to him, but he hadn't left her any choice. And it wasn't like she hadn't tried to save the money left over from her wedding budget, because for the first three months of their marriage, she hadn't spent one dime of it. She'd tried her best to live the way Phillip wanted them to live, but it hadn't been long before she'd started driving over to Chicago and frequenting upscale department stores the same as she'd been doing since she was a child. She'd been shopping at Saks, Neiman's, and Marshall Field's flagship location on State Street for as long as she could remember, well before Marshall Field's was bought out by Macy's, and she didn't see why Phillip had a problem with it. Maybe the fact that she'd spent five thousand dollars of her money every month for three months straight, and the fact that she only had five thousand left, hadn't been the best decision she could have made, but the most important fact still remained: It was her money. It was all hers, and she had the right to do whatever she felt like doing with it.

Alicia pulled the plush tan and purple comforter toward the head of the king-size bed, positioned the pillows and shams, and then sat down on the posh-textured chaise adjacent to it. Just yesterday, she'd received notification from QVC about their white gold sale this morning, and she couldn't wait to see what they were going to be offering. She'd been thinking about it the entire time she and Phillip were having breakfast and was glad he'd left when he had.

She reached to the bronze and glass designer table sitting to the side of her to pick up a notebook and pen. Then, she turned the channel to QVC and waited for the host of the white gold segment to introduce the first item. But when Alicia saw the gold and diamond bracelet, she wasn't all that impressed and decided it wasn't worth the selling price.

As she continued watching, though, she couldn't help thinking about Phillip and how unreasonable he was being and how he really could be making over six figures at another church. If he did, it wouldn't matter how much money she spent on clothes, jewelry, and whatever else. He seemed so proud of the money her father paid him, and yes, he was right, seven thousand dollars per month was a very decent living, but it wasn't enough. Actually, he wouldn't even be earning that amount if Deliverance Outreach hadn't grown to just over two thousand very loyal members, many of whom were tithe givers, and was now having to hold two services back-to-back on Sunday morning. Alicia couldn't deny that she was very grateful that her father had chosen Phillip to serve as his assistant pastor and that he was paying him more than he'd paid the previous interim pastor, but she also knew that Phillip had so much more potential. He could probably earn double what her father had earned back when he was first starting out because not only did Phillip deliver great sermons, he was a good and honest man. He was faithful to her, and he genuinely cared about people in general.

"Now, here's a stunning white gold and diamond ring that is sure to be sold out in no time," the QVC host announced, and Alicia agreed with her completely. It was beautiful and very classic. It was a neat little band with diamonds covering the entire circumference and she had to have it.

She pressed the speed-dial number she'd assigned to QVC

and the representative answered immediately. Of course, her shipping and credit card information were already in the system, and since she was calling from her home phone number, the representative had already identified who she was.

"Will we be shipping to the Lampley Cove address?"

"Yes."

"Your first item number, please?"

Alicia read the number she'd written down in her notebook and told the rep she needed a size seven.

"Next item," the woman continued.

"That will be it for now . . . no, wait." Alicia stopped when she saw a pair of hoop earrings on the TV screen. She already had a pair that looked similar, but these were a bit smaller and would look great when she wasn't dressed up and wanted to wear a T-shirt and jeans. So, she quickly spoke the item number and the woman confirmed her order.

Alicia thanked her and then heard the call waiting signal. Someone was calling from the church and while she knew it could either be Phillip or her father, she had a feeling it was Phillip and debated whether she should answer.

She waited but then muted the television and pressed the Flash button. "Hello?"

"Hey, I just wanted to call to say I'm sorry and that I hate when we argue like this."

Alicia had prepared herself for combat, but her face softened when she heard him apologize. "I hate it when we argue, too."

"I know I get upset about the way you spend money but in the end I hope you know how much I love you. I love you with all my heart and, baby, you really do mean the world to me."

"I love you, too, sweetie," she told him and suddenly felt her eyes watering. Phillip made her so angry when he ragged on her about money, but she did love him and even after only being married to him for a short period of time, she already knew she didn't want to live without him.

"Truce?" he offered.

"Truce."

"So, what were you doing before I called?"

"Working on the outline for my novel."

"Well, that's good news. You haven't worked on that in a while now."

"I know, and it's really time I started taking my writing a lot more seriously, because the sooner I finish the outline, the sooner I can get the entire manuscript written, and then start submitting it to literary agents."

"Once you finish it, you'll be published in no time."

"You really think so?"

"Of course. Your short stories and articles are excellent, so now all you have to do is write an actual book."

"Yeah, but a full-length book is a lot more time-consuming, and it takes a lot more character developing and plotting."

"But you can do it if you truly want to."

Alicia watched the QVC host displaying a diamond, oval-shape pendant hanging from a dainty chain. It was another must-have, and she hoped Phillip wasn't planning to be on the phone with her much longer. She'd already lied to him about what she was doing, and she didn't want to tell another lie just so she could end their conversation.

"Well, I guess I'd better get going, but again, baby, I'm sorry."

Alicia's prayers had been answered. "So am I. And I love you."

"I love you, too, and happy writing."

"Bye."

Alicia dropped the phone to the side of her and quickly jotted down the item number of the necklace. Then, she jotted down the information for a second pair of white gold earrings, except these were a lot dressier than the hoops she'd purchased earlier. She waited to see what the next item was going to be, however, when she saw it, she decided she wasn't interested and called to place her next order. Right after, though, she flipped to the Home Shopping Network and smiled when she saw this fabulous-looking, mustard-colored leather jacket. It must have been the sharpest thing she'd seen in months, and she could already see herself wearing it with a cute white short-sleeved top and matching pure white pants. It was only February, but just a matter of time before it would be warm outside.

After another hour of not seeing much of anything that was worth her while, Alicia turned off the television and decided it really was time for her to work on her outline. She'd put it off long enough, and the more she thought about it, if she could finish writing her first novel and was blessed enough to get it published, she'd have a chance at earning her own six-figure income. Which would be good because then Phillip wouldn't have a single reason to complain about anything. She'd have her own money, and this problem they were having would be over with.

Alicia tore out the notebook pages she'd written her item numbers on and went into her office and shredded them. She did this because the last thing she needed was for Phillip to see her notes and then instigate another argument. This was also the reason she was glad he worked all day, Tuesday through Friday, because for whatever reason, not many of the packages she received tended to come on Monday or Saturday. Those were Phillip's two off days, and it was just better if he didn't see most of the things she ordered. There was an occasional delivery every now and then on both of those particular days, but thankfully they were very rare.

The Best of Everything

When Alicia sat down in front of her computer, the phone rang and she smiled when she saw that it was her mother.

"Hey, Mom."

"Hi, sweetie. How are you?"

"I'm good, and you?"

"Fine."

"And James?" Alicia asked, referring to her stepfather.

"He's doing fine as well."

"I can't believe I haven't seen you in almost two weeks."

"I know, and that's pretty unusual for you."

"It is, but I'll see you this week for sure. I've been a little busier than normal with some of our church activities, but this month will be a lot more open," Alicia told her but felt somewhat guilty because she knew her statement was only partly true. The real reason she hadn't stopped by to see her mother and James was that the last couple of times she'd driven over to the Chicago area, she'd spent so much time shopping, it had become too late for her to head out to the suburb where they lived and still get home early enough to keep Phillip from asking questions—suspicious questions relating to her whereabouts and the kind she didn't want to have to answer.

"Honey, you know I understand, and there's no need to explain. You have a husband now that you need to spend time with, and even though we're only ninety miles away from you, that's still a pretty good ways to drive on a regular basis."

"I know, Mom, but I miss you."

"I miss you, too, but your husband comes first, and you should never forget that."

"I know."

"So, what have you been doing this morning?"

"Oh my goodness, Mom, I bought this amazing yellow jacket. It's dark like mustard."

"This early? Did one of the stores have a thirteen-hour sale or something?"

"No, I ordered it from HSN."

"The Home Shopping Network?"

"Yep."

"Alicia," her mother said, sounding disappointed.

"What, Mom?"

"I know you're grown and that we've talked about this before, but honey, you really need to cut back on some of your spending."

"Why?"

"Because you know Phillip isn't happy about it."

Alicia loved her mother with all her soul, but she didn't like any of what she was saying. It was true that they had had this conversation before, but Alicia was getting a little sick of everyone, specifically her mother and Phillip, making such a big deal about nothing. She was sick of people telling her what she should and shouldn't do, and she wasn't sure how much more of it she could take.

"Mom, everything is fine. Things are not as bad as you think. Believe me."

"Maybe it's time you considered finding a job. Even if it's only part-time."

"But if I do that, I won't have time to work on my novel."

"Of course you will. You can write before you go to work or after you get home. I'm sure other writers do that all the time."

"Maybe."

"You really should, and just a few weeks ago, your dad was telling me that he wants you to come work at the church. He said something about a public relations position, so has he talked to you about it yet?"

It still amazed Alicia that even though she was twenty-two, her parents still discussed her life like she was a child. They were divorced, but they always seemed to stay in contact so they could talk about her and what she was doing.

"Yes, he mentioned it but I told him I'd think about it."

"Well, I think you should take him up on it. You'd be good at promoting the church to the public, and it will be a good way for you to start building your résumé."

"I'll talk to him again," Alicia agreed and thought about how maybe this was a good idea after all. Partly because once she'd spent the money in her bank account, she'd still have an income and even more so because she knew her father would pay her much more than the job was probably worth.

"You can work part-time and still get a lot of writing done because Phillip makes more than enough to support both of you. Especially if you stop buying things you don't need."

Alicia rolled her eyes toward the ceiling and decided it was best she ended this stressful dialogue with her mother.

"Well, Mom, I'd better get back to my outline, but I'll talk to you later or tomorrow, though, okay?"

"Sounds good. Tell my son-in-law I said hello."

"I will."

"Love you."

"I love you, too, Mom," Alicia said and hung up the phone.

Then, she turned off her computer and called her best friend, Melanie, to see if she wanted to meet her at the mall. If so, her outline would just have to wait.

Chapter 2

Y ou are such a cheapskate," Alicia said to Melanie after locking her silver-blue ragtop BMW, the one her father had bought her for graduation. Then she hugged her best friend.

"Call me whatever you like, but if I shopped the way you did, I'd be broker than two mules. Plus, we just went to the mall two weekends ago, anyway."

"And?"

"It means there's no reason for me to go back until a long time from now."

Alicia pulled open one of two elegantly carved wooden and beveled-glass doors, and she and Melanie walked inside the restaurant. She loved The Tuxson, a gorgeous restaurant that sat on the river, but she was still a little disappointed about not being able to head to the mall the way she'd wanted to. Of course, she had tried her best to talk Melanie into it, but Melanie had quickly resisted the whole idea of it and had told her she would gladly meet her for lunch instead.

"You kill me," Alicia said, smiling.

"No, you kill me."

Next, the maître d' escorted them to a linen-covered table,

right at a window overlooking the water, and they took their seats. Alicia was glad that for the first time in a while, they hadn't gotten much snow all winter and that even today, the river wasn't frozen. It was a bit chilly outside, but still above freezing range.

"Gina will be your waitress and will be with you shortly."

Alicia smiled at him. "Thank you very much." Then she turned her attention back to Melanie, who was one of the few people she knew who still looked great even without makeup. She didn't even wear lip color most of the time, and her skin was so unblemished, she didn't even need powder. Her only fault was that she was just so doggone cheap. "I just don't understand how you can spend so much time worrying about money when you work all those hours and earn such a great salary."

"I worry because from the time I was a child, my mother and my grandmother were telling me I should always save for rainy days."

"That's all fine and well, but you and I both know that tomorrow isn't promised to any of us."

"It might not be promised to us, but based on life expectancy for most Americans, there's a good chance we're going to be around for a lot of years. And if that ends up being the case, I want to be prepared. I want to be okay and living as comfortably as I can. Not extravagantly, but living in a way that will allow me to pay for food, clothing, and shelter."

Alicia snickered. "Girl, you sound like some eighty-year-old woman who's struggling to make ends meet on a fixed income from Social Security."

"Laugh if you want to, but if you don't change your thinking, I'll be eating breakfast, lunch, and dinner seven days a week, and you'll be homeless and trying to find some soup line to stand in."

"That'll never happen."

"Well, you know what they say. Never say never."

"That might be true, but in this case that saying doesn't apply."

"One day you'll eventually get what I'm talking about."

Alicia doubted it and looked at her menu. She just didn't understand Melanie. Here she'd gotten a bachelor's degree in nursing, graduated near the top of their class, and worked in the heart center at the area's largest hospital, yet she was acting as though she had no formal education and barely made minimum wage. Worse, she worked no less than four twelve-hour days and even picked up a few additional hours through the home health-care agency she worked for on the side. To be honest, Alicia had been pleasantly surprised to learn Melanie wasn't working today, because over the last couple of months, she had been working six-day weeks and there were a couple of weeks when she'd worked seven.

The short-haired, middle-aged waitress walked over and greeted them and then took their orders. Alicia ordered a shrimp appetizer, Melanie ordered a cup of butternut squash soup, and they both ordered field green salads dressed with raspberry vinaigrette and then broiled tilapia as their entrées.

"Oh, and just so you don't have to worry about who's paying for this, I've got it covered," Alicia teased.

"No, actually, I'm paying for both of us. You paid last time, and you know I'm definitely no freeloader."

"You're right, lunch or dinner is one thing you don't mind taking care of."

"I really don't. It's only unnecessary stuff that I don't like wasting money on. Things I don't have to have or need. Plus, my goal is to save as much as I can before I settle down to get married and have children."

"Well, if you end up marrying Brad, you won't have to worry about paying bills at all. The man is only thirty-two and here he's already made partner at his law firm. He's beyond successful."

Brad was Phillip's handsome and highly intelligent best friend, and as soon as Alicia and Phillip had begun dating, they had introduced Brad and Melanie.

"Yes, he's doing very well, but when it comes to taking care of myself, I always remember three things."

"Oh, no." Alicia feigned disgust. "Not the three 'always' rules again."

But Melanie repeated them anyway. "Always be able to stand on your own two feet, meaning be able to take care of yourself with or without a man. Always save at least ten to fifteen percent of whatever you earn with no exceptions. And always pay your bills on time, preferably well before the due date and even if it means you don't have a lot of money left to blow away."

"I think you're working in the wrong career field."

"Please."

"You are. With the way you talk, you should be working for Suze Orman or somebody like that. Because you're really caught up, woman."

"You know what?" Melanie said when the waitress set down their appetizers. "Maybe you're right. Maybe there's no way you'll ever get what I'm talking about."

Probably not, was all Alicia could think and she wondered how she and Melanie could be best friends for life, love each other like sisters, yet be as different as Milan, Italy, and Barnesville, Georgia. They viewed life as a whole so dissimilarly, but thankfully it never affected the caring way they felt about each other. And actually, Alicia didn't totally disagree with Melanie's financial philosophy because she did believe in saving, when she was a lot older, and she did believe in paying bills on time as long as Phillip was the one who did it. To her, it was the man's responsibility to do whatever he had to in order to make sure his wife was happy and comfortable, the same as her father had done for his first two wives and was now doing for Charlotte.

But Alicia decided it was best to keep her current thoughts to herself because in the end, she knew their discussion on this subject could go on and on without any possible resolution and there was no way they'd come to any real agreement.

After Alicia and Melanie had finished their appetizers, the waitress brought their salads to them. "Is there anything else I can get for either of you?"

Melanie looked up at her. "No, I think we're fine."

"Then please enjoy."

Alicia took a couple of bites. "I love this dressing."

"So do I. It's probably the best in the city."

"I think it is."

"Brad would come here once every week if he had time."

"So, how is everything with you guys? Is he starting to talk more about marriage yet?"

"We talk about it, but neither of us wants to rush into anything."

"Well, he's always telling Phillip how in love he is with you, and I know you love him, so I don't see what you guys are waiting for."

"We just want it to be right and make sure we're definitely ready. Marriage is a serious commitment and when we take our vows we want it to be forever and without question."

Alicia would never admit it openly to Melanie, at least not today, but she didn't blame them for taking their time. She didn't blame them because while she did love Phillip, she didn't like all the arguing or the restrictions he was constantly trying to impose on her. She didn't like the idea that to a certain extent, he was trying to control her. He might not have been doing it intentionally, but that was what his complaints and demands were starting to feel like, and she wasn't happy about them.

Alicia sipped some of her water and then set the glass back down on the table. "Did you ever think either one of us would end up falling in love with men who were ten years older than us?"

"No, not really," Melanie said, chuckling. "Although I guess we shouldn't be all that surprised because we're both so much more mature than the average twenty-two-year-old."

"Isn't that the truth. But with a father like mine, I had no choice but to grow up, fast and in a hurry," Alicia said and they both laughed. "From the time I was seven, I saw and heard just about every adult situation there was, whether I wanted to or not. And when that happens, you sort of bypass a lot of your childhood years. I even think my father's history with women and the way he slept around all the time had a lot to do with why I ended up surfing around on the Internet and meeting that guy who ended up raping me. I was way too young to be meeting any boy I didn't even know but at the time, I was searching for love wherever I could find it because my father was always busy with the church or sneaking around with his mistress."

"I'm so sorry that that happened to you." Melanie spoke with saddened eyes.

"It was bad, Mel. It was the worst. And sometimes it seems like only yesterday when it happened, even though it was nearly nine years ago."

"I can't even imagine, and I wish I'd known you back then so I could have been there for you."

Alicia's voice trembled but then she smiled. "I know. But the good news is that you're here for me now, and I'm so glad we met when we did."

"I am, too. It was a good thing you decided to spend part of the summer here with your dad and Charlotte before we left for college."

"You're right," Alicia said, remembering how she and Melanie had connected at church and had clicked immediately. Alicia had seen Melanie from time to time whenever she visited her father on weekends, but she and Melanie hadn't truly gotten to know each other until the summer before their freshman year in college and, as it had turned out, they'd enrolled at the same university without even knowing it.

During the first semester, though, Melanie had lived in a dorm room with a roommate, and Alicia had lived in a four-bedroom apartment with three other roommates herself. But by the time their second semester had rolled around, Alicia had explained to her father that she didn't like sharing space with three other girls and that she wanted a much nicer apartment, off-campus, for her and Melanie. Melanie's parents had said an apartment like the one Alicia had chosen wasn't in their budget, however, Alicia had talked her father into paying the total amount.

Then, during the last semester of their senior year, Melanie had wanted to live closer to the hospital where she was doing her clinical work, and once she moved out, Alicia had let another friend of theirs, Sonya, move in. Alicia had been fine with the idea of living alone for those last few months, but when she'd learned that Sonya was having financial aid problems, she'd offered to let her stay with her free of charge. She'd liked Sonya a lot, but it hadn't been the same without Melanie.

Melanie took a bite of her tilapia and then patted her lips with a napkin. "You know, you're not the only one who was exposed to adult drama when you were growing up, because my parents had just as many problems. They bickered like enemies all the time and it wasn't until my father had that car accident and almost died that things changed between them. His illness really woke them up and by the time I entered high school, they'd started going to marital counseling and also to church every Sunday. Then, when your father founded Deliverance Outreach, they joined as charter members and they've been happy with each other ever since."

"That always trips me out when you talk about the way they used to be because the Mom and Dad Johnson I know are so much different from that. They're the ideal couple and the kind of people you can't help but look up to and want to be like."

"I'm proud to call them my parents but because they said whatever they wanted in front of me whenever they got into it, it was only natural for me to act a lot older than most of my friends. I can even remember one time when my mother told my father he should worry less about those porn movies he liked watching so much and spend more time trying to figure out how to satisfy his own wife. She told him that what he needed to do was take a class or something because his sexual skills were just plain pathetic. Then, she went on to say that what she needed was a man who was packing something a lot bigger than what he was carrying and someone who knew how to make her scream."

Alicia almost choked on her food and then giggled under her breath. "She said that right in front of you?"

"Well, not directly in front of me, but it wasn't like we lived in some huge mansion, so my bedroom was right next door to theirs. I heard everything they said, all the time, even when our doors were shut."

"How old were you then?"

"Seven at the most!"

"Wow."

"But like I said, they've definitely changed, and I'm really happy they did."

"I am, too, and actually my father has changed a great deal as well. I really believe him now when he says he's done committing adultery and doing all the other terrible things he used to do. At first, I was a little leery, especially after Curtina was born and his ex-mistress starting causing so many problems, but he's definitely different and trying his best to prove to Charlotte that all he wants is her. He's also doing everything he can to build up Deliverance Outreach and create as many ministries as he can to help as many people as possible. It took years for him to get to this point, but I'm very proud of him, the same as you are of your parents."

Melanie pulled out her wallet and removed one of her credit cards, and Alicia couldn't resist messing with her. "I'll bet this is the first time you've used it in months, isn't it?"

"Whatever," Melanie said, smiling, and then she slipped her card inside the leather folder on top of the check.

Soon after, the waitress processed the payment and brought back the receipts. "Thank you so much, and please enjoy the rest of your day."

"You, too," they both said. Melanie wrote in the gratuity amount, signed one of the copies, and they left for the parking lot. When they arrived at their automobiles, they hugged each other, said their good-byes, and drove in opposite directions.

Melanie went to her condo.

Alicia rushed to the mall.

Chapter 3

*P*hillip tried his best to concentrate on the sermon he was writing, but he just couldn't do it. Not with all the problems he and Alicia were already having. He loved his wife, more than life itself, but he hadn't counted on her being so stubborn about her ridiculous spending habits. He'd been trying to reason with her, but no matter what he said, she didn't seem to be happy living a normal life. To her, normal meant expensive worldly possessions, it meant top-of-the line luxury, it meant Donna Karan, Dolce & Gabana, Ralph Lauren, and dear God, just yesterday he'd even seen an outfit by St. John. He hadn't wanted to search through her closet, but his curiosity had gotten the best of him and he hadn't been able to help it. But then, a part of him was glad he had, because he'd seen loads of clothing that he'd never seen before and he knew it was all brand new. Alicia had quietly and cleverly, or so she thought, removed every one of the price tags, probably hoping he wouldn't notice one way or the other, but Phillip knew for sure that she'd just purchased most of it over the last two months. He knew because this wasn't the first time he'd sneaked into her closet. He'd felt bad about doing it all the other times, too, but now his top-secret closet explorations had become commonplace. He'd become almost obsessed with seeing what she was going to buy next; however, it was that sixteen-hundred-dollar off-white St. John's pantsuit that pushed him over the edge. Shoot, if you asked him, she was way too young to even like St. John's clothing styles, but then again, Alicia had very high standards and for all he knew, she'd purchased it mainly for status and also because of how much it cost. The tags were missing from that outfit, too, but Phillip had found it online and was quickly able to confirm the dollar amount. He hadn't wanted to believe his eyes when he'd seen the actual numbers, but now he knew his wife had a problem—he knew she was a shopping addict.

Phillip glanced over at the bronze-framed wedding photo sitting on his desk, then picked it up and drew it closer to him. The day he'd married Alicia had been the happiest day of his life, and he'd known for sure that they would remain happy with each other for the rest of their lives. And they still could if only Alicia would come to her senses and realize all the trouble she was causing them. If only she'd take a long look at all the money she was tossing away and recognize the damage it was doing to their marriage. If only she'd think about the negative effect it was already having on their plans to have children in a couple of years or so.

Phillip could still remember the first day he'd laid eyes on Alicia and how he'd known right away that he was going to marry her. He'd known this with everything in him because he'd never been more attracted to anyone so quickly. It was true that she was a beautiful young woman, but he'd been drawn to everything about her. He loved her smile, her mannerisms, the way she talked, the way she walked, the way she laughed; even now, he still felt the same way—that is, with the exception of her spending habits.

Phillip sighed deeply, returned the photo to his desk, and

leaned back in his chair. He was so frustrated and wondered what it was going to take to get through to Alicia. Maybe he could convince her to talk to a counselor. Maybe there was some sort of local support group meeting like Alcoholics Anonymous, Narcotics Anonymous, or Gamblers Anonymous she could go to. He'd referred some of their church members to a couple of those affiliations, but he wasn't sure he'd ever heard of anything that could help people who couldn't stop shopping.

Or maybe it was time he confided to Curtis what was going on with his daughter, because there had been a couple of instances while they were dating when Phillip had heard Curtis telling Alicia that she liked to shop just a bit too much and that at some point she was going to have to think more about her future. He'd even told her that once she was married, he was ending her monthly allowance because he wanted her to become a lot more responsible and a lot less dependent on him. Of course, Alicia hadn't cared about her father's comments or concern in the least, but still, just remembering what Curtis had said led Phillip to believe that Curtis was starting to think she might have a problem or was eventually going to.

When Phillip heard a knock at the door, he looked up. "Come in."

"Hey," Curtis said, entering the office and taking a seat in front of Phillip's desk.

"Hey, how's it going?"

Phillip smiled when he saw the tailor-made, navy blue suit Curtis was wearing because it sort of explained, just a little, as to why Alicia had such expensive taste in clothing. Curtis always looked tip-top, and Charlotte was the exact same way, so in at least some fairness to Alicia, Phillip understood why she did some of the things she did. She'd gotten used to what she'd gotten used to, and it was hard for her to change that.

But the thing was, she'd spent the majority of her childhood growing up with her mother and stepfather, and they certainly didn't have a lavish lifestyle. They did live in middle-class comfort, but that was pretty much where it ended with Tanya and James—they were normal people. But even so, Alicia had somehow adopted the same tastes as her father and stepmother.

"I'm well, and how's everything with you and my baby girl?"

At that very moment, Phillip wanted to tell Curtis about the difficulties he and Alicia were having and how he didn't know how to go about fixing them. But he didn't. He debated whether he should or not but instead he said, "We're good."

"I'm glad to hear it. You're a fine man of God, and while I know I've told you this before, I'm proud to have you as my son-in-law."

"I appreciate that and of course I'm proud to have you as my father-in-law and as my pastor. I often wonder how I'll ever repay you for everything you've done for me. I mean, first you blessed me with this wonderful opportunity to serve as your assistant pastor and then you offered me your blessing when I asked for Alicia's hand in marriage."

"That I did, but you don't owe me a single thing. All I want is to see you continue to grow as a minister and be a good husband to my daughter. That's all I ask and nothing more."

"And I will. I'll do my best all around."

"I know you will. I have no doubt about it. I love the people of this church, and I love my baby girl, and that's why I've entrusted you with both of them."

Phillip was glad Curtis had so much confidence in him, but now he knew he couldn't tell him about the trouble he was having with Alicia. He wanted to, but he couldn't chance the outcome. For all he knew, Curtis might somehow think his "baby girl" was right and Phillip was as wrong as wrong could be, and he didn't want Curtis holding any animosity toward him. He didn't want him reconsidering the position he'd given him or the approval he'd given him as his son-in-law. So, no, it was better to pretend that life couldn't be better between him and Alicia and to simply leave well enough alone.

Phillip repositioned his body in his chair. "So, the elder board meeting is still on for tomorrow, right?"

"It is, and it'll be good having the architects join us so they can give us an update on the designs for the new church."

"I can't wait to see them."

"I'm pretty anxious myself, and it makes me think back to exactly where I came from. When I first became a minister, it was only a short period of time before I became a pastor in Atlanta and had three hundred members. Then, I came to Chicago to lead a congregation of three thousand. Then, I led another large church and then came here to Mitchell and founded Deliverance Outreach. I'm not sure I thought we'd have over two thousand members in only six years, especially since Mitchell is a much smaller city than Chicago, but it just goes to show what God can and will do when one vows to become a better person and works hard at doing the right thing."

"You've gone through a lot, and your entire life is such an amazing testimony."

"I've gone through a lot but it's mostly because I took other people through a lot. I did some horrible things that some people would have never forgiven me for, but thankfully God is a forgiving God and He believes in second chances. Truth be told, in my case, He believed in multiple chances because He gave me a lot of them. He never gave up on me, and I'll always be thankful for that."

"Like I said, your life is an amazing testimony."

"That it is."

"Oh and hey, I got your voice message yesterday, saying that you were going to be out of town next Sunday."

"Yeah, that's one of the other things I came in to talk to you about. I'm speaking at a church conference in Houston on Saturday evening, but Charlotte and I won't be flying back until Sunday."

"So, how many people are they expecting?"

"I hear twenty thousand."

"Unbelievable."

Sometimes Phillip still had a hard time believing that his father-in-law was *the* Reverend Curtis Black. He had a hard time believing he was actually married to the daughter of a world-renowned pastor and speaker, not to mention a bestselling author, but here Curtis was, clear as day, and sitting right in front of him.

"I wish you and Alicia could travel out there with us but, unfortunately, I need you to cover both services here on Sunday."

"I wish we could go, too, but I know I have a job to do."

"And you do it very well, too, because whenever I'm gone, all I hear is how much everyone loves you and how much they enjoy your sermons. So, you know there's going to come a time when you'll either have to lead Deliverance Outreach or head up another location because at the rate we're going, we'll definitely need to branch out to another city."

Phillip wasn't sure he'd heard Curtis correctly, so he didn't say anything.

"What?" Curtis asked.

"Nothing."

"You look shocked."

"Well, actually I am."

"Why? Because I know you don't think I'm spending all this

time grooming you just so you can stand in the background. You're my assistant pastor now, but, Phillip, you're a true leader. I knew it when I first hired you, and as long as you stay on track and live according to God's Word, you'll do great things. You're a much better man than I was when I was your age, so the sky is the limit in terms of what you can do. And from where I'm sitting your future looks extremely bright."

"I'm glad you feel that way, and I just hope I don't let you down."

"You won't. Because it's like I just told you a little while ago, all I want is to see you continue to grow as a minister and be a good husband to my daughter."

Phillip couldn't have been happier when it came to knowing exactly how Curtis felt about his potential. But the idea that Curtis had repeated himself, word for word, made Phillip a little nervous. Phillip had no problem working as hard as he could so he could in fact continue growing as a minister, but he wasn't so sure he could continue being a good husband to Alicia. Well, actually, he had no problem being a good husband to her, but he wasn't so sure he could make her happy.

In the end, all he could do was try his absolute best. That was all he had to offer, but if for some reason that ended up not being enough, he knew he could lose everything.

Not just his wife, but his job, too.

Chapter 4

Alicia rolled her car to a complete stop, just outside their local mall entrance, and waited for the light to change. What she'd really wanted to do was head over to one of the larger malls that carried the higher brand-name labels, but at the same time, she didn't want to chance driving all the way to Oakbrook or downtown Chicago because in a couple of hours, traffic would be treacherous. Then, if she wasn't able to get back home until early evening, she'd have to deal with Phillip and all of his questions. And she didn't want that. They'd finally called a truce, and she wanted to keep it that way. She wanted them to have peace, love, and understanding in their household, and she wouldn't do anything to ruin it. Not today, anyway. She couldn't promise him total cease and desist when it came to the amount of money she spent, but she was going to try her best to do better than she had been. She wouldn't buy cheaply manufactured items, not under any circumstances, but what she would do was try to buy less in quantity.

When the light turned green, Alicia proceeded into the parking lot and drove around to Macy's. When she found an open stall, she pulled in it, turned off her ignition, and got out of her car. After locking it, she was striding toward the building when she heard someone calling her name.

"Alicia," the male voice yelled again, and when she turned around, she saw that it was Levi Cunningham, one of Deliverance Outreach's former but biggest financial supporters—and one of the biggest drug dealers in the region.

"Hey, how are you?" she said as he walked closer to where she was standing.

"I'm good, and I see you're looking as fine as always."

"Thank you." She wanted to tell him the same thing because he'd always been one of the finest men she'd ever laid eyes on, but as a married woman, she knew it would be inappropriate so she said nothing.

"So, I hear you're married now," he said as if he'd been reading her mind.

"I am."

"Happily married or just married?"

"Happily."

"Is that right? Well, I'm really sorry to hear that."

Alicia smiled and looked away.

"Come on now, you know I always wanted you to be my girl but your father wasn't having it. Not one bit."

"Oh, well."

"So, is this husband of yours treating you like royalty? Is he treating you the way a princess like you deserves to be treated? Because from what I hear, he's working as your father's assistant. Now, I'll admit that I don't have a clue about what the going salary is for an assistant pastor, but somehow I can't imagine it being enough to take care of you. Not Pastor Black's daughter. Not the woman who's used to the good life and all its splendor. I mean, he might be able to pay a few bills around your house and what not, but can he buy you all the things you love and need? Can he do all of that? Can he give you everything you want and then some?"

"Good-bye, Levi," Alicia said, and started walking away.

"Well, if you ever need anything, you can find me at my mom's restaurant over on Chestnut. I hang out there just about every evening for dinner."

"Good-bye, Levi," Alicia repeated, and walked inside the doorway. A few seconds later, he walked in behind her, but thankfully all he did was smile and stroll past.

Alicia stopped in the first department she came to, which was shoes, and browsed through the sandal section. She couldn't stop thinking about Levi, and she felt guilty. She couldn't deny the attraction she had for him, not years ago when she was a lot younger, and not now that she was twenty-two and married to someone else. She knew Levi was bad news, and this was the main reason her father had told him his daughter was off-limits.

It was also the reason that a couple of years ago, her father had sat him down and told him that Deliverance Outreach could no longer accept his generous donations. Levi rarely attended service, but he'd told her father that he admired him, that he loved all the things her father was doing for the community, and that he wanted to support all his efforts. Which had been fine until her father had changed for the better and decided it wasn't right for the church to benefit from drug money. Levi had never talked about what he did for a living and her father had never asked him one way or the other, but everyone *knew* what Levi did. They knew he ran a major conglomerate—an illegal conglomerate for sure, but a conglomerate nonetheless. They knew he had lots of people working for him, everyone from narcotics officers to petty street dealers, and that he never physically moved any drugs or used them. Everyone knew he was basically as clean as a whistle, essentially untouchable as far as the law was concerned, and that he was a very wealthy man.

Alicia picked up a pair of strappy sandals, checking to see what the price was, but as soon as she did, she felt someone rub their hand across her back. She jumped to the side, then realized it was her stepmother.

"Oh. Charlotte, it's you. You scared me."

"Well, I certainly didn't mean to do that. How long have you been here?"

"Not long. Not long at all."

"Neither have I. But I'm getting ready to head up to the Ralph Lauren section if you wanna come."

"That's fine. I sort of like these sandals but . . ."

"But what?"

"I already have a pair sort of just like them. The heel is a lot shorter, but they look pretty similar."

"And since when do you care about anything like that?" Charlotte teased as they headed toward the escalator.

"Since Phillip started complaining about how much money I spend."

"Uh-oh. You know I've already been there and done that with your dad, and it definitely wasn't a happy time in our marriage."

"I know."

"We argued all the time, and it even got to the point where I stopped showing him any of the things I bought."

"I stopped showing Phillip pretty much as soon as we got married."

"I know it's tough, but the good news is that I'm sure things will get better. Phillip will eventually earn a lot more money than he does now, and then he won't care about what you buy. I remember how upset your dad used to get when I shopped for myself, for you, and even for Matthew, but as soon as he got his first major book deal and started earning a lot of royalty dollars, his whole attitude about my spending changed for the better. Then he started earning thousands from every speaking engagement he scheduled, and the ministry grew larger every single year. Although, since your father earns so much from outside sources, he doesn't take as much of a salary from the church as he could, because he wants all the money from tithes and offerings to go back into the ministry."

"Well, I just hope Phillip finally wakes up and starts being a lot more ambitious. I keep telling him that what he needs to do is work toward moving into a senior pastor position at a megachurch in one of the major cities."

"Hmmm."

Alicia frowned. "What?"

"Well, don't you say anything to Phillip until he tells you himself, but I was talking to your dad a little while ago and he was saying how he'd just had a conversation with Phillip and that he let him know that he was grooming him for either the top position at Deliverance Outreach or at a future location in another city. So, as much as I know you don't want to hear it, I doubt Phillip is going to be looking for anything else anytime soon. He's always been happy working for your dad, but now that he knows the actual plans that Curtis has for him, I'm sure he's even more content."

"Well, that's just great."

"Everything will work itself out."

"I don't see how. Not when Phillip makes less than a hundred thousand dollars."

"But it won't always be that way. He'll eventually make a lot more."

"When?"

"I don't know, but he will."

Alicia picked up a sleek-looking black jean blazer and matching jean pants by Ralph Lauren but quickly placed them back on the rack.

"You like that?" Charlotte asked.

"Yeah, but I promised myself I'd cut down my spending just to keep peace between Phillip and me, and I'm really trying to stick to that."

"Is it your size?"

Alicia checked the labels and saw that both were a six. "Yep, but oh well."

"Give them to me," Charlotte told her, and took them away from her. Then, she walked over to the checkout counter.

"You really don't have to do that."

"I know, but I want to. I know exactly how you feel, and it's the least I can do for you."

Alicia hugged her stepmother, who, at only nine years her senior, was more like a friend. "Thanks for everything."

"You're quite welcome."

When they headed back down the escalator, they hugged again, exited through separate doorways, and out to their respective parking areas. Alicia was so excited about the outfit Charlotte had purchased, but just in case Phillip still had a problem with her buying something new, even though she hadn't paid for it herself, she decided it was best not to bring it into the house until later. Or tomorrow if that ended up being a better bet.

She walked toward her car but stopped in her tracks when she saw Levi driving toward her in a shiny black, freshly washed Lexus LS 460. He drove behind her car and rolled down his window. "Don't forget what I told you. If you ever need anything, you can find me at my mom's restaurant."

Alicia opened her trunk, placed her new clothing inside it, and then closed it back down.

"Hiding your own stuff from your own husband?"

How in the world did he know? Did she look that obvious?

"Shame, shame. A gorgeous-looking woman like you, hiding what she bought because her husband doesn't think she deserves to wear quality clothing."

"That's not it at all," Alicia tried to explain, but she knew her words were unconvincing.

"Then why'd you just put that Macy's garment bag in your trunk and not inside your car?"

"Does it matter one way or the other?"

"No, but I'm just calling things as I see them. I'm an analytical kind of guy, and I pay attention to even the smallest of details."

"Apparently so. But you're wrong about me."

"Is that right?"

"Yes, it is."

"Hey, whatever you say. But seriously, though, I hope you'll call me if you need me because I really am here for you. Your dad ended my relationship with the church, and I totally respect his reasoning behind it, but I still care about him, his family, and especially you. I know you're married, and I guess I'm going to have to respect that as well, but I can't help the way I feel about you. I've always been attracted to you, and I think you've always felt the same way about me."

"Levi, please. We've only seen each other maybe five or six times over the last four years. We barely even know each other."

"I know what I like, and it doesn't take a hundred meetings for me to recognize that."

Alicia felt her stomach fluttering. "I have to go."

"That's fine, but you just remember what I said, okay?"

He watched her for a few lingering seconds and then drove away.

The Best of Everything

Alicia sat inside her car and leaned her head against her headrest.

She sat there, feeling more guilty than she had earlier, and then she prayed that Levi would never approach her again.

She prayed and then drove home to her husband.

Chapter 5

Alicia slipped on a baking mitt, eased open the stainless steel oven door, and pulled out the dish of orange roughy she was preparing for dinner. She set it on top of the stove, uncovered it, took a careful look at one of Phillip's favorite dishes, and then re-covered it so that it would stay warm. It was finally done, and now all she had to do was sauté the asparagus, remove the salad she'd made, and place a few rolls inside the dish sitting on the island.

During her drive home from the mall, Alicia had done a lot of thinking and had decided it was time she worked a little harder on her marriage. She'd decided this mainly because of the tense encounter she'd just had with Levi—tense because she hadn't liked the feelings she'd had around him and tense because for a split second, and only a split second, she hadn't thought about Phillip. She hadn't thought about her husband, the man she loved, the man she'd taken vows with, the man she'd promised to cherish always. And that scared her. It scared her because the last thing she wanted was to be unfaithful . . . or be like her father used to be. She couldn't deny that she certainly was her father's daughter in a number of different ways, but she didn't want to follow anywhere close in his footsteps when it came to having affairs or hurting innocent people.

Which was why she'd rushed over to the grocery store and picked up everything she needed so she could prepare Phillip a nice dinner. They'd already called a truce earlier, but Alicia was hoping that the gesture she was making now would help validate her efforts even further.

Alicia heard the garage door shutting and then saw Phillip walking inside the house. He smiled at her in silence and strode over to where she was standing. Then, he stepped directly behind her, wrapped his arms around her waist, and kissed her on her neck. Alicia closed her eyes and felt more at ease than she had in weeks.

Phillip held her close and then squeezed her tightly. "I love you so much. I love you so much that it hurts."

Alicia turned around to face him and smoothed her hand across his cheekbone and down toward his chin. "I love you, too."

Her husband was truly a handsome man. His complexion was flawless, his teeth were pure white and perfect, and he actually reminded her of her father. She remembered watching a talk show once and hearing a relationship expert speaking about women who sometimes choose husbands who have similar physical characteristics as their fathers, and while she hadn't paid much attention to it before, right now she could see the similarities as plain as day.

Alicia and Phillip locked eyes with no words to speak and then kissed forcefully and passionately. They shared such a beautiful moment, and it reminded Alicia of the way things had once been between them while they were dating and then during their first four months of marriage.

"Maybe we should just skip dinner," Phillip finally suggested while still holding her in his arms.

"You think?"

"Well, maybe not skip it altogether but maybe put it on hold so to speak."

Alicia double-checked the stove, making sure it was off, and Phillip grabbed her hand and led her upstairs.

Phillip slipped on his plush blue terry-cloth robe and then helped Alicia into a matching one, but when she started to walk away, Phillip stopped her. "Hey. Come here, you."

Alicia slid closer to him and Phillip kissed her again.

Then he gazed into her eyes. "Baby, whether you realized it or not, I really, really needed to make love to you. I thought about you all day, and while I found myself feeling every emotion imaginable, mostly I felt a lot of sadness and pain."

"I felt the same way, but I promise you we'll do whatever we have to to keep our marriage strong. We love each other, and I'm just going to believe that love is what will always sustain us in the end."

"And it will. It has to."

After lighting two candles in long-stemmed holders, Alicia and Phillip sat down at the dining room table and held hands while Phillip said grace.

"Dear Heavenly Father, we just want to take a moment to, first, thank You for just being You. Then, we thank You for our marriage, for the wonderful life You have given us, for keeping us in great health and for the food my beautiful wife has prepared for us to eat. These and many other blessings I ask in Your son Jesus' name, Amen."

Alicia squeezed her husband's hand. "Amen."

"This smells delicious."

"It does, but I hope it tastes good."

Phillip was in the midst of eating his salad but reached his fork into the dish of roughy and sliced a small piece of it. He took a bite and nodded. "It's very good. Excellent."

"I'm glad."

"You know I love baked fish."

"Yeah, and that's why I wanted to make it for you."

"And I appreciate it."

Alicia tore her dinner roll in half and glanced over at her husband, who looked so happy and more content than he had been in days. She watched him and prayed that their marriage would be okay. She was willing to work hard at making things right on her end, but she prayed that Phillip would at least meet her halfway. She prayed that he would eventually come to understand why she couldn't simply dress in an average sort of way or simply be pleased with the idea of only shopping maybe once a month. She knew Phillip was fine with living that way, but she hoped that maybe he'd come to realize that no two people were alike and that they each had different wants and desires when it came to certain material possessions.

"So, I was chatting with your dad today, and from the way he was talking, he wants to keep me around for a very long while. He even talked about my possibly heading up Deliverance Outreach at some point or maybe a new location in a different city."

Alicia thought back to what Charlotte had told her earlier and while she wanted to be happy for Phillip, she felt somewhat indifferent because if he continued working for her father, it would be years before he made the kind of money she needed him to make. But she kept her thoughts and ideas to herself because she didn't want to ruin the wonderful evening they were having.

"Really? So, when is he talking about starting a new location?"

"Well, right now the focus is on the construction of the new building, so I'm sure his plans for me will be a little while off. But that's more than fine with me because I love my current position, anyway. I love what I do, and when you can do what you love for a living, there's nothing much better than that."

"I know you have a lot of loyalty toward my dad, but I also hope you don't lose sight of what some of your other options might be. I know you don't want to leave Deliverance and that you feel you earn a fair salary, so all I'm asking is that you keep an open mind."

"There's so much I can do right here, though, and I'm so excited about it. We meet with the architects tomorrow, but even when we saw the preliminary designs a few months ago, they looked out of this world. I'm just happy to be a part of a church like Deliverance and be a part of something a man like your father founded only a few years ago. As a matter of fact, the church is growing so quickly and we're adding so many new ministries and programs that I really wish you would reconsider taking the PR position. The church has always hired a PR firm to market and promote our ministries and events, but your dad, along with the rest of the elder board, all agree that we also need someone in-house working a lot more closely with the people inside the church."

"My mom and I talked about that this morning, but I'm worried that if I take the job, I won't ever get my novel written."

"I think you can do both."

"Maybe, but with so many new programs starting up at the church, it won't be long before that PR position switches from part-time to full-time and that means I'll be working eight hours or more every day."

"I think that's a long time off, and the important thing is

that this would be great experience for you, and while I know this is a touchy subject, it wouldn't hurt for us to have the extra income. To be honest, it would be kind of nice."

Alicia didn't like where the conversation seemed to be heading, so she continued eating and didn't respond. Maybe, though, it was as she'd been thinking earlier—if she did take the job, she would have her own money to spend any way she chose. She could buy whatever she wanted, and there would be no reason for Phillip to become angry about it. He'd have not a thing to complain about, and their problems regarding money would be over for good.

But she still didn't want to talk about any of this in detail because she didn't want to take a chance on them discussing the job, money, her spending, and then end up disagreeing and ultimately arguing. So she changed the subject entirely.

"So, what's up with Brad these days? And when is he finally going to ask Melanie to marry him? I had lunch with her this afternoon, and she was telling me something about how they want to make sure marriage is right for them. But if Brad loves her, then what is he waiting for?"

"I'm not sure, but actually I don't blame them for waiting because the last thing I'd want to see them do is rush into marriage before they're both one hundred percent ready. It would be a big mistake for them to do so and then end up regretting it."

"I guess."

"They're both very intelligent people, so when the time is right, they'll move forward. Actually, if more people did that, the divorce rate would be a lot lower than it is."

Alicia wasn't sure if what he'd just said was a hint to her or if he was just speaking generally. "Are you saying we should have waited?"

"No. I mean, of course, when you get married as quickly as we did, there will always be certain things you won't find out about each other until after the fact, but for the most part we got to know each other pretty well right away. We knew what we liked about each other right from the start."

"But what about what we disliked?" Alicia had been thinking this question but hadn't planned on saying it out loud.

"I don't think it was ever a matter of not knowing what we disliked as much as it was that we didn't think the tiny things we disliked would ever cause us to have marital problems."

Alicia could feel a sense of resentment building inside her, and for some reason, she was having a hard time controlling it. "Well, Phillip, you knew I liked nice things when you met me, and you knew what I was used to. As a matter of fact, you even bought me quite a few expensive pieces of clothing yourself while we were dating. And what about this ring? The center diamond is two carats just by itself, let alone the other diamonds inside the mounting."

"You're right. But the truth is, I always thought it was way too expensive, and the only reason I bought it was that I knew you wouldn't be happy with anything less than that. Not that you don't deserve the ring you have, because you deserve that and so much more, but, baby, we have a mortgage to pay, car payments, and utilities; we have to buy food and other necessities and still save for our future. But nonetheless, I should have talked to you before we got married and told you how I feel about saving money and how I don't believe in overspending."

"We both should have shared how we feel, because even though I knew you didn't like to do a lot of shopping and that you were always waiting for sales or comparing prices on everything you bought, I just figured that was your philosophy and I respected it. But not once did I even consider that you might expect me to live the same way. I never expected that you would want me to change who I've always been."

"Okay, let's just stop. And how on earth did we end up on this subject, anyway?"

Alicia wondered the same thing, but she knew it was because they both felt so strongly about their positions on this.

"Baby, let's not do this," he said. "I know we have to figure out a way to work this out and come to some sort of an agreement, but not tonight. Please."

Alicia's face and heart softened because she didn't want to argue anymore, either. So she stood and began removing the dishes from the table.

Phillip helped her and they went back and forth between the dining room and the kitchen until everything was placed in either the refrigerator or dishwasher.

Phillip pulled Alicia toward him and kissed her more passionately than he had earlier, and she felt good all over again. Things were great right at the moment, but she couldn't help wondering when she and Phillip would find themselves yelling at each other like enemies again. Would it be later tonight? Tomorrow morning? Tomorrow evening? She felt like they were on some crazy roller-coaster ride, but the more she rode it, the more she realized that all these hills and valleys were starting to get old. She was trying with all her might to love her husband as hard as she could. Trying to understand him. But was he really trying to understand her? Was he trying to see her point of view, or was he pretty much just dead set on changing her into the person he thought she should be?

She sincerely hoped that wasn't the case because she wouldn't be controlled by him or anyone else she could think of. She would never be controlled because it was like she'd been thinking earlier: she was her father's daughter. She was Curtis Black's daughter, and as far as she was concerned there was no other explanation needed.

Chapter 6

They'd made beautiful love last night, and Phillip was glad that he and Alicia were back on good terms again. Things had been perfect throughout most of last evening, sans the rocky discussion they'd somehow slipped back into toward the end of dinner, but other than that, Phillip couldn't have asked for a better time. Then, this morning, they'd made love once again, and he'd felt so close to her. So in tune with her soul and so miraculously in love with her that he could hardly stand it. He was even at the point where he didn't think he could ever love anyone the way he loved Alicia, and it was almost as if their disagreements made their intimate moments even more satisfying. He wouldn't say they had a love-hate relationship because that wasn't the case, but there was no question that they loved making up. They loved it, and they did it very well.

Phillip flipped his Bible from one scripture to another, jotting down various verses, so he could insert them into the sermon he'd been writing since yesterday. He hadn't preached the main sermon in three weeks, and he was looking forward to ministering to the congregation on Sunday. Whenever Curtis was in town, he normally delivered the sermon for both services, but whenever he was gone, he never thought twice about giving Phillip the opportunity. Every now and then, they'd bring in a guest minister, just because it was good to give people at least some variety, but for the most part, Curtis expected Phillip to take over whenever he was out of town.

Phillip heard a knock at the door. "Come in."

"Uh, Pastor, I'm sorry to interrupt you, but I just wanted to check to see if you needed anything before I head out to lunch."

"No, I think I'm good. Thanks, Linda."

"And don't forget about the Kings. They're coming during Mrs. King's lunch hour and should be here shortly after noon. Also, I believe she took an extra hour so they could spend two hours with you."

"That'll be fine. And when you confirmed the appointment with Mrs. King, did she give you any more details? I know she said they were having marital problems, but I was just wondering if there were any specifics."

"No, all she said was that it would be best if they spoke to you directly."

"Okay, sounds good. Enjoy your lunch."

"I will."

Linda left the office, but Phillip still wondered what kind of issues the Kings were having and hoped they weren't too serious. He also wondered why they'd asked for him and not Curtis, because Phillip hadn't done much marital counseling since he'd signed on at Deliverance. When he'd held the position of associate minister at his previous church, he'd consulted with couples on a regular basis, both for premarital counseling and marital in general, but, again, he hadn't done it a lot lately. He had to admit, though, he did appreciate the vote of confidence Mr. and Mrs. King were obviously willing to offer him.

Phillip's cell phone rang, and he saw that it was his mother. "Well, isn't this a pleasant surprise."

"Hi, son. How are you?"

"I'm fine, Mom. How are you? And how's Dad?"

"We both couldn't be better. And how's that new bride of yours?"

"She's doing fine, too."

"So, what's new?"

"Right now, I'm working on a sermon for this weekend and then I have a counseling session in about twenty minutes or so."

"You're preaching this Sunday?"

"I am. For both services."

"Well, why didn't you call to tell us? Because you know we love to hear you speak. I know you've preached a few times since we were last over for a visit, but we figured we'd give you and Alicia some time to honeymoon before we came down and intruded on you again."

"Mom, you and Dad are never an intrusion. Alicia loves you both, and you're always welcome."

"We love her, too, and I was just telling my friend what a cute little thing my daughter-in-law is. She's just a doll, Phillip. A true sweetheart."

"That she is. And hey, why don't you and Dad come down on Saturday so you can spend the night with us?"

"Are you sure it's okay with Alicia?"

"She'll be fine. She'll be excited to know you're coming."

"Okay, then that's what we'll do."

"I'm really looking forward to seeing you and Dad. I miss both of you a lot. When I was at the church in Chicago, I saw you all the time, but now that I'm out here in Mitchell, it's a lot harder for me to visit as often as I'd like to."

"We completely understand. You've got a job to do, and

there's nothing wrong with that. You couldn't be working for a more well-known minister in the country and what are the chances of someone as well known as Curtis Black living in a smaller midwestern city."

"I know. There was a time when he was in Chicago, but founding a church out here was the best thing he could have ever done. Deliverance Outreach is on its way to gaining megachurch status in terms of the size of its membership, and it will be the first in this area. Then, he's eventually wanting to start a new location somewhere else."

"Is that right?"

"Yeah, and I might be the pastor overseeing it."

"Honey, that's wonderful. Curtis really has been a wonderful blessing to you."

"He has and continues to be all the time."

"Okay, well, I won't hold you because you know I like to get all my chores and errands done pretty early on Wednesdays so we can attend Wednesday night Bible study."

"We've got Bible study tonight as well but since I'm doing the sermons on Sunday, Curtis asked one of the associate ministers to lead it."

"Okay, then, honey, I guess I'll talk to you later."

"Tell Dad hello. And by the way, where is he?"

"He went to lunch with some of his retiree buddies."

"Good for him. I'm glad he still connects with them."

"I'm glad, too, because with both of us retiring right at fifty-five this year, I was worried that your father was going to become a little bored. I have tons of stuff that keeps me busy, but your father doesn't like to participate in much outside of the house."

"Well, he's way too young not to be involved in anything, so I'll see if I can think of some things he might be interested in doing."

"That would be good, son."

"Okay, Mom, well, I'll let you go."

"I'll talk to you later, and I love you."

"I love you, too."

Phillip pressed the End button on his phone and then dialed Alicia.

She answered on the second ring. "Hey, what's up?"

"You. The love of my life."

"Is that right?"

"It is. But the reason I'm calling is to let you know that I just spoke to Mom and she and Dad are coming down for church on Sunday. But I invited them to come on Saturday, though, so they could spend the night, so I hope that's okay with you. Mom wanted me to ask you first, but I told her you'd be excited."

"Of course I'm excited. We never get any company, and you know I love your parents. I can't wait."

"Neither can I."

"I just hate that my dad and Charlotte will be out of town, because it would have been great if we could have all had dinner together. I would even invite my mom and James, but they're taking a short vacation up in Wisconsin and they're leaving on Friday."

"It would have been nice having them here."

"But that's okay. Having your parents by themselves will still be a great time."

Phillip heard a knock at his door and saw the Kings waiting there. "Sweetheart, I have to go, but I'll call you later, okay?"

"Talk to you then. I love you."

"I love you, too."

Phillip switched his ringer off, set his phone inside his desk, and then stood up. "I apologize for being on the phone. Come right in and have a seat."

Mr. King reached his hand out and shook Phillip's and so did Mrs. King.

Mrs. King eased her purse onto the floor and wasted no time getting to the point. "Thank you so much for seeing us, Pastor, and I think it would best for me to let you know up front that I'm only days from contacting my attorney and filing for a divorce."

Phillip looked at her and then at Mr. King, but since Mr. King seemed beyond embarrassed, he returned his attention to Mrs. King. "If you don't mind, may I ask why?"

"Because my husband is a low-down, adultery-committing, lying, no-good fool."

Phillip was stunned by her statement, and now Mr. King seemed even more humiliated.

"This son of a gun, Lord forgive me"—she paused, as if she'd spoken words of profanity—"this son of a gun had the nerve to come to me late last week, talking about how he's got some baby on the way and that it'll be here any day now. Can you believe that, Pastor?" She looked her husband up and down, but kept her conversation steered toward Phillip. "I mean, can you believe his old and corroded seventy-year-old behind had the audacity to have sex with another woman behind my back? Can you believe that?"

Phillip was speechless. Partly because of what she was telling him and partly because of the way she was expressing herself.

"I tell you, I'm just sick over this, and over the last few days, this whoremonger right here has made me want to lay my religion all the way down. I just want to lay it down long enough to beat him silly. I want to pay him back so badly, Pastor. I know the Bible speaks against this, but he deserves whatever he gets."

Phillip opened his mouth to speak, but Mrs. King kept on talking.

"And the thing is, Pastor, if you think this is bad, just wait until I tell you the best part."

Phillip couldn't imagine Mr. King doing anything worse than what he'd already done, and he regretted having to hear whatever it was.

"The woman he got pregnant is my thirty-year-old niece. A low-life piece of trash who's young enough to be his grand-daughter."

Phillip watched Mr. King's demeanor, and there was no doubt he wanted to vanish. But the thing was, he couldn't. There was no escaping this awful situation, and he had no choice but to deal with it. He had to deal with his wife, the family member he'd taken on as a mistress, and soon a brand-new baby.

"I tell you, Pastor, I'm just plain numb. This situation right here has cut me straight to the core, and I just don't see how I'm ever going to get beyond it. I'm so angry, and all I seem to be able to think about is violence and how nice it would be to inflict the same kind of pain on this joker right here and also on my niece."

"Well, Mrs. King, I won't sit here and tell you that I know how you feel, but what I will say is that it's prayer time. I'm going to be praying for you, and you have to pray as well. I know that what you're going through is very difficult, but you've got to take this to God. You've got to pray for peace and understanding."

"Well, you know I don't mean any disrespect, Pastor, but for the first time in my life, I'm not sure God can help me. I'm not sure anyone can help me."

"Believe me, God can and will help you. It may not seem like it right now, but He will. And, Mrs. King, if you don't mind, I'd like to ask Mr. King a couple of questions."

"Go ahead."

"Well, first of all, Mr. King, how do you feel about all of this?"

"Pastor, I made a terrible mistake, I'm sorry, and I'll do anything I have to in order to save my marriage. I'm just a naive old fool who made a horrible mistake, but I still love my wife."

"Mrs. King? Do you believe him when he says he's sorry?"

"Actually, I do. But it's too late for sorry."

"Well, before we go any further, there is one thing I'd like to mention. Because Pastor Black and his wife experienced a similar scenario and he openly talks about it in sermons and during interviews, I'm wondering if maybe he might be the better person for you to counsel with."

"No!" Mrs. King spoke quickly and loudly. "I disagree. And it's because Pastor Black and his wife went through the same thing that I don't believe he'll be able to remain neutral. It's my feeling that Pastor Black will automatically expect me to do what his wife did, which is to forgive my husband and accept his out-of-wedlock child."

"Okay, fair enough. But what I do want to clarify is that as a minister called by God to preach, my responsibility must first rest with trying to keep the two of you together as husband and wife."

"I understand that, but I should let you know that I've pretty much made up my mind about filing for a divorce. The only reason I asked for us to meet with you is because as a Christian woman, I decided it was only right to at least try to see if something could be worked out. But the more I sit here looking at this joker, I don't see where there can ever be a solution."

"Well, you definitely made the right decision about getting counseling, and I'm going to do everything I can to help you."

Mr. King forced a smile. "We really appreciate your time."

"You speak for yourself! I do appreciate Pastor, but from now on, don't you even think about using the word *we* when it comes to you and me. Because there is no *we* as far as I'm concerned."

Phillip asked them both a few more general questions and then asked if could meet with them again two days from now, on Friday.

Mrs. King picked up her handbag. "That's fine, Pastor."

Mr. King agreed. "Yes, that'll be fine. And thank you again."

"You're quite welcome, and that's what I'm here for. On Friday, I'd like us to go more into what your marriage has been like since the beginning. Mr. King, I want you to think about your marriage and just how you've felt about it the entire forty years you've been with Mrs. King, and I also want you to think about why you decided to have an affair. Then, Mrs. King, I want you to think about the same exact things but from your point of view."

"I'm not sure what good it's going to do, but I'll do what you're asking. I'm not sure because I'm not the one who went out sneakin' and sleepin' around."

"You're absolutely right, but please just think about it so we can discuss it on Friday."

Phillip gave both of them all three of his phone numbers— church, cell, and home—and told them to please call him anytime, day or night.

Mr. King grabbed his hat. "Thank you again, Pastor, and we'll see you again on Friday."

"See you then."

Phillip escorted them to the doorway and said good-bye to them, but as he watched them leave, he wondered what it must be like for them when they were alone. The whole scenario was a dreadfully painful one, and it made him appreciate his own marriage. It made him realize that compared with the Kings, he and Alicia actually had a wonderful union and one they should be thankful for.

Chapter 7

Woodfield Mall was only about an hour's drive from Mitchell, and since it was the middle of the week, there wasn't a lot of traffic or as many people shopping as there would be on the weekend. This morning, right after Phillip had left for work, Alicia had debated back and forth whether she should make the trip but had eventually decided against it. She'd told herself that if she wanted a happy marriage, she had an obligation to at least try to resist all the temptation she was constantly feeling—particularly her yearning for a new pair of princess-cut diamond earrings she'd seen a week ago.

But then, Phillip had called her on the phone, announcing that his parents were coming to town, and there was no way she could let them see the same old, drab-looking comforter set they'd had to sleep on when they'd stayed with them the last time. Actually, the only reason she'd purchased the one they had was that Phillip had gone with her when she'd bought it and had insisted it was perfect. But Alicia knew he'd chosen it more because it was on sale and less because he loved it.

However, today, she was going to replace not only that cut-rate comforter set but also the bathroom accessories with plush bath towels, a soap dish, toothbrush holder, as well as tissue and garbage containers. She would buy everything top of the line, and she couldn't wait to dump every bit of the old stuff into the trash bin.

Alicia entered through Nordstrom's north entrance and proceeded through the store and down to the home department. She looked at one set after another, searching for the best one she could find, and then spotted an elegant dark lavender comforter. It was beautiful and, more important, very expensive-looking and she could already picture it in the guest bedroom with four pillows, three shams, the bedskirt, and each of the three decorative pillows that were on the display model.

So, she went down the aisle, found a queen-size comforter along with everything else that went with it, and she and the sales lady helping her carried all of it to the counter in three trips. But then she realized how there was no way she could bypass purchasing a matching sheet set, so she added that to her pile also.

The fiftysomething woman signed in to her cash register. "This really is one of our most popular bedding sets, and I just love it."

"I do, too, and I think my in-laws will like it as well."

"I'm sure they will."

As the woman scanned each item, Alicia glanced around the surrounding area, but unfortunately nothing else caught her eye, so she waited for the clerk to finish.

When she did, she told Alicia the total. "That'll be one thousand, one hundred forty-seven dollars and fifty-nine cents."

Alicia swiped her Nordstrom credit card through the portable machine. "Actually, that was a little bit less than I thought it was going to be."

"Yes, most of the items were twenty percent off, so that's always nice."

When her information processed, Alicia signed the plastic screen and tapped the Enter button.

"Would you like me to call someone to help you with your bags? Or better yet, I can have someone take everything out to our loading dock area and you can drive around and pick it up there.

"That would be great. Thank you."

"No, thank you for your business and have a wonderful rest of the day."

"You, too."

After Alicia pulled in front of the shipping and receiving doorway and one of the employees had piled everything into her trunk, she drove back out to the general parking lot and parked. She hadn't been thinking about the diamond earrings she'd wanted to get, but now she wondered if there was time for her to check them out. She'd seen them at one of the first-floor jewelry stores the last time she'd come to the mall, and they'd been on sale for forty-nine, ninety-nine—which was a steal since they had a two-carat total weight with excellent clarity and were regularly priced at seventy-five hundred dollars.

She knew, though, it probably wasn't the best idea for her to buy them because if she did, she'd have to use the remaining five thousand dollars in her checking account. Not to mention, Phillip would certainly go through the roof once he found out about them, and as it was, he was going to be livid about the thousand-plus dollars she'd spent on the comforter set—which was the reason she was going to store everything in the guest-bedroom closet and then wait until Friday to set all of it up. This way, there would be a chance he wouldn't pay much attention to it until his parents arrived. It would also mean she wouldn't have to hear any of his complaining because he would never do that in front of them.

But as far as the earrings, maybe she would just take another look at them and then wait awhile before actually making a purchase. Yes, that's what she would do and then she'd be on her way home in less than an hour.

Alicia pulled her car into the first open spot she could find and then went back inside the mall. This time, though, she went through one of the main entrances and not through one of the anchor stores, which was a lot safer because rarely could she walk through Nordstrom, Macy's, or Lord & Taylor without finding something to buy, even if it was only a bottle of cologne.

She walked past one specialty store after another and had a mind to stop at Victoria's Secret, but remembered how she'd only come in there for one reason. She passed a few more places she sometimes patronized and then walked inside the jewelry store.

She smiled when she saw the same distinctive-looking salesman who had shown her the earrings the first time she'd looked at them.

"You're back."

"Yeah, but basically I just want to see them again."

"Of course."

The salesman pulled them from the glass case and passed them over to her.

Alicia sighed. "I just love these."

"Then you should get them."

"They have so much fire, and I really want them, but I'm thinking I should wait."

"I can understand that, but just the fact that you came back only one week later means you haven't been able to stop thinking about them."

He was right because in actuality, when she'd purchased

those few pieces of jewelry from QVC yesterday, she'd been hoping they would suffice and that she'd no longer feel the need to own the earrings she was holding right now. But she knew they'd never left the back of her mind.

"You only live once."

He was right about that, too, because with all the terrible things going on in the world, it was like she'd tried to explain to Melanie, tomorrow wasn't promised to any of us.

"I'll take them."

"Good for you."

Alicia pulled out her debit card and waited for the salesman to process the transaction. When everything was complete, he boxed them up, slipped them into a bag, and gave them to her.

"A beautiful pair of earrings for a very beautiful lady."

"Thank you. And take care."

"You, too, and come again."

Alicia felt like she was on a high, and she couldn't wait to sport her new diamonds. She wouldn't do it right away and would have to be careful when it came to choosing the best time to wear them in front of Phillip, but once she did, she would enjoy them on a regular basis, that was for sure. It was true that she already had a pair of diamond earrings, but they were round, smaller, and not as noticeable, so she hadn't worn them in a couple of years.

After Alicia had exited onto I-90 West, her cell phone rang. It was Phillip and she was hoping he hadn't left the church yet and was already at home. It was almost dusk, but she'd been counting on his staying late for Bible study.

She answered in a cheerful and unsuspicious tone. "Hey."

"Hey, yourself."

"Are you still at the church?"

"No, I'm on my way home. I decided to leave early."

That's exactly what she'd been afraid of, and now she'd have to keep everything she'd purchased in the trunk overnight and wait for him to head off to work in the morning.

"Well, I'm out running some errands and then I'm planning to stop by the bookstore to browse the writing and publishing section, so if it's okay with you, I probably won't be home for a couple of hours or so."

She hated lying to him again, but he never left her much choice and she just couldn't bear another evening of arguments.

"That's fine. Do what you need to do and take your time. But did you want me to pick up some carryout?"

"That'll be good, or I can grab Chinese once I leave the bookstore."

"That'll work."

"Did you need me to get anything else?"

"No, but I'll be waiting patiently for you to get here, if you know what I mean."

"You're bad."

"I know."

They both laughed, and Alicia loved the mood her husband was in. She loved when he was happy. When they were happy. And that's why she had to hide everything as planned.

"I guess I'll see you soon."

"See you later."

As Alicia drove farther down the highway, traffic eventually began to slow down a bit. She'd been expecting it, though, and that was the reason she'd told Phillip she wouldn't be home for another two hours. That way she'd have time to get through traffic, arrive back in Mitchell, and still drop by the bookstore to pick up any book she could find—just to prove that she'd actually gone there.

The Best of Everything

She didn't like living this way, but she had to do what worked and what was best for the sustenance of their relationship. And what was wrong with telling a little white lie every now and then as long as it was for the betterment of her marriage? She was sure some people would beg to differ, but the way she saw it, stretching the truth was a lot smarter than doing nothing and then heading to divorce court.

When Alicia arrived back in Mitchell, she went to the bookstore as planned, purchased three books on writing, two novels, and one memoir. She hadn't planned on buying as much as she had, but she'd ended up seeing a lot more interesting titles than she'd expected.

Next, she drove about twenty minutes to their favorite Chinese restaurant, went inside, placed the order, and then waited for them to get it ready. Like most times when they ordered takeout from this lovely establishment, it didn't take more than fifteen minutes.

Now, Alicia walked through the parking lot, which wasn't lighted nearly the way it should have been, and approached her vehicle. As she unlocked the door . . .

"Open up your trunk and give me that jewelry you purchased."

Alicia thought for sure her heart and lungs were going to collapse. She was scared to death, and it felt like the man who spoke was pointing a gun into her back.

"Do it!"

"Oh my God. What are you talking about?"

"Look, do you think I followed you more than fifty miles, just to play games with you? Now, please don't make me hurt you."

"Oh dear God, please. Please don't do this."

The gunman snatched her by her shirt and dragged her

toward the back of the car. "Now, for the last time, I said open it!"

Alicia fumbled her keys, trying to find the correct button on her keyless-entry gadget, and then pressed it.

The trunk door flew open and the gunman pulled out the jewelry bag and fled to a car that was waiting a few feet away. When he jumped in on the passenger side, they sped off like nothing had ever happened. Alicia could barely move, but she looked around and didn't see a soul. Not one person had witnessed what had happened and while she was a nervous wreck and terrified for her life, she knew she could never report this. She couldn't call the police and she would never tell her husband because if she did, she'd have to disclose exactly what the gunman had taken from her. She'd have to confess to Phillip that he'd taken her newly purchased, five-thousand-dollar, princess-cut diamond earrings, and there was no way she could do that.

She stood there a few more seconds and finally burst into tears. Then, she slammed down the trunk and sat inside the car. This was insane. She'd been robbed right in the heart of Mitchell and in the parking lot of a quaint little Chinese restaurant and there was nothing she could do about it. Then, the idea that someone had cased the jewelry store, watched her make her purchase, followed her out to her car, saw her place the bag in her trunk, and trailed her back to Mitchell and even to the bookstore sent chills through her body.

She was beyond upset, but she started her engine and slowly drove away.

She drove but she couldn't help thinking . . . why couldn't the gunman have taken her purse, with the little bit of cash she had inside of it, and just been satisfied? Why couldn't he have taken something that she hadn't even spent a thousand dollars on?

Chapter 8

No matter how many times she replayed the entire scenario, Alicia still couldn't fathom what had just happened to her less than an hour ago. She'd actually been robbed. What were the chances that today would be the day she'd choose to stop at a restaurant that normally had very few customers during the weeknights? On top of that, it had just gotten completely dark only minutes before she'd gone inside of it. Although, that would explain why the gunman hadn't confronted her at the much busier bookstore while it was still light outside and had decided to wait until later.

On her way inside her house, she was glad she'd thought to stop at the pharmacy to get a bottle of eye-makeup remover and cotton balls so she could fix her face before seeing Phillip. She'd bawled all the way to the store, and the last thing she needed was Phillip asking her what she'd been crying about. She was also glad she never left the house without her eyeliner, mascara, pressed face powder, and lip color and liner. During college, she'd gotten in the habit of always carrying them in her purse and today that habit had paid off.

Alicia set the bags of food on top of the counter, dropped her goldish-tan Coach handbag, the one that had cost her nearly eight hundred dollars, across the back of one of the island chairs and gathered her composure. Then she called out to Phillip. "Honey?"

But he didn't answer.

"Sweetheart, I'm home."

Phillip finally walked into the kitchen, holding a document in his hand. "Alicia, what in the world is this?"

"What are you talking about?"

"This. This Visa statement and all these charges you made last month."

"Oh, not tonight. Pleeease, not tonight."

"Why do you insist on trying to ruin everything for us?"

"I'm not doing this with you right now. I'm not, Phillip."

"Just tell me why. Why do you keep buying all this unnecessary stuff?"

"I needed everything I bought, but don't you worry. I'll take care of it first thing tomorrow."

"How?"

"I'll pay it by phone through my checking account. It's only eight hundred dollars."

"*Only?*"

Alicia turned away from him, but then it dawned on her that she'd already spent the last five thousand dollars she had to her name on those stupid earrings.

"How many other credit cards have you been making charges on? That's what I wanna know."

"I told you I'm not doing this with you. I don't wanna argue with you, Phillip," she said matter-of-factly and then grabbed her purse and headed upstairs.

But Phillip followed behind her and tossed another statement onto their dresser. "And what about this?"

Alicia saw that it was from Victoria's Secret and was furious.

"Why are you opening my mail? That's my account and my account alone."

"It's not like I wanted to but after I saw the Visa bill, I couldn't help myself. And I'm glad I did because you charged over five hundred dollars just in the last month and the balance is over fifteen hundred."

"You had no right opening anything of mine. My business is my business, and it has nothing to do with you."

"No, it has everything to do with me. We're married, remember? When you mess up, it affects me and vice versa."

"That's beside the point, and I'm telling you now, you'd better stop trying to control me."

"I'm not trying to control you. I'm just trying to get you to see what you're doing."

"You *are* trying to control me, and I think it's time you stop and realize that I'm your wife and not your child."

"I know you're my wife, and that's why I'm so concerned about this. Alicia, we can't afford your excessive spending habits and it's going to have to stop. Period."

Alicia raised her eyebrows at him and then dropped down on the bed and turned on the television.

"Oh, so now you're just going to ignore me?"

Alicia flipped through the channels.

"Why can't you see how damaging all of this is eventually going to be for us? I'm doing everything I know how when it comes to being a good husband to you, but you act as if you don't care about me or our marriage. You act as though you couldn't care less."

Alicia never even looked at him.

Finally, he walked out of the bedroom and back downstairs to his study, she guessed. To be honest, she didn't care where he was and was just glad he was no longer harassing her. He was really starting to get on her nerves, and he'd certainly gone way too far when he'd opened her mail. Mail that wasn't even addressed to him. And how dare he confront her like he was her boss or like he owned her.

Alicia reached for her purse and pulled out her wallet. Then, she removed the MasterCard that she'd just received in the mail a couple of weeks ago, the one that she'd signed Phillip's and her name to right after the preapproved letter had come last month. She hadn't planned on using it unless there was some dire emergency, but now Phillip hadn't left her any choice. Now, she'd have to take it to the bank tomorrow and get a cash advance so she could pay off the Visa he was whining about. She'd also have to visit the post office first thing tomorrow morning so she could rent a P.O. box and then notify her bank and each of her credit card companies that she had a new mailing address.

She slipped the MasterCard that had a five-thousand-dollar line back into her wallet and then went back downstairs. She picked up the Visa statement and then tossed the actual card onto the island.

"I'll be paying off your precious little Visa by noon tomorrow and just so you know, I won't be using it again. Oh, and I've decided to take my father up on his offer to come work for the church so from here on out, I won't be asking you for another dime."

"Baby, you're taking this too far and all I'm asking is that you stick to buying only things that you really need and things that are priced within reason."

"No. You keep your money and your Visa. You can have your American Express card back, too, because I don't want anything that has your name on it."

"But I'm not asking you to stop using our credit cards completely. Those cards belong to both of us, so keep the American Express card in your wallet and take back the Visa, too."

Alicia gave him a dirty look and then went back upstairs again.

But this time, she went into her office and shut the door. She was steaming, and she couldn't stand the way she was feeling. So she turned on her computer and then called her dad.

"Hey, baby girl. How are you? I haven't talked to you in a couple of days, have I?"

"No, and I'm fine, but I've decided that I do want to come work at the church."

"Good. You know that makes me happy, and I'll run it by the elder board for final confirmation. They already know that I've been trying to convince you to take the position, but I just need to have them approve your salary. There won't be any benefits offered, so I'm sure they'll approve at least two thousand dollars per month."

Alicia quickly did the math in her head and realized that this wasn't bad at all because what it meant was that she'd be averaging about five hundred dollars a week and only working about twenty hours. The more she thought about it, it was great, considering this was her first real job since graduating.

"I really appreciate this, Daddy. I was worried about taking it because I still want to have time to write, but now I know I can do both."

"Of course, you can. Easily. Now, the elder board won't meet again until next week, but you should be able to start right away. Probably next Wednesday if you want."

"That'll be fine."

"We'll have you spend time with the PR firm that does contract work for us now, and then you, Charlotte, Phillip, and I and a couple of the elder board members can all sit down to see exactly what direction we want to take our PR and marketing efforts in."

"Sounds good to me."

"So, you're doing okay?"

God, how she wanted to lie in her father's arms, cry her eyes out, and tell him what had happened to her earlier this evening. She wanted to tell him because she needed him to console her the way he'd done since the day she was born. But she couldn't.

"I'm fine."

"I'm glad. I was talking to Phillip yesterday and no matter how many weeks and months pass, the one thing I can tell you is that you've been blessed with a great husband. He's a good man, baby girl, and a good, decent man is what every father hopes his daughter will end up with. And with Phillip, I definitely got my wish."

"He is a good man" was all Alicia could muster, because in all honesty she couldn't stand her "good husband" at the moment. She didn't even want to look at him.

"Have you spoken to your mom this week?"

"I talked to her yesterday morning, but I'm hoping to go visit her next week sometime. They're headed out of town for the weekend, and then Phillip's parents are coming here to stay with us on Saturday and Sunday."

"Phillip mentioned that to me when we were leaving the church this evening, and I'm glad both of you will get to spend some time with them."

"I am, too. Well, Daddy, I'd better get going. But I'll talk to you tomorrow. Oh, and tell Charlotte I said hello."

"I will. Love you, baby girl."

"I love you, too, Daddy."

Alicia hung up and burst into tears again. She sat there for a few minutes trying to calm herself, but she couldn't stop thinking about the gun that had been pointed into her back. She'd tried to block her memory of it, but now she could practically feel the gun touching her body. She cried because it hadn't really dawned on her until now that the gunman could have killed her in cold blood. He could have taken her life and all because he wanted to steal her jewelry. And it was only the jewelry that he must have wanted because he hadn't asked for anything else. Not her cash, credit cards, or even the comforter set, towels, and other accessories that were also packed inside the trunk.

Alicia wiped her face with both hands and then wiped her hands on the sides of her jeans. She knew she'd gotten makeup on them, but that was the least of her worries because right now, all she wanted to do was feel better. She needed a pick-me-up, so she went onto AOL and pulled up the Neiman Marcus website. She browsed from one category to the next but stopped when she saw those elegant-looking Manolo Blahnik four-inch classic black pumps that she'd been trying her best not to purchase for some time. But now, since she had a job, she'd have more than enough to pay her Neiman's bill when it arrived next month. Not to mention, she needed these pumps to go with some of her business suits, because she wanted to look classic and professional whenever she had business meetings to attend. Then, after adding the shoes to her shopping cart, she clicked on the accessories link and saw the Cole Haan black leather satchel she'd been eyeing for a while. It was only three hundred seventy-five dollars, so she added that to her basket as well.

She was glad she'd treated herself to some of the things she'd been wanting because she felt 100 percent better than she had a half hour ago. Shopping was good for the soul, and she deserved to have nice things. Everyone did, whether they realized it or not.

After processing her Neiman's order and receiving confirmation, she pulled up the Saks website to see what suits were on sale. She'd had her Saks and Neiman's cards forever, and it wasn't like she had huge balances on either one of them because while she'd been in college and up until the last three months, her father and Charlotte had paid them off like clockwork. They'd paid them every single billing cycle, and once they'd stopped, Alicia had been able to pay them herself with the cash she'd had left over from her wedding budget. As of today, though, that money was gone, but she'd still be fine because she'd soon be working at the church, and maybe in a few months, she would finish and sell her novel.

She would do whatever she had to do in order to be happy, and Phillip had no choice but to accept that. She loved him and wanted to stay married to him, but she wouldn't change who she was as a person. She wouldn't limit herself in any way, not for him or anyone else.

She would do what she wanted to do, and there was no room for discussion.

Chapter 9

She actually went out and bought a brand-new, ridiculously priced comforter set, simply because my parents were coming for an overnight visit, Phillip thought, and that was all he'd been able to focus on for two days straight. And though he was standing in the pulpit preparing to give his sermon, he couldn't stop replaying that same thought, over and over again.

The whole idea of it was senseless and the reason he knew exactly how much Alicia had spent was that he'd eventually gotten her to tell him where she'd purchased everything from. Then, he'd called up Nordstrom's 800 number and checked all recent charges. He'd even listened to the amounts more than one time before finally hanging up and was just sick over it. Because it wasn't as if she'd be able to pay off the entire balance when the statement came. He would have to do it, and he was getting tired of all the debt she kept accumulating.

They'd been arguing on and off ever since he'd confronted her about those Visa and Victoria's Secret statements, but the Nordstrom purchases had made things worse. They'd been at it all evening on Friday, which was the day he'd come home and seen everything, and the only reason they hadn't argued the rest of yesterday or any today was that his parents were in town.

Phillip was beyond angry with his wife, and what bothered him the most was that she didn't seem to care about his feelings in the least. All she cared about were her own, and it was as if she didn't see one problem with that. Then, the other thing he didn't like was the way he was now standing before the congregation, trying to keep a smile on his face and trying to pretend that life just couldn't be better for him. He didn't like doing this, and he wasn't sure how long he'd be able to continue, which was why he hoped and prayed that he and Alicia would find some sort of common ground and end these issues they were having.

"You know, church, not every day is a good day."

"No, it's not, Pastor," one lady responded.

"Some days are wonderful, but there are some days when you wish you could crawl back into bed, pull the covers over your head, and never get back up again."

"He's definitely telling the truth," an older gentleman told another man sitting next to him.

"But then, we all know that life wasn't meant to be perfect. Life wouldn't be normal if we didn't experience a few problems from time to time. It wouldn't be real if we didn't hit a few bumps in the road every now and then."

The majority of the members nodded in agreement.

"It wouldn't be real and the truth of the matter is, if we didn't have problems, some of us would never, not once, get down on our knees and pray."

"Boy, you know you're speakin' today," another elderly gentleman offered.

"He's so right about that," Lena added. She was Curtis's assistant.

Phillip locked eyes with Alicia. "Some of us think we deserve to have everything we want, when we want it, and never even bother to give thanks or consider how selfish we're being. Some of us care only about ourselves and we don't care at all about who we step on in the process."

Phillip could tell how annoyed Alicia was, just by the look on her face, but he didn't care because he knew he was telling the truth. He was telling the kind of truth she very much needed to hear.

"Then, there's the institution of marriage. Now, this particular subject has very little to do with the topic of the sermon I'll be delivering today, but I really feel like I need to share a few marital observations for all the married people who are here today."

He looked across the congregation and smiled when he saw the Kings because even though he hadn't made much progress with Mrs. King when they'd met for the second time on Friday—mainly because her husband and niece's baby had been born the day before—he was glad to see that she'd at least come to church and was sitting with her husband.

But then Phillip looked at Alicia again.

"Just last week, I was reading an article about the number of divorces that take place in this country every year, and I was truly saddened by it. There are way too many of them, and a lot of it has to do with the fact that people don't take the time to find out enough about the person they're marrying, they don't communicate the way they ought to, and they have no idea that marriage involves a huge amount of give-and-take. Marriage is about two people who have become one in the eyes of God, and it's up to both parties to act accordingly—meaning each party should always consider how their individual actions will affect his or her spouse. Always."

Phillip looked at his parents, who seemed as proud as any parents could be, and he smiled at both of them. This time he didn't bother looking at his wife again because he didn't want to see the dirty looks she kept giving him.

"None of us is without fault, and we all make mistakes. Sometimes the mistakes are small, and sometimes they're so huge they may seem unforgivable. But if God forgives us, then we have a responsibility as Christians to forgive our fellow man or woman exactly the same way."

Phillip glanced at Mr. and Mrs. King but only for a short second.

"Forgiveness, especially when we've been hurt, isn't always the easiest thing to offer, but it is possible and it is the right thing for us to do. Sometimes, forgiving the people who have wronged us, the people who have betrayed us, well, sometimes it seems like we just shouldn't have to forgive them for anything. Sometimes all we want is for something bad to happen to them so we can feel like justice has been served. But I'm here to tell you that revenge is not of God. Revenge is wrong and something we should work hard to separate ourselves from."

"Amen," a woman toward the back agreed.

Phillip knew all that he'd said would help at least someone, but sadly his words weren't helping him one bit. He was still furious with Alicia, and he was having a very difficult time forgiving her.

"So, married people, if you're happy and truly enjoying each other, then I say God bless you, but if you're married and having one problem after another, then please think about what I said. Refer to your Bibles because there are some wonderful scriptures in there on marriage that will truly help you. Then, sit down and just talk to each other. Pay attention to what your spouse has to say, and do what you have to in order to work things out. Realize that your relationship is not just about *you* but about both of you."

"Amen," members of the congregation said in unison.

"Now, before I move on to begin my message, I would be

remiss if I didn't acknowledge my parents who are here visiting with us from Chicago. So, Mom, Dad, please stand up."

Phillip's parents stood, turned toward the audience and waved, and everyone applauded. Phillip smiled when he thought about how well they looked and how they could easily pass for ten years younger than their actual ages.

"Needless to say, I'm very happy to have them here with me today, and I thank all of you for giving them such a wonderful welcome as always. Then, if I could ask Ms. Brittany," he said, turning toward the youth choir and searching for his favorite fifteen-year-old soloist, "if I could ask you to sing 'His Eye Is on the Sparrow,' you would really make my day."

The young girl smiled at Phillip and then made her way to the microphone.

Phillip took a seat and waited for her to begin. As the introduction of the music played, Phillip scanned the pews and did a double take when he spotted Shandra Keyes, a woman he'd gone to high school with in Chicago—the woman he'd dated his entire senior year and thought he would marry. He was actually very shocked to see her and wondered why she was visiting all the way here in Mitchell, because as far as he knew, she still lived in the Chicago area.

He looked away but then glanced in her direction again and instinctively, they smiled at each other. Although, when Phillip saw Alicia peering toward the area where Shandra was sitting, that told him that Alicia had seen him acknowledging someone. Phillip was upset with his wife, but now he felt bad because, right or wrong, he couldn't deny that he was happy to see his ex-girlfriend. He felt worse when he thought about all the great times he and Shandra had shared and remembered that the only reason they'd broken up was because they'd gone to separate colleges and the distance had proven to be too great for both of them.

Phillip returned his attention to Brittany who was singing as beautifully as every other time she sang, so he closed his eyes and enjoyed her amazing voice. Then, when she finished, he delivered his sermon as planned, welcomed a few new members who'd decided to join the church, and then he and Alicia stood at the entrance, greeting parishioners who were on their way out.

"I really enjoyed everything you had to say today, Pastor," a twentysomething young man told Phillip and shook his hand.

"I'm glad to hear it."

"That really is a gorgeous suit you have on, Ms. Alicia," one of the mothers of the church said, complimenting the expensive navy blue outfit Alicia was wearing. Phillip could barely stand it.

"Why thank you, Mother Jacobs. You're too kind."

"Pastor," Elder Jamison, the head of the elder board, said, "when you finish here, I'll meet you in your office so I can give you a few more proposals that we received a couple of days ago from potential contractors. Pastor Black asked me to give them to you so that you and he can review them sometime tomorrow when he's back in town."

"That's fine. Of course."

Phillip shook one hand after another and so did Alicia, but he felt a bit nervous when he saw Shandra, standing only a few feet away. There were only four people in front of her, and he wasn't sure how Alicia was going to take their meeting each other. If he could have gotten by without introducing them, he would have, but he already knew that there was no way Shandra had waited all this time just to say hello and pretend like she didn't know him.

So, he greeted the next four members and then prepared himself to speak to her.

Shandra's smile was wide and genuine. "Oh my goodness, Phillip, it's so good to see you."

"It's good seeing you, too. How have you been?"

"Wonderful. And you?"

"Very blessed."

"I'm visiting Donna, a close friend of mine, who's actually a member here at the church." Shandra turned and pointed to the woman directly behind her and Phillip recognized her right away. He didn't know her personally but he'd seen her a few times in passing. "She'd told me about a year ago that you were the new assistant pastor. I was so excited for you, and I'd always said that if I ever got some time to spend the weekend with her, I was going to come to service."

"Well, we're glad you did. Come anytime. How are your parents?"

"They're doing fine."

"Please tell them I said hello."

"I will. And is this your wife?"

Phillip looked at Alicia who'd obviously been taking in every word of the conversation. "Yes, this is my wife, Alicia, and, baby, this is Shandra."

Alicia shook Shandra's hand. "Nice to meet you."

"It's nice to meet you as well. Phillip and I went to high school together."

"Really?"

"Yes, we go way back."

"And how long are you in town for?"

Phillip looked straight ahead but wondered why Alicia was asking this.

"Just until this afternoon. I have to get back for work tomorrow."

"Well, you have a safe trip back," Alicia told her and then

looked away and struck up a conversation with one of the members standing on the other side of them. It was at that moment that he knew he and Alicia were going to have words about his ex.

"Well, Phillip, it really was good seeing you, and you take care, okay?"

"I will and you, too."

Phillip watched her walk away but then caught himself as he realized Alicia was staring him straight in the face. He shook hands with the next person in line but couldn't help thinking about the way Shandra looked. They were both thirty-two, but she appeared not a day over twenty-eight, and she was even more beautiful than he remembered.

But he knew it was wrong for a married man to focus on the beauty of any woman who wasn't his wife and he was sorry. *Lord, I apologize.*

He'd heard Dr. Frederick K. C. Price give a sermon on television one time about thoughts, ideas, and suggestions and how any of the three could get you in a lot of trouble if you weren't careful. Now, Phillip knew Dr. Price was right.

He knew because even though he'd apologized to God for the thoughts he was having and was still standing right next to the woman he was married to, he couldn't get Shandra out of his mind.

He couldn't stop thinking about her—and that scared him.

Chapter 10

Alicia wasn't sure who this Shandra person was and why she'd suddenly decided to drop in at Deliverance Outreach, but just as soon as Phillip's parents were on their way back to Chicago, she was going to find out. The woman had claimed she was visiting a friend who just so happened to be a member of the church, but Alicia didn't believe it. She suspected it was more because, one, the woman had no sign of a ring on her finger, and, two, Alicia hadn't liked the way the woman looked at Phillip.

Then there was that pre-sermon tirade about marriage that Phillip had conveniently decided to share with the entire congregation even though he was clearly speaking specifically to his own wife. Alicia had wanted to walk right out of the sanctuary, and there was a chance she would have, had she not been sitting next to her in-laws. They were such nice people and exceptionally kind to her, so she didn't want to make a scene or ruin their visit. But she was at the point where she'd had just about all she could take of Phillip and his self-righteous attitude, and she was going to let him know precisely how she felt right after she found out what this Shandra chick was really up to.

Mom Katherine took another bite of her dessert. "This cake is simply divine. It's even better than the last time we were here."

Alicia ate a bite as well. "It really is good. And actually, I think it's the best German chocolate cake you can find in the city."

Dad Phil leaned back in his chair. "I like it myself, so, Kat, maybe we should have gotten a whole one so we could take it back with us."

"I thought about it but then I realized how you and I would eat the entire thing by sundown tomorrow and that would be just terrible."

"Well, it's not like either of you has a weight problem," Alicia added.

"No, sweetie, but we want to keep it that way, too."

Alicia laughed. "I hear you, and I don't blame you about that at all."

Mom Katherine looked around the family room. "Alicia, I just love that painting you have hanging over the fireplace. It's so exquisite."

"Thank you. I bought it at an art gallery near downtown."

"Here?"

"No, near downtown Chicago."

"Well, it's perfect. Everything in here is beautiful, and you've certainly done a lot of decorating in a very short period of time."

"That's pretty much all she did the first three months we lived here."

Alicia wanted to kill Phillip for making that comment. He was being rude, but she was going to ignore him. For now.

"Well, it definitely shows," Mom Katherine continued. "And, Phillip, you should be very proud of your wife and all the good taste that she has. And you definitely should appreciate how clean and in order she keeps every room."

"I do appreciate her—and the housekeeper who comes and cleans every Monday, too."

How dare he try to diminish the compliment his mother had given her. But Alicia knew he was only doing it because he was still upset about those new bedroom and bathroom items she'd purchased. But so what? So what if she had because it wasn't like he could take any of it back to return it. The best thing he could do was get over it.

"Well, that's fine and well," Mom Katherine said. "But your wife is the one who's keeping things clean the other six days. Right, Alicia?"

"That's right, Mom Katherine. You tell him."

Phillip looked toward the television and acted as though he hadn't heard any of what his mother had just said.

"So, son, when will you be preaching again?" Dad Phil asked.

"It's hard to say. Sometimes I do the early-morning service even when Curtis is in town. It just depends on how busy he is and what else he has going on. Then, of course, like today, when he's gone for the entire day, I normally preach the sermons for both services."

"Well, you let us know when you'll be doing it again because we'd love to come hear you."

"I definitely will."

Mom Katherine set her plate down on the coffee table. "We really did enjoy being here this weekend. It was nice to go to church today and nice to be here relaxing with both of you."

Alicia stood up and grabbed her in-laws' dishes as well as her own. "Is there anything I can get for either of you from the kitchen?"

"No, I couldn't eat or drink another thing," Mom Katherine said.

Dad Phil patted his stomach. "No, daughter, neither could I."

Alicia loved when her father-in-law called her that and some-times her mother-in-law called her that, too. They'd accepted her right from the beginning, and she'd liked them both imme-diately. She was glad she didn't have to deal with a horrid mother-in-law because she had certainly heard stories from so many other women she knew.

When Alicia returned to the family room, she sat down on the sofa and curled her legs under her. "Phillip, did you want anything?"

"No."

Phillip's answer was short and curt, and he hadn't even bothered looking at her. Maybe he was angrier than she'd thought, but what he didn't know was that she was angry, too. Angry, irritated, and feeling like she was living with some prison warden.

Mom Katherine could obviously tell something was wrong. "Son, is everything okay with you? You've been so quiet since we got home, and you seem distant."

"No, Mom, everything is fine."

Phillip's parents looked at each other, and Alicia could tell they knew different.

Alicia changed the subject. "So, Mom Katherine, in a couple of weeks, maybe I'll drive over to the city so that you, my mom, and I can have lunch together."

"I'd really like that. I haven't seen your mom since you and Phillip got married, but the two of us had such a great time that whole weekend."

"She talks about that, too."

"You make sure you tell her I said hello."

"I will."

After another two hours passed, Phillip's parents gathered their garment and overnight bags and Phillip helped his dad load everything into the car.

Mom Kathrine hugged Alicia and then Phillip. "Well, I guess it's time to head back home."

Dad Phil hugged them next. "Yeah, we'd better get going before it gets too late."

Phillip stood with his arms folded. "You know I hate to see you go, but I understand."

"You two take care of yourselves, and we'll be talking to you," Mom Katherine said, smiling.

Alicia smiled back. "You, too, and we love you both."

"We love both of you, too."

Alicia and Phillip stood in the front doorway, waving until his parents had left the driveway and were on their way down the street. Then, once they were back inside the house, Alicia shut the door and wasted no time giving Phillip a piece of her mind.

"What I want to know is why you were trying to make me look bad in front of your parents. Because I didn't appreciate that little snide remark you made about the housekeeper one bit."

"Look, Alicia. I'm tired, and all I want to do is enjoy the rest of my Sunday evening in peace. If you want to argue with someone, then by all means, please feel free to argue with yourself. But leave me out of it."

Alicia followed him back into the family room. "Excuse me?"

Phillip sat down on the sofa and resumed watching the basketball game he'd sort of been watching while his parents were still there. But what pissed her off was that he acted as though she wasn't even in the room with him. He acted as if she didn't even exist. But she was going to make him talk to her one way or the other.

"So, who was that tramp you introduced me to today?"

"What? What tramp?"

"You know exactly who I'm talking about, Phillip. That tramp Shandra."

"Didn't you hear her say we went to high school together?"

"Oh, I heard her loudly and clearly but with the way she was looking at you, I have a feeling that you were a lot more than just schoolmates. And I also saw how you were looking at her, too."

"You're making something out of nothing."

"Am I now? So, you never dated her?"

Phillip didn't say anything.

"Hello?"

"What?!"

"Did you or did you not date that woman?"

"Okay, fine. Yes, we dated but that was a long time ago. Years and years ago."

"I knew she was more than just some acquaintance. I knew it as soon as I laid eyes on her and saw how she was acting around you."

"We were practically kids, Alicia, so why are you harping on this?"

"I'm not. But I do think it's just a little bit strange how she just sort of showed up out of the blue, even though she lives over in Chicago."

"Alicia, people visit Deliverance all the time. And you know that."

"Not women you used to date."

"Well, it's not like I can control who visits the church."

"And what was all that garbage you were talking this morning about marriage? You spent all that time explaining what it takes to have a good marriage, yet there you were, using your position in the pulpit as a way to try to get back at me, your own wife. You acted like you were speaking to the entire congregation, but you and I both know that you were talking directly to me. Then you had the nerve to talk about forgiveness, but at the same time, here you are walking around holding a grudge simply because I made a few charges on some credit cards."

Phillip turned up the volume on the television.

Alicia stood there for a few seconds, wishing she had something she could throw at him, but gave up and went upstairs instead.

Entering the bedroom, she slammed the door and threw herself across the bed. Then she called her mother. But when she didn't get an answer, she tried her cell phone.

"Hey, Alicia."

"Hi, Mom. Where are you?"

"James and I are headed back from Wisconsin."

"Oh yeah, that's right. Did you have a good time?"

"We did and we were just saying how we'll have to start going up there a lot more often than we do."

"I'm glad you enjoyed yourselves. But, Mom, I really needed to hear your voice."

"What's wrong? Are you okay? Because you sound like something's wrong."

Alicia broke into tears.

"Alicia, honey, what is it?"

"It's everything."

"Honey, you have to try to calm down and tell me what you mean by that."

Alicia sniffled a couple of times and took a deep breath. "Phillip and I aren't getting along at all. And it's getting worse all the time. It's getting so bad that I'm starting to think we never should have gotten married."

"Oh, Alicia. What's going on?"

"Well, for one thing, he's still mad because I bought a new comforter set and some bathroom accessories for the guest bedroom, but Mom, who gets mad and stays mad over something that petty?"

"Well, you know how he feels about the money you spend, and that's why I tried talking to you about that the other day."

"But it's not just that anymore, because today some ex-girlfriend of his showed up at the church, claiming she was visiting a friend of hers who's a member."

"How long ago did he date this woman?"

"Back in high school or so he says."

"You don't believe him?"

"It's not so much that I don't believe him. It's more the fact that I think that woman showed up for a lot more reasons than Phillip is willing to acknowledge."

"Like what?"

"I don't know. Maybe she wants to sleep with him."

"Did you talk to Phillip about this?"

"We just had a big argument about it a few minutes ago."

"And what did he say?"

"That she was someone he knew from high school and that he can't control who visits the church."

"And he's right. I mean, don't get me wrong, who's to say whether this woman has ulterior motives or not, but the bottom line is that if Phillip hasn't been communicating with her since high school, then I don't think you have anything to worry about. Plus, even if she does want to mess around with him, it'll be up to Phillip to put her in her place."

"But what if he doesn't? Because even though I've never said this to you before, that was one of the reasons I was sort of hesitant about marrying Phillip."

"Meaning?"

"Meaning, I didn't want to end up hurt like you were. I'm only twenty-two years old, but for as long as I live, I'll never forget all the women Dad had affairs with while he was married to you. And Mom, I'm telling you, I could never take that for as long as you did. I could never take it for even a few weeks."

"I understand why you feel that way, and I don't want to see you go through the same thing I went through, either. But at the same time, I really believe that Phillip loves you and that you should try talking to him again. Tell him how you feel about everything."

"I don't know . . . I'm tired of arguing with him."

"Well, how mad was he about this comforter set you bought?"

"He's real mad, and it's so uncalled for."

"Alicia, you really are going to have to stop blowing money the way you do. And you should apologize to Phillip. Because, honey, if you don't stop soon, not only are you going to ruin your credit, but you're going to cause your marriage to come to an end. And I know you don't want that."

Alicia didn't like what her mother was trying to insinuate. "Ruin my credit? How am I going to do that when I pay all my bills on time and my credit is excellent?"

"If you continue down this path you're riding on, it won't stay that way."

"I don't see how, because my spending isn't any worse than what it's always been."

"That might be true, but it was different when you were growing up and while you were in college because your father paid all of your bills. But now that you have a husband, you have to make better choices and act a lot more responsibly."

"Mom, why are you siding with Phillip?"

"I'm not siding with anyone. You're my daughter and Phillip is a wonderful man who really loves you, and I just want to make sure you consider that. I want the best for you, Alicia, and more than anything I want to see you happy."

"You know what? I have to go."

"That's fine, Alicia, but I hope you'll think about what I said."

"Yeah, right. I'll think about it. Bye, Mom."

Alicia threw the phone on its base and turned on the television. She flipped through a few movie channels, watched CNN for a few minutes, and then decided to check out QVC. Very rarely did she watch shopping channels on Sundays, but from the looks of the citrine and diamond ring they were showing, she was very glad she'd tuned in on this one. This ring would go perfectly with the mustard-color leather jacket she'd purchased not very long ago.

She watched and listened to the host as she described the details and thought about her mother and how she'd actually sided with Phillip against her own daughter. But Alicia wasn't going to let that bother her because she knew her mother was only trying to keep peace between her and Phillip. Either that or she just didn't get what Alicia had been trying to tell her. She didn't understand that Phillip was being unreasonable and was only trying to control her and that she wasn't having it. He kept acting as though Alicia had a problem and now her mother sounded as though she might be thinking the same thing, but they were wrong.

However, in the end, the only thing that really mattered was that Alicia was a grown woman, and she didn't have to listen to anybody she didn't want to listen to. Not Phillip, not her mother, not Melanie, not anyone.

And for the rest of the evening, she wasn't going to think about any of the problems she and Phillip were having. What she was going to do instead was relax, enjoy the QVC precious stones broadcast, and see what else she liked in addition to the ring she was now getting ready to order.

She did what made her happy, and there wasn't a single thing wrong with that.

Chapter 11

This past weekend had been by far the worst weekend of Phillip and Alicia's marriage, but now that he'd finally awakened and was watching her sleep so peacefully, he was reminded of just how much he loved her. He didn't understand why she did the things she did and why she couldn't seem to stop, but there was no denying that he loved his wife with everything in him. He hated arguing with her as if they were mutual enemies, but she made him so angry sometimes—and lately on a pretty constant basis.

What he wished was that they could rewind to the first day they'd met and start over again, because for him, life couldn't have been more perfect. He'd been beyond taken with her, and it hadn't mattered to him that she was ten years younger. In the past, he never would have even considered dating a woman that much younger, but Alicia was out of the ordinary. She was a very young woman who had a very old soul, and he never noticed their age difference. He'd thought she was perfect for him, but now with the way they weren't getting along, he couldn't help wondering if maybe they'd made a mistake. He wondered if maybe they'd married too quickly because it just seemed that no matter what he said or did, he couldn't stop her from overspending like some madwoman. She was digging a very deep ditch for herself and also for them as a couple, and he wasn't sure what to do about it. Maybe it was finally time he did tell Curtis what was going on so that maybe Curtis could offer him some much-needed advice. He didn't want his telling Curtis to backfire, but he wasn't sure who else he could turn to for help.

Phillip continued admiring his wife until finally she opened her eyes. He wasn't sure how she was going to react, but he smiled at her. To his surprise, she smiled back and he felt relieved.

"Hey, I'm sorry. I'm sorry for getting so angry at you and for using the pulpit as a platform to purposely say things that I was mainly directing toward you. I'm also sorry I wouldn't talk to you when my parents left and that once again, we went to bed not speaking. It kills me when we're like that but, baby, I was so upset."

"I know, and I'm sorry, too. I'm sorry that we can't seem to agree on anything, and that we're at each other's throats all the time."

Phillip pulled her into his arms and looked deeply into her eyes. "We still have to figure out a way to settle our differences, but the one thing I don't ever want you to forget is how much I love you. Because I *do* love you."

"I love you, too, Phillip, but I have to tell you that I'm not happy about your ex-girlfriend showing up out of nowhere."

"I'm not sure why she came, but I promise you, I haven't had any contact with her or seen here in years, and I definitely had no idea she was going to be there yesterday."

"I hope you're telling me the truth because I could never deal with you having any outside affairs."

"And you won't ever have to. I'm committed to you and our marriage, and the idea of my being with another woman is completely out of the question."

"I'm glad to hear you say that because I'm nothing like my mother, my first stepmother, or even Charlotte. I would never stay with a man who sleeps with one woman after another, year after year."

Phillip understood how she felt and now that they'd cleared all of that up, he desperately wanted to discuss the real problem at hand. He wanted to try to reason with her and maybe discuss them sitting down and figuring out a monthly spending allowance, something fair and one she could try to stick to.

But he decided not to because he didn't want to risk having another falling-out with her. He simply didn't have the emotional energy that would be required to deal with the kind of quarreling they always fell into—that is whenever this particular subject came up, and, today, it just wasn't worth it.

Today, all he wanted to do was feel close to his wife and share the kind of intimacy they'd shared at the beginning of their marriage—intimacy without animosity, resentment, or excessive anger.

He just wanted to make love to her and be happy.

Alicia smiled as Phillip turned the black BMW SUV, the one she'd talked him into buying just before they were married, onto the winding driveway and drove up to the garage area. No matter how many years passed or how many times she visited her father and Charlotte, she always felt like it was her first time seeing their home. It was nearly a mansion and probably was one by most people's standards, and Alicia loved it. So much so that she lived for the day she could have one built just like it. Of course, at the rate she and Phillip were going financially, it wasn't going to happen anytime soon, but it would happen at some point. She couldn't say exactly when, but she knew she was destined to live in one of the best kinds of houses money could buy. She knew this because she refused to believe that God would bless her with a father who was rich, allow her to live in great wealth her entire childhood, and then force her into an average, middle-class lifestyle as an adult. The God she knew didn't work that way, and she was counting on Him to come through for her the same as He always had.

When Phillip turned off the vehicle, they both stepped out of it and walked around to the front door. Her dad and Charlotte had flown back from Houston last night and had called this morning to invite her and Phillip over for lunch. Her dad and Phillip were both off on Mondays, so her dad liked spending time with just the four of them whenever he could. Alicia wished Matthew, her baby brother, had been home, but he was already at school. She even wished she could see her baby sister, Curtina, but since she lived with Tabitha, her mother, Alicia never saw her as often as she would have liked to. Tabitha had told her she could visit Curtina anytime she wanted, but Alicia still wasn't all that fond of Tabitha. She felt sorry for her because she had HIV, but the idea that she had slept around with Alicia's father, all while knowing he was married to Charlotte, didn't sit too well.

After ringing the doorbell, Agnes, the housekeeper and cook, opened the door and smiled.

"Why hello, you two."

Alicia walked in first. "Hi, Agnes. How are you?"

"I'm fine, Ms. Alicia. And you?"

"I'm good."

"And how are you, Mr. Phillip?"

"Very well, thanks."

"Your parents are in the dining room, and I'll be serving lunch very shortly."

Alicia dropped her Louis Vuitton shoulder bag on one of the tables in the entryway. "Thanks, Agnes."

Alicia liked Agnes, but she still missed Tracy. Matthew missed Tracy, too, and if it hadn't been for their father having an affair with Tabitha and Tabitha blackmailing Tracy the way she had, Tracy never would have been forced to betray Alicia's dad and Charlotte. It still made Alicia sad when she thought about all the scandals her father had been involved in and how his actions had affected and hurt so many different people. He'd hurt people intentionally and unintentionally, directly and indirectly, but Alicia tried her best not to think about any of it because now she really was proud of the good person her father had become. He was a true man of God and worked a lot harder than he used to at doing the right thing. Alicia was also glad that he and Charlotte were finally very happy with each other.

"Hey, baby girl," her father said, hugging her.

"Hi, Daddy."

Phillip spoke to and embraced Charlotte and then Alicia did the same.

Alicia sat down at the long wooden table that seated twelve. She was adjacent to her father, and Phillip sat next to her. "So, Daddy, how was the trip?"

"The best. Such a powerful conference and so many people."

Charlotte was across from Alicia. "Your dad was good. He had the entire arena more motivated than I've ever witnessed before, and there were thousands and thousands in attendance"

Phillip shook his head in awe. "Amazing."

"It was a memorable trip," Curtis said. "But I think my wife had just as good a time at The Galleria as she did at the conference."

Charlotte playfully rolled her eyes toward the ceiling. "I did not."

"You know it's true because I practically had to drag you back to the hotel. The woman shopped so much after we got there on Friday, she ended up sleeping almost twelve hours that evening. That's why she wanted to take an early morning flight into Houston. So she could shop."

"He's making it sound worse than what it really was."

"She bought so many items that we would have had to buy additional luggage just to bring them home, so thank God for FedEx, UPS, and all the other shipping carriers."

They all laughed, but deep down Alicia wished she could have been there with Charlotte. She still remembered the one time she'd gone to The Galleria and how huge and magnificent it was. She'd gone there with her mom on a business trip a couple of summers ago while she was home on break from school, and she'd shopped for hours. She remembered how she'd been glad her mom was tied up with meetings because that had allowed her the freedom to browse like she'd wanted to and without any criticism.

There had been so many fabulous stores, she hadn't known which ones she should go in first, but by the time she'd left the building, she'd spent well over three thousand dollars. Sadly, though, this had been one of the times her father had told her that she'd charged way too much money on her cards for one month's period of time and that she wasn't to ever do that again.

But it had been worth having him scold her about it because her reward had been the most gorgeous pairs of shoes, the sharpest designer jeans she'd ever owned, and better-looking dresses than she'd seen in a long while. Just the thought of that particular day gave her an incredible rush, and she could barely hold back the excitement she was feeling.

"Alicia. Baby. Are you here?" she heard Phillip say and then realized she'd been daydreaming for longer than she should have.

She smiled sheepishly. "Oh, I'm sorry."

"What were you thinking about?"

"A really great story idea I want to write about, so I guess I got a little caught up."

She lied without missing a beat, and from the look on her father's face he, at least, had believed every word.

"That's why I wish you would spend a lot more time with your writing and that you would take it a lot more seriously. Ever since you were a little girl, your imagination has been vivid and that's why I've always encouraged you to be a writer."

"I am, Daddy. I'm really going to get serious, and that's why I'm glad the position at the church is only twenty hours."

"Oh and by the way, the elder board is meeting tomorrow, so you could probably start on Thursday if you wanted or even next Tuesday, which is the beginning of our workweek."

"That's fine."

"This will be good all around," Curtis said.

"It really is, Alicia," Charlotte agreed. "You'll be good doing PR."

"I hope so."

Phillip placed his arm across the back of Alicia's chair. "You will, baby. Once you get started, you'll have everyone lining up to join Deliverance Outreach."

Agnes brought in four trivets to sit each of the dishes on, then came back with everything she'd prepared. It all smelled wonderful, and in this house, lunch seemed more like dinner because on the table were cucumber salad, stuffed shrimp, chicken fettuccine, and hot, buttered rolls.

Once Agnes left the room, Alicia's father said grace, and they dug in. They laughed and chatted about everything imaginable and it was a wonderful day. Alicia was happy she and Phillip were back on good terms and that they'd come to visit her dad and Charlotte, but there was one thing that she sometimes couldn't help thinking about and that was the fact that after all these years, she still wished her parents were still together. She loved her stepmother and certainly loved her stepfather, but there was this aching part of her soul that longed to see her parents married again. She'd accepted the fact that, years ago, they'd both moved on with their lives, but who could blame her for still holding on to her childhood fantasy? What child wanted his or her parents to live in separate households or file for a divorce? Not one she could think of. She knew not every couple was meant to be together, but her parents' divorce had caused her more pain than the two of them had ever realized. They didn't know because she purposely tried not to talk about it and had decided it was her responsibility to be a big girl and just be mature about the whole situation. But being mature hadn't helped her emotionally. All it had done was make her grow up much faster than she'd wanted to.

When they finished eating, Charlotte suggested they see what afternoon movies were playing so they could take in a show. Her father agreed as did Alicia and Phillip, but now Phillip's phone was ringing.

"Hey, Mom, how are you?"

Alicia couldn't hear what her mother-in-law was saying but from the look on Phillip's face and the frantic tone of his voice, she knew something was gravely wrong.

"Is he breathing?"

Alicia covered her mouth in horror.

"Mom, Dad is going to be fine, and we're on our way."

Phillip hung up, slid his chair back, and stood up. "We have to get to Chicago. My father has had a heart attack, and it doesn't sound good."

Chapter 19

As soon as they all arrived at the south suburban hospital and walked into the ER waiting area, Mom Katherine rushed over and hugged Phillip. "Honey, what am I going to do if something happens to your father?"

Phillip led her over to one of the long settees and tried calming her down. "It won't, Mom. So, please don't talk that way."

Mom Katherine was a nervous wreck, and Alicia could tell she'd been crying for the last couple of hours.

"Mom, what happened? What was Dad doing?"

"Nothing. We'd just finished eating some sandwiches I'd made for lunch and were laughing at some sitcom and the next thing I knew, your father was grabbing his chest and starting to keel over. So, I went over to him and then quickly called 911. And now, he's in surgery having a quadruple bypass because four of his arteries are blocked," Mom Katherine explained. Then she started crying again, and Phillip pulled her into his arms.

Alicia rubbed her husband's back, trying to console him, because she knew exactly how he felt. She was sorry for him and couldn't imagine what it would be like if her own father had a massive heart attack. But she knew it would be devastating because she remembered how hard it had been on her years ago when one of her father's ex-mistresses had shot him right while he was standing in the church pulpit. She'd been so shaken up and so terrified she was going to lose him, she'd prayed she would never have to experience anything like that ever again.

Mom Katherine lifted her head and stood up. "I just don't know what'll I do if he doesn't make it."

"Mom, please don't do this. What we have to do now is keep our faith as strong as possible."

Charlotte walked over and hugged her.

Alicia's dad followed behind. "That's right, Katherine. Faith is what we have to focus on and as a matter of fact, let's join hands so we can have a word of prayer."

There were other people in the waiting area, but Alicia knew her father didn't care where he was or who was around when he thought group prayer was necessary.

"Dear Heavenly Father, we come right now just thanking You for what You've already done for each of us, thanking You for the knowledge and skill You've given the doctors who are now performing surgery on Brother Phil, and we thank You for bringing him through it. We know that when everything is all said and done, the final decision always rests with You and that You never, ever make any mistakes. We know that everything is for a reason, good or bad, even if only to draw us closer to You. Then, Lord, give Sister Katherine the strength and understanding that she needs during this difficult time. These and all blessings, I ask in Your son Jesus' name, Amen."

They all sat down again, but no one said anything. Alicia prayed that her father-in-law was going to be all right. She understood that sickness and death were a natural part of life, but she didn't understand why things like this happened to good people because her father-in-law, mother-in-law, and husband were three of the kindest people she knew. Good, decent people and it bothered her because it seemed like bad people, say like the thief who'd robbed her at gunpoint, seemed to get away with whatever they wanted. They did fine in life, for the most part, and that confused Alicia.

After another five hours passed, the surgeon finally walked out and asked if they were the Sullivan family. He introduced himself as Dr. Nicholson and directed them into a nearby consultation room.

He sighed and then pulled off his surgical hat. "Mrs. Sullivan, your husband is a very sick man, but the surgery went a lot better than I expected it to and that has me very hopeful."

"Will he be okay?" she asked.

"Right now, he's in critical condition and we're sending him to the intensive care unit, but we won't have a better idea until maybe forty-eight hours from now."

"How did my dad end up with four blocked arteries? He's not even overweight."

"It's hard to say, but the good news is that your mom was there with him when this happened and was able to call the paramedics as soon as she did. Mrs. Sullivan, you helped save your husband's life."

Mom Katherine nodded and tried to force a smile but didn't say anything. Alicia's dad and Charlotte looked on sympathetically.

But then Mom Katherine asked, "When can I see him?"

"In a little while. He's in recovery and then once they get him up to coronary ICU, they'll need some time to get him situated. But after that, you can see him. You won't be able stay in with him long, but you can visit for a few minutes."

Everyone looked back and forth at each other and then at the doctor again.

"Well, unless you have other questions, I think that's all I have for now."

"Thank you so much, Doctor," Mom Katherine told him.

"You're quite welcome. We're going to do everything we can for your husband. That I can promise you."

"Thanks again."

Phillip stood up and shook Dr. Nicholson's hand. "Yes, thank you, Doctor."

When he left, the rest of them stayed seated.

"Mom, I'm going to spend the night here, but I think you should go home and get some rest," said Phillip.

"And I can go with you," Charlotte offered.

"No. I'm not leaving my husband. I can't do that."

"But, Mom, you look tired and you're going to need all your strength as we go through the next few days or so."

"That's fine, but I'm not leaving here."

Finally, when Phillip saw that his mother wasn't going to change her mind, he relented.

Alicia's father slid back from the table. "Katherine, is there anything we can do? Anything we can get for you?"

"No, just your being here, both of you, is more than enough."

Charlotte got up and went around to where Mom Katherine was and hugged her.

"We'll definitely be back over tomorrow, once the elder board meeting is over, but if you need anything before then, we're only a phone call away."

"I know that and thank you."

Alicia looked at Phillip. "Honey, since we all rode in Daddy's car, I should go back with them so I can pick up one of our vehicles."

"That'll be fine and why don't you just sleep at home tonight and then just come back in the morning."

"Are you sure? Because I don't mind driving back if you want me to. I really want to be here for you, anyway."

"No, Mom will be here, so we'll just see you in the morning."

Alicia hated leaving him, especially since she could tell how sad and worried he was, but it was getting pretty late and it probably was best for her to rest at home and then just plan on driving back over and spending the entire day here at the hospital tomorrow. So, they all left the consultation room and said their good-byes.

Alicia hugged Phillip, and they held each other longer than usual. "I love you, and call me on my cell once you go in and see your dad."

"I will."

Alicia's father and Charlotte hugged Phillip and Mom Katherine, and then the three of them headed out of the hospital.

Inside the intensive care unit, Phillip slowly walked toward the bed his father was lying in and, without warning, broke down like a child. He'd told himself he wouldn't do this because he needed to be strong for his mom, but he couldn't help the way he felt. He'd held things together for as long as he could, but now that he'd given in to the terrible pain that was eating at him, he was glad his mother was back out in the waiting area. She was already upset herself, but if she found out he was just as distraught, she'd feel even worse. She'd lose hope, faith, and everything else she needed to deal with the situation.

He stood over his father's bed, observing every tube, monitor, and sound and shook his head in disbelief. If he hadn't seen all of this for himself, he would have refused to believe that *his* father was fighting for his life. Not the man that meant everything to him. Not the man who, when Phillip was a small boy, took his only child just about everywhere he went. Not the man who had worked as hard as he could, making sure

Phillip and his mom had everything they needed, yet still found time to come to every one of his son's baseball games. Not the man who'd found and worked a part-time job just so his son could attend an out-of-state, private university. It was true that Phillip had gotten a partial scholarship all four years, but his father and mother had done whatever they had to in order to make up the difference, something that couldn't have been easy.

"Oh, God, please don't take my father," he whispered. "Please make him well."

Phillip caressed his dad's forehead, leaned over and kissed him on the cheek, and then stood watching him for a few more minutes.

Finally, he went back out and sat next to his mother.

She held her son's hand. "He doesn't look good, does he?"

"He's been through a lot. A quadruple bypass is very serious."

"My mother used to say how we can be up one day and down the next, and she was right."

"Has he been complaining about any chest pains or saying he doesn't feel good?"

"No, you saw how well he was all weekend. He was fine."

"I just don't understand it. Maybe he needs more exercise."

"Maybe, because I've been telling you how he doesn't like to do much except sit around the house. And that's not good for anybody."

"Well, after this, he's going to have to make some changes. He's going to have to join a health club and even though he doesn't have a weight problem, he's going to have to start eating a much stricter diet."

"I agree, but he won't like it. He loves high-fat, high-calorie food and because he can eat what he wants without gaining a lot of weight, he doesn't see any problems with it."

"I remember the last time I was over. He ate a big bag of pork skins and drank two cans of soda and never thought twice about it."

"His metabolism is very high, but now we know that even thin people who don't eat right or move their bodies on a regular basis can be unhealthy."

"This is true, and Dad's heart attack has me thinking about the things I eat as well. I work out every single morning except on Sunday, but I don't necessarily watch what I eat when it comes to fatty foods. I love steak, I love anything cooked in butter, and I love dessert."

"It's definitely a wake-up call and, sweetheart, I'm really scared. Your father and I have been together for thirty-five years, and he's the only man I've ever loved. We were only twenty years old when we married, and I'd just graduated from the community college. He's all I know, and I'm all he knows."

"I know, Mom, and I've always been very proud of how happy you and Dad have always been with each other."

"Don't get me wrong, we've had our share of problems the same as anyone else, but for the most part, we really have had a very happy marriage."

"I'd always hoped to have the same thing when I got married, too, but, lately, I don't know."

He wasn't sure why he was burdening his mom with any of this right now, but he needed to tell someone the truth about his relationship.

"Is everything okay with you and Alicia?"

"Sometimes, yes, sometimes no. It just depends."

"Your father and I talked about you and Alicia on the way home yesterday because we could tell you weren't happy about something. But I just figured you'd had your first argument or something, and that it was probably nothing."

"Mom, Alicia spends money like a person who has unlimited access inside the Federal Reserve."

"Well, most women like to shop, so maybe this is just some little phase she's going through."

"No, I don't think so. She buys things that millionaire wives can afford."

"Oh come on, Phillip, it can't be that bad."

"It is. Mom, I found a sixteen-hundred-dollar St. John suit in her closet."

"A St. Who?"

Phillip chuckled. "St. John. It's an expensive designer that anyone in their right mind would know we can't afford. Actually, the only reason *I* know some of these names is because of Alicia."

"But sixteen hundred dollars? You must be mistaken."

"No. I checked the price online."

"I just can't believe that. For one outfit?"

"Yes. And she buys all sorts of jewelry, purses, shoes, suits, dresses, and just like you saw this weekend, she even buys expensive stuff for the house."

"I will admit, she does have high-class taste when it comes to decorating."

"And you know that comforter set you couldn't stop talking about on Saturday?"

"Mm-hm."

"Well, in all total, including the bathroom towels and other accessories, she paid nearly twelve hundred dollars for it."

"No, Phillip. There's no way."

"It's true. She thought the other one was too cheap and that you and Dad deserved a lot better than that. We argued all night on Friday and we barely spoke on Saturday morning, and that's why I wasn't myself by the time you and Dad got there."

"Son, I am so sorry."

Phillip sighed in a defeated manner. "I just don't know what I can do to make her stop. And actually the more I've thought about it over the last few days, I don't think I can because Alicia has always been used to getting whatever she wants since she was a child. Curtis always earned good money, even before he became as wealthy as he is now, so all my wife has ever known is brand-name clothing and fine jewelry. She thinks it's a crime to even look at costume jewelry or sterling silver unless it's designed by John Hardy or Judith Ripka, which are both very expensive."

"Have you talked to her—not just while arguing, but seriously?"

"Until I'm blue in the face, but that doesn't even faze her. She still does whatever she wants to do, and she resents me for talking about it. She says I'm trying to control her."

"Maybe it's time the two of you went to see a marriage counselor, because if you allow this problem to get worse, you might not be able to fix it or save your marriage."

"I agree, because if Alicia continues spending money the way she has been, we'll be drowning in debt in no time."

"You need to find a counselor and make an appointment as soon as possible."

"I have thought about it before, but I sort of told myself things weren't bad enough to warrant seeing a counselor. Which is strange because as assistant pastor, I counsel members of the church from time to time and I encourage it, but I guess we all look at things a little differently when we're dealing with a problem ourselves."

Phillip's mom patted his hand. "Everything will work out. You just make that appointment so you and your wife can get the help you need."

"I will. Just as soon as Dad gets better," Phillip agreed and felt a new ray of hope where he and Alicia were concerned.

Chapter 13

Alicia had called her mother a little earlier, letting her know about Phillip's father, and her mother had told her that she and James would stop over at the hospital when they left work. Now, she was dialing Phillip's cell to see how everything was going. She'd spoken to him last night, once she'd gotten home and then again first thing this morning, but she hadn't heard from him in the last couple of hours.

"Hi, baby."

"How's your dad?"

"He's still about the same but thankfully not any worse, and Dr. Nicholson was in not long ago, saying that this was a good sign."

"I've really been praying for him, Phillip, and my mom and James will be by this evening."

"That's very kind of them. And your dad called and said that he and Charlotte will be here before five."

"You know, of course, I'm worried about your dad and your mom, too, but how are you holding up?"

"As well as can be expected, considering the circumstances."

"I know this is hard, and I just wish I could make things better."

"Praying is the most any of us can do, and you're already doing that, so you're fine."

"Do you need me to bring anything other than the bag you wanted me to pack?"

"No, I don't need much. Just some extra clothing and my toiletries."

"What about your mom?"

"Her best friend has a key to the house, so she went by to pick up a few things for her."

"Miss Thelma?"

"Oh, that's right. I forgot you met her at the wedding. She's just like a sister to Mom and since Mom's brother and sister are deceased, she's the only sisterlike person she has in her life. Then, you know Dad's only brother is in a nursing home, suffering from Alzheimer's disease, so it's not like we have a lot of family."

"It's pretty much the same for me because my mom is an only child, and even though my dad has a sister, they don't have a relationship."

"I know. Your dad has talked to me about that before, and that really bothers him."

"Well, hey, I guess I'll let you go so I can get going. But call me if you remember something you need before I get there. I'm planning to leave the house in a few minutes."

"Thanks, baby. And hey, I miss you."

"I miss you, too, and I'll see you soon."

"You drive safely."

"I will."

Alicia ended the call, dropped her phone on the seat, and felt bad. Terrible, guilty, and less than the person her parents had raised her to be was more like it—because she was nowhere near home. She'd told Phillip she was going to be on her way to

Chicago but in all honesty, she was already there—sitting in a mall parking lot, waiting for the stores to open in about ten minutes. She'd known it was wrong for her to stop here, what with her husband needing her by his side, but since he seemed to be doing okay, she didn't see where stopping at the mall for a couple of hours was going to make much difference. Plus, had Phillip told her that his father wasn't doing well or that he was worse, she would have immediately told him the truth, that she was only about twenty minutes away.

She didn't like lying to him the way she'd been doing as of late, but he made her feel like she had to. If only he'd stop micromanaging her spending the way he did, she wouldn't have to sneak around or lie about anything. If only, he'd finally come to the realization that it was crazy to save every dime for an uncertain future and not enjoy some of the good things in life before it was too late. His father was genuine proof that tragedy or illness could strike at any time, and all she could hope was that maybe now, Phillip would finally see things differently. Maybe he'd realize that enjoying life to the fullest should be their priority.

After exactly two hours had passed, Alicia left the mall and was proud of the fact that the only items she'd purchased were a Nike sweat suit, something she would need in a couple of months when it was warm enough to get back out on the bike path, and a matching pair of Nike athletic shoes. Even better, she'd gotten all of it for less than two hundred dollars.

Now, she was in the car, turning the ignition, but for some reason, her car wouldn't start. She turned the ignition again. And again and still nothing happened. It made no sound at all, and all she could hear was a slight click. She didn't know a lot about cars, but she did know that if there was no sound, there was probably something wrong with her battery or there was some sort of electrical problem. So, she sat there for a minute, trying to figure out what she should do next because there was no way she could call Phillip and tell him where she was stranded.

She sat for another couple of minutes and then opened the glove compartment. She pulled out the thick leather case, pulled out the service card, and dialed BMW's toll-free number. She gave them her name and all of the other information they needed, and they told her they'd send a tow truck out right away. They'd also said they'd send someone out from the dealership to pick her up so she could ride back with them to get one of their loaner vehicles, which actually, she was very happy about because if she hadn't owned a car manufactured by a company like BMW, she'd have had to rent some pitiful-looking rental car.

In the meantime, while she waited, she thought about going back inside the mall to browse around a few more stores but figured she'd better wait for the tow truck. Instead, she called Melanie.

"Hey, girl, I just got a chance to listen to your message and was about to call you."

"Can you believe Phillip's father had a heart attack?"

"No, and I'm really sorry to hear it. I see cases like your father-in-law's all the time, and it's never an easy situation."

"But he's not going to die, is he?"

"I won't lie to you. People have died, but there are so many people who recover from quadruple bypass surgery and go on to have normal and very productive lives. He'll probably have to be on heart and cholesterol medication for the rest of his life, but that's a small price to pay when we're talking life or death."

"I just hate that this is happening. Phillip is extremely close to his father, and his mother isn't taking this very well herself."

"That's totally understandable, but I'm sure he's in good hands."

"Yes, he's at one of the hospitals that specialize in heart surgeries, so we're really happy about that."

"Are you there now?"

Alicia paused at first. "Um, no, I was on my way but my car broke down, so now I'm sitting here waiting for the tow truck."

"That's not good. What do you think is wrong?"

"I don't know. But BMW is having it towed to one of their Chicago dealerships, so I'm sure they'll get it taken care of pretty quickly."

"Are you going to have Phillip come pick you up?"

"He doesn't have his truck because yesterday we rushed over with my dad and Charlotte, and then I came home with them last night so I could get my car and come back over to the hospital this morning."

"Oh, then how will you get there?"

"They're having someone from the dealership pick me up so they can take me back to get a loaner vehicle, but I'm hoping the dealership isn't too far away because, right now, I'm only twenty minutes away from the hospital, and I really want to get there as soon as I can."

"Well, let me know if there is anything I can do. I have to work the next four days straight but you know I'll take off in a second if you need me to be there for you."

"I know that, but for now I think we're okay."

"And don't hesitate to call me if for some reason Phillip and his mom have medical questions that they're not getting answers to, and I'll connect them with one of the doctors here at our heart center."

"I will, and I'll definitely keep you posted on what's going on."

"Please do, and I'll check in with you as well."

"Okay, well, I guess I should go because it looks like the tow truck is already here. They must have been very close by."

"Take care, and call me."

"See ya."

Alicia waited for the truck to make its way around to the aisle where she was parked, and then she stepped out of her vehicle.

Two handsome young men got out, and the driver walked closer to her. "Are you Alicia Sullivan?"

"Yes, that's me."

"Sorry about your car."

"Thanks, but it happens."

"Here's our card and on the back of it is the address of the dealership where we'll be taking your vehicle to."

Alicia glanced over it. "Thanks."

"Do you have everything out of it that you want to take with you?"

"Just a couple of bags and my purse but that's pretty much it."

"Well, while you're getting that, we'll go ahead and start the hook-up process."

"Sounds good."

Alicia gathered her belongings from the car and stood to the side. It didn't take them very long to load her car onto the flatbed and, thankfully, a representative from the dealership was just pulling up. Soon after, the towing company employees finished what they needed to do and waved good-bye to her.

The salt-and-pepper-haired man from the dealership greeted her and then opened the passenger side of the car for her. She asked him how far they had to drive and he told her about thirty minutes. Which wouldn't have been such a big deal, except now it had been almost three hours since she'd spoken to Phillip, and she knew he was probably wondering where she was. But she guessed there was no sense worrying herself about it because it wasn't like she had any other options.

About an hour later, Alicia drove away in a silver BMW and headed straight for the hospital. Within minutes, her phone rang. It was Phillip, but she was now okay to talk to him because she had her story ready. Actually, she'd left him a message about fifteen minutes ago, and she was glad he was calling her back.

"So what happened to the car?"

"I don't know. It just wouldn't start?"

"And it stopped on you right in the middle of traffic while you were driving on the expressway?"

"Yes, and these two men had to stop and help push it to the side of the road."

"Are you okay?"

"I'm fine. But it took a while for the tow truck to come, and then I had to go to the dealership. I'm finally on my way now, though."

"Good. And the reason I didn't answer when you called earlier was that Mom and I were talking to the doctor."

"What did he say?"

"Not much, except that nothing's changed and that no news is good news. Oh, and your dad and Charlotte are here. They decided to miss the elder board meeting so they could come back over."

"I'm surprised they didn't call me."

"They thought you were already here. And actually, I told them you should be arriving any minute, but then I figured maybe you didn't get to leave home right when you said."

"Actually, I left a little later but not by much."

"It's been good having them and Miss Thelma here for the last couple of hours because, baby . . . this is hard. And I really need you right now."

"I'm only about a half hour away or less, and I'm sorry the car broke down. Otherwise I would have already been there."

"You can't help what happened, so don't feel bad about that. But, baby, just get here as soon as you can because, like I said, I really need you. I wanted to tell you that so badly when you called me this morning. I kept thinking how if for some reason Dad got worse and he didn't make it, I really wanted you here. But I didn't say anything because I didn't want to sound like some wimp. Plus, I wanted you to get as much rest as you could and take your time getting ready because I knew we'd have to be here all day and all night."

"I'm really sorry I didn't leave home earlier, but I'll be there shortly."

"I love you, Alicia."

"I love you, too."

Alicia drove about ten miles and then cringed when she saw that traffic was starting to back up. It wasn't even three o'clock yet, so she hoped there hadn't been an accident. If that was the case, it would take her forever to arrive at her destination. She coasted along and then changed lanes, but that didn't help much. She did this for forty minutes, and then finally she saw flashing lights. There really had been an accident.

Finally, though, it only took her another twenty minutes to drive beyond it, and fifteen minutes after that, she pulled into the hospital lot. After parking, she hurried into the building, and took the elevator up to the fifth floor.

But when the doors opened, and she walked toward the waiting area, she saw Charlotte wiping away tears and a regretful look on her father's face.

"We didn't want to call you while you were driving, but, baby girl, he's gone."

"What?"

"Your father-in-law is gone."

"Where's Phillip?"

"He and his mom are in with him, saying good-bye."

"No. But I just talked to Phillip, and he said nothing had changed."

"I know, but as soon as he hung up we heard a code being called on the PA system, and then we found out it was for him. But come on, you need to go in there because Phillip isn't taking this well at all. Charlotte and I only left him and his mom because we wanted to tell you as soon as you got here."

Alicia followed her father's direction, but all she could think was that if she hadn't stopped at the mall, she would have gotten to see her father-in-law before he passed, and she would have been there for Phillip when it happened.

She already felt guilty for lying to him in the first place, but this was the absolute worst.

Chapter 14

*P*hillip finally knew what it meant to have the wind knocked clean out of him because that's exactly how he'd felt when the doctor had pronounced his father dead. His father had flat-lined without warning, and although the ICU medical staff had tried their best to revive him, they hadn't been able to do so. Phillip had stood at a distance, studying them as they worked frantically and he was glad his mother had chosen to remain in the waiting area. As a matter of fact, he was sure he wasn't sup-posed to be inside the unit either, not while a code was being handled, but with all that was going on, he guessed they hadn't paid much attention to him.

Now, though, one day later, he wished he'd waited outside like everyone else, because he would never forget what it was like, physically watching his father die. It had been horrible, and the only solace he'd been able to find last night was in the arms of his wife. It was true that he'd never been more hurt, felt more empty, or felt more alone, but it had helped having Alicia right there with him. Loving him, caressing him, consoling him. And then, while he hadn't wanted anyone to see him in such a sad state, he was thankful to Miss Thelma and Curtis and Charlotte for being with them at the hospital and then coming to his parents' house. He was thankful to his other set of in-laws, too, Tanya and James, as well as a few of the members from his parents' church because they'd dropped by and kept his mother's spirits up as best they could.

It was a rough time in Phillip's life, and it was only going to get worse as the day went on because in a few hours they'd have to head out to the funeral home to make his father's arrangements. Phillip already dreaded going near that place and couldn't wait for that part to be over with.

Phillip went into the newly remodeled kitchen, the one his parents had finally decided to upgrade after more than thirty years, and sat down at the table. His mother, Miss Thelma, and Alicia were eating breakfast.

His mother smoothed the side of his face. "You okay?"

"Not really, but . . ."

"Can I fix you something to eat?" Miss Thelma asked.

"No, thank you. I'm not really hungry."

"Well, you're going to have to eat sometime, and it may as well be now."

He could tell Miss Thelma wasn't planning to take no very easily, but his stomach was tying itself in knots and he just didn't have an appetite.

"You know we have to meet with the funeral director in a couple of hours."

Phillip nodded and then looked down at the table.

"Son, I know this is hard, but there's no sense putting off what we know we have to do."

"You're right, but I'm just dreading this, and it's almost like this isn't real."

"I feel the same way, and this morning when I first woke up, I turned to look at your father and then realized he wasn't there. I realized he was never going to be there ever again." Phillip's mother shed a few tears, but then quickly got control of herself. "I felt like I wanted to die, too, but then I thought about how the last thing your father would want us to do is fret over him. He always used to say that just as surely as we come here, we're going to leave here, and there ain't no sense in trying to maneuver your way around it."

Miss Thelma smiled. "That sure is what he would say. He said that all the time."

"Then he would go on to talk about how he knew he was never going to be a rich man but that whenever it came time to put him away, he wanted to go in style. He would talk about how he wanted all the stops to be pulled so he could have a memorable send-off. He even made sure he got an extra insurance policy just to cover his funeral expenses."

Phillip wasn't interested in any of what his mother and Miss Thelma were talking about, but he pretended that he was. He knew they were trying to stay positive, look on the bright side of things, and he didn't want to hurt their feelings. "Then we'll do exactly what Dad would have wanted."

"That we will."

"I think I'm going to get dressed."

"Go ahead, son. Do what you need to do."

Phillip left and went back into the bedroom and Alicia followed behind him.

"I just don't see how this is ever going to get better."

"I know, honey, but it will."

"My parents have always been everything to me but now my father is gone. Then, on top of that, I'm worried about my mom. She hasn't been alone in all these years, so who's going to look out for her?"

"We'll look out for her. Miss Thelma will and other people, too."

"But it won't be the same. It won't be the same as having someone here with her day in and day out. It won't be the same at all."

Alicia didn't say anything but reached out to hug him. He felt so secure when they embraced this way, and it was the only thing keeping him going.

"I'm having a tough time with this, too, though, because I'm so hurt that I didn't get to see him again. Not ever did I think that when he and Mom Katherine left Mitchell on Sunday that that would be the last time I would see him alive."

"But, baby, we already went over that, and there's no reason for you to feel bad. You didn't leave home until late morning and then with the car quitting on the expressway, you couldn't help not being there. It would have been nice for you to have seen him, but you had no control over that."

"I know, but I still feel bad. I should have been there for you when it happened."

"I wish you could have because while I was trying to console Mom, I still couldn't wait for you to walk through those doors. I mean, if there was ever a time when I needed you, it was then and now. But like I said, there was nothing you could have done that would have gotten you to the hospital any earlier, so stop beating yourself up."

"I'll try, and I just want you to know that I'll do anything you want me to do. For you or your mom."

Phillip hugged her and was glad he had such a compassionate wife, the kind any man needed at a time such as this.

Mom Katherine browsed through the catalog but then turned back to the page that showed a casket designed in cherry wood. It was beautifully polished and looked every bit worth the three thousand dollars the coffin manufacturer was charging.

"This is the one. This is the one Phil would want, and I even think one time he showed me a picture of one that was pretty similar."

She passed the catalog over to Phillip, and he took a closer look. "Whatever you want is fine with me. It's definitely a nice one, if there is such a thing as a nice casket."

The funeral director, who sort of looked dead himself, spoke up. "It's one of our top sellers and one of the best you can buy in this category. It's an excellent choice."

Mom Katherine took the catalog back and looked at it one last time. "What do you think, Thelma?"

"It's beautiful. Very elegant."

"Then we'll take it. Phil wanted something exquisite, and I think this will do very nicely."

Alicia sat listening to the way Mom Katherine and Miss Thelma carried on about the casket, but to her it sounded more like they were shopping for high-priced living room furniture. Maybe she was just too young to understand it but from the look on Phillip's face, he didn't get it either.

Then, the place in general gave her the creeps. The atmosphere seemed morbid, as did the music that was playing in the background, and Alicia couldn't wait to get out of there.

"Now, you're sure this is okay with you?" Mom Katherine asked Phillip again.

"Yes, really, Mom, it is."

Actually, Alicia was a bit surprised that Phillip hadn't made any objections because when it came to anything else, including her, he was very money conscious and was always worried about paying too much for everything. But maybe he was okay with this because he didn't have to pay anything out of his own pocket.

After deciding on which vault to go with, something Alicia had no idea about because she'd always thought the casket itself went straight into the ground and didn't need anything to protect it, they ordered a limousine to serve as the family car, and then decided on the day and time of the funeral, which would be three days from now on Saturday. The visitation would take place three hours before the service started.

When they finished, they headed over to the flower shop and ordered a flower blanket for the casket as well as family wreaths. One would have a ribbon that said, "husband," one would say "father," and the other two would say "father-in-law" and "brother."

They were finally headed home but when Mom Katherine remembered that she'd forgotten to pick up the clothes she'd dropped off at the cleaners a couple of days ago, Phillip took her by there to get them. While she was inside, the dealership called Alicia's cell phone.

"Hello?"

"Hi, is this Alicia?"

"Yes, it is."

"This is Richard Freeman calling from Jay Carson, the BMW dealership your car was towed to, and I wanted to let you know that we have it ready for you."

"Oh, thank you. We'll pick it up in a little while."

"You had some electrical issues going on, but now you should be good to go."

"Sounds good, and thanks again."

"See you soon."

Phillip looked at her. "Your car ready?"

"Yep."

"Well, as soon as we drop Mom and Miss Thelma at home, we can swing by and pick it up."

When Mom Katherine came out of the cleaners, Phillip asked her if she needed him to get out and help her but when she said, "absolutely not, you stay where you are," apparently trying to prove her independence, he popped the trunk with the interior latch, she laid the clothing inside, and then got back into the car. It only took ten minutes to arrive at the house and then Alicia and Phillip headed out to the dealership.

There had been some traffic but thankfully not enough to slow them down to a crawl the way that accident had caused her to do yesterday.

Phillip pulled into the parking lot, turned off the ignition, and they walked inside.

Alicia smiled at the service guy. "We're here to pick up a car for Sullivan."

"Yes, I'm Richard, the one who called you," he said extending his hand to both of them.

"So, she shouldn't have any problems after this?" Phillip asked.

Richard passed Alicia the key that had a service tag attached to it. "No, not at all. It was electrical, but she's all set. And it was completely under warranty, so there's no charge."

"Sounds good."

"You two take care."

They went back outside, and Alicia walked around to the passenger door. "Do you wanna drive?"

"That's fine, but you know what? Mom didn't take her clothes from the cleaners out of the trunk of the loaner, so let me run back in to get the key."

"Oh yeah, that's right."

Alicia got in the car and turned on the radio. Beyoncé was singing one of her older singles, "Me, Myself and I," and Alicia loved that. She even started singing some of the lyrics but then stopped midsentence when she saw Phillip heading toward her, carrying two Macy's bags. With everything that had gone on with her father-in-law, she'd totally forgotten about them and all she could hope was that Phillip hadn't looked inside them. If she was lucky, maybe he'd just assume these bags were just part of the stuff she'd brought with her from home yesterday.

But when she saw the outraged look on his face and the receipt he was carrying in his hand, she knew he'd figured out everything.

Phillip bypassed the driver's side and walked around to where she was sitting. "What's this, Alicia?"

"What?"

He pushed the receipt closer to her. "This. This receipt from Macy's that has a time of ten twenty A.M. on it."

Alicia saw a couple of customers looking over at them. "Phillip, please just get in the car. You're making a scene."

"That's the least of my worries, so just tell me. How could you have made a purchase twenty minutes after the store opened, if you were still in Mitchell right before ten? Because last I checked, Mitchell is easily an hour and forty-five minutes from the mall listed on this receipt."

"It's not what you think."

"*Not what I think*? Then what is it exactly? Explain it to me."

"If you get in the car, I will."

"No. I want you to tell me now. But you can't, can you, because you know you've been caught in your lie?"

"Will you please stop all this yelling? This is crazy."

"So, now I guess I'm wondering where the car really broke down. Were you really on the expressway like you said?"

Alicia turned away from him and looked straight ahead.

But Phillip opened up the bag that contained the athletic shoes and pulled out the receipt for those and scanned it as well.

"Did you even try this stuff on? Because it looks like you bought these barely twenty minutes later."

Alicia didn't want to make him more neurotic than he was, so she would never tell him that she hadn't tried any of it on and that she didn't have to because she knew her sizes.

Two of the service men stood a few feet away. "Sir, is everything okay?"

Phillip opened the back door of the car and threw the bags on the backseat. "Everything is fine, and I'm sorry for the disturbance."

Then he finally got in the car and drove away.

"Honey, I am so, so sorry."

She waited for Phillip to say something, but he drove in silence. He never even looked at her.

"Phillip, please listen to me. I wasn't there very long, and I was only twenty minutes away from the hospital."

Still he wouldn't say anything.

"Please don't be mad at me. I now realize that I shouldn't have stopped there, but I promise it won't happen again. I'm really, really sorry, and I'll never forgive myself for what I did yesterday."

Phillip finally turned and looked at her. "Oh yeah? Well, that's good because neither will I."

Chapter 15

$\mathcal{A}$s soon as Alicia and Phillip walked inside his parents' house, he went straight into the bedroom.

Mom Katherine frowned and then called out to him. "Phillip? What's wrong?"

But Alicia heard him close the door.

"What's wrong with him?"

"We had an argument."

"Oh. Well, sometimes that's what married people do."

Miss Thelma laughed. "Isn't that the truth? I argued with my Johnny all the time, God rest his soul. But we wouldn't have traded each other for anything."

Mom Katherine patted her hand on the table. "Go ahead and sit down, sweetheart. He'll be fine, and maybe you should just give him some time alone. He's probably just a little on edge because he's hurting so badly over his father."

Alicia took a seat and hung her Gucci shoulder bag over the back of the chair, the one she'd bought herself for graduation. Her mother-in-law and Miss Thelma were sorting through photos.

"Is there anything I can do?"

"Well, once we pick out a few good photos of Phil and also

some family photos we can use, we'll still need to pick out a suit for your father-in-law so we can get it over to the funeral home by tomorrow. Then, we need to put together the obituary information and the way we want the order of service to go, so the church can get the programs formatted and printed."

"I can do that, but maybe Phillip will want to help you pick out a suit for his dad."

"Maybe, but I don't know because he's just not himself."

That was putting it lightly. Alicia had seen him angry in the past, plenty of times over the last few weeks, but she'd never seen him quite this infuriated, the way he'd been this afternoon. He'd acted as though she'd killed somebody. Yes, she was wrong for stopping at the mall, and yes, she was wrong for lying to him, but it wasn't like she'd gone out and slept with another man. She was guilty as charged but not of the kind of crime he was making this out to be. She was sorry—more than sorry—but Phillip was taking this too far.

"If you have some paper," Alicia said, "we can just stay in here to figure out the program, and that way, you can keep going through the photos while we do it. I could just write everything down and then go into the den to type it up."

"That would be good. There should be a pad of paper and some pens in the desk that the computer sits on."

Alicia got up and went to get the paper and came back to the kitchen. Then she pulled out her black Mont Blanc pen to write with. She'd seen some generic pens, the same as Mom Katherine had told her, but Alicia preferred using her own. She'd gotten used to the feel of it and rarely used anything else. At three hundred dollars, her writing instrument had cost her quite a bit, even in her opinion, but she loved it so and was glad she'd bought it.

"I guess we should start with the obituary," Mom Katherine

said. "Because we'll also need to get this to the funeral home so they can submit it to our suburban newspaper."

Alicia opened the notebook. "I'm ready when you are."

"I have a number of sample funeral programs that I kept when certain friends at the church passed away, so you can use them as an example."

"Okay."

"We'll need his full name, his age, and the day he died and that he departed after a short illness. Then, we can list where he was born, his parents' names, where he worked and for how long before retiring, and that he was a faithful member of Shiloh Missionary Baptist Church as well as a member of the male chorus there."

Alicia jotted down everything her mother-in-law was saying and once she finished with the family section, which wasn't very long, she added the name of the funeral home and the cemetery location.

"For the service, we can use the same format as one of the samples I'm going to pull out for you, but I do want to make sure that the two solos are 'The Lord's Prayer' and 'His Eye Is on the Sparrow.'"

Alicia smiled when she thought about how much Phillip loved that song and how he'd just requested that one of the teenagers in the youth choir sing it this past Sunday.

"Your father-in-law loved that song and so do I. We've loved it for years, and I guess that's why it's one of Phillip's favorites, too."

"I was just thinking how he'd asked Brittany to sing it when you and Dad Phil were in town."

Mom Katherine rested her hands on the table and sighed. "I know. And who would have guessed that two days later Phil would be gone. Just like that."

Alicia rubbed the side of her mother-in-law's arm.

"I'm okay. Just having one of my moments is all."

"And there's not a thing wrong with it," Miss Thelma added. "I've been in your shoes and know just how you feel, but time really does heal all wounds. Most people think that's just some saying, but I'm here to tell you, it's really true."

"Well, I sure hope so because what I'm feeling now is so painful. It's the kind of pain that reaches deep down in your soul and feels like it will never get better. Not even twenty years from now."

"But I promise you, Kat, it does. It took me a long time, and while I'm still not over it, even after a whole decade, I've learned to accept it and go on with my life."

Alicia listened to them talking about the loss of their husbands and it made her want to go check on Phillip—beg him to forgive her—although, earlier, he'd sounded as though he was never going to do that. But maybe it was like his mother had said, he was only acting this way because he was having a hard time dealing with his father's death.

When Mom Katherine finished giving Alicia all of the details, including the scripture she wanted typed on the back of the program, 2 Corinthians 5:6–8, Alicia went into the den and turned on the computer. She smiled when she saw her and Phillip's wedding photo as the screensaver. Phillip's parents really were proud of their only son, and they really were glad to have her as a daughter-in-law. She already knew this, but for some reason seeing their wedding photo seemed special.

Alicia looked in the bottom right-hand drawer and pulled out a couple of the sample funeral programs her mother-in-law had told her about and then opened Microsoft Word.

She set her font type and size to Times Roman 10 and began entering the information. She'd majored in English and minored in public relations, but she was glad she'd taken typing classes her last couple of years in high school and also at the community college the summer before she'd left for the university. She was also glad she'd learned a few of the business software programs because it had made all the difference when she'd had to write papers and create presentation materials. It would also make all the difference when she finally buckled down and started writing her novel. She didn't know why she kept putting it off, but once things settled down with Phillip and they made sure his mother was okay, she would finally go ahead and get started. She had a ton of ideas floating through her head, but it was time she picked one of those ideas and went with it. Especially since she was the one who'd chosen writing over going to law school, so now she needed to follow through on it.

When Alicia finished the program, she reread it a couple of times, did some editing here and there, and then printed it out so her mother-in-law could take a look at it. But before she took it to her, she went down the hall and walked into the bedroom where Phillip was.

He immediately said, "How could you be so selfish? How could you actually lie about what time you left home, lie about where you were when the car broke down, and worst of all, how could you go shopping, when you knew my father was in critical condition? You knew that, and you knew how upset I was."

Alicia shut the door, hoping her mother-in-law and Miss Thelma hadn't heard him, and then she let her tears fall. "Phillip . . . honey . . . I'm sorry. I'm really, really sorry. I wish I could take back what I did, but I can't."

"You're right. You are sorry. You're sorry and you're pathetic, and I hate the day I ever laid eyes on you."

His words sent scores of chills through her body. "How can you say that? And all because I made one mistake?"

"One mistake? Alicia, my father is dead! Gone! And you didn't even bother to be there for me. You weren't there for your own husband."

Alicia sniffled and took a step toward him but he stopped her.

"Don't even think about it. And as a matter of fact, I think it would be best if you just left here."

"You don't mean that."

"You think I don't? Get out. Get out and stay out."

"Honey, please. Please don't do this, because I really want to be here for you. I want to be here for your mom. You know how much I loved your dad. I loved him a lot."

Phillip laughed out loud. "You loved him, huh?"

"I did. You know I did."

"Yeah, you loved him all right. You loved him enough not to come see him before he died. You loved him so much that you stopped at some stupid mall to buy a sweat suit and some gym shoes."

"I know I was wrong for doing that, but I wasn't thinking. I wasn't thinking, and I thought he was going to be fine."

"Well, he's not fine, Alicia. He's dead. Now, for the last time . . . get out."

"Phillip, please. I'm begging you not to do this."

Phillip stood up. "I want you out of here! Not later, not tomorrow, not even the day after! I want you out now!"

He was now yelling like a crazy man, so Alicia opened the door and walked out of the room. Her mother-in-law met her in the hallway.

"Alicia, sweetheart, what's going on?"

"Phillip wants me to leave."

She walked to the front of the room and Alicia stood behind her. "Phillip, baby, what's wrong?"

"I don't want her here."

"Why?"

Phillip looked at Alicia. "Tell her. Tell her what you did."

"I'm sorry, Mom Katherine, but I'm leaving."

"No, tell her how you lied all day yesterday and that while we were sitting at the hospital, praying that Dad would be okay, you were out shopping at the mall like it was nothing. Tell her how you made up that story about the car being stopped in traffic when you were actually sitting in the mall parking lot. And then you had the audacity to dream up two men who supposedly stopped and helped you push the car to the side of the expressway. It's bad enough that you lied about where the car broke down but to turn the lie into this whole detailed story, well, that's just being deceitful. It's just plain dishonest."

"Phillip, I know you're hurting but you really need your wife right now and she needs you," Mom Katherine said.

"No, I needed her yesterday."

"I realize that, but whether you want to realize it or not, there's nothing Alicia could have done to save your father. There's nothing any of us could have done."

Phillip walked away from his mother and over toward the window. "Mom, I definitely don't mean any disrespect to you, but I'm done talking about this."

Mom Katherine shut the bedroom door. "Honey, he just needs to cool down. And when he does, he'll see that the only reason he's lashing out at you is because of all the pain he's feeling. This is the first time Phillip has ever lost anyone this close to him, and I just don't think he knows how to deal with it. Just give him a little time."

"I want to be here for him, but maybe it really is best for me to drive home and then just come back tomorrow."

"I truly hate to see you go but if you think that's best."

"I do because I've never seen him this angry before. It's almost like I don't even know him."

"Everything will be fine. You'll see."

Alicia hugged her mother-in-law and hoped she was right. Because if she wasn't, she wasn't sure what she could possibly do to fix this.

Chapter 16

*P*hillip slowly opened his eyes, glanced over at the clock sitting on the nightstand, and saw that it was seven in the
evening. He hadn't meant to fall asleep and had never been a
nap taker, but after arguing with Alicia and thinking about his
dad, he guessed the emotional strain had taken its toll. Not to
mention, he hadn't slept much at all the night before and when
he had dropped off for a few minutes here and there, he'd had
vivid dreams about his father. He would dream something
happy about him, but then he'd wake up and realize his father
was gone, and the continuous cycle of dreams only depressed
him even more.

Then, there was this thing with his wife. The woman he
loved and would do anything for—yet here she'd acted as though
his father's illness hadn't even mattered to her. She'd acted as
though she had no obligation to stand by her husband, and Phillip now saw her in a totally different light. Her obsession and
addiction to shopping had been one thing, but this was something much worse, and he didn't know how they'd ever get past
it. He didn't know how he'd ever be able to look her in her face,
without immediately thinking about the low-down way she'd
treated him. She'd actually wasted precious time at some mall,

looking for athletic gear, for God's sake, and he couldn't see where any decent person would do something like that.

Phillip sighed and then sat up on the side of the bed. He sat there for a few seconds with his hands covering his face and then reached over and picked up his cell phone. He saw that he had three voice-mail messages and wondered how many of them were from Alicia.

But when he went through his call log, he didn't see her number. Instead there were numbers for Curtis and his best friend Brad, and a number he didn't recognize.

He dialed into the system and listened to them.

"Phillip, this is Curtis, and I just wanted to check in to see how things are going and to let you know that our prayers are still with you. I tried calling Alicia's phone, too, but I guess you guys are busy right now. I also wanted to know if you'd decided on Saturday as the day for the funeral, so give me a call when you get this message. Take care."

Phillip deleted the message and played the next one.

"Hey, Phil, man, this is Brad. I was in court all day today and I have to prepare for tomorrow, but then I'll get over to see you and your mom sometime tomorrow night. Also, I know when we talked early this morning, you'd said you were probably going to shoot for Saturday as the day to have the funeral, so let me know. I'm there regardless of what day it is, but I just wanted to confirm. Also, I just want to say that I can do whatever you need me to do, and all you have to do is say the word."

Phillip deleted Brad's message and then played the last one.

"Hi, Pastor Phillip, this is Linda. Pastor Black told all of us here at the church about your father, and we're just sick over the news. But please know that we're all thinking about you and praying for you and your family. You don't have to call me back unless you need something, anything at all, but if not we'll see you at the funeral. I haven't heard when that is yet, but I'm sure Pastor Black will let the entire administrative team know, and of course you'll be hearing from the bereavement ministry by no later than tomorrow, and we'll be announcing the news about your father at Bible study tonight. Now, you take care of yourself and also your mom and we'll see you soon, okay? We love you."

He deleted his assistant's message and smiled at how kind Linda always was to everyone. She went out of her way to do the best work she could for him and he was glad he'd hired her.

Next, he called Curtis.

"Hello?"

"Curtis, hey, how are you?"

"I'm good. And you?"

"Hanging in there."

"And your mom?"

"She's doing pretty well. She's handling this a lot better than I expected her to and a lot better than I am."

"She's a strong woman. There's no doubt that she's hurt, but she seems like the type that will do whatever she has to do, no matter how bad things are."

"She is. But she was so sad and afraid while Dad was undergoing surgery that I just assumed she would fall to pieces if we lost him."

"I'm sure she's still afraid. Anybody would be if they'd been with someone for most of their life and then now find themselves alone."

"That's true."

"Hey, before I forget, is the funeral on Saturday?"

"It is. We made the final arrangements today, and everything is all set."

"Good. And why isn't Alicia answering her phone?

Phillip hesitated answering. He wasn't sure if he should just say she wasn't there or go ahead and tell Curtis the truth.

"She's not here, so I'm not sure."

"Did she say where she was going?"

"No, she didn't."

"How long has she been gone?"

"Maybe three or four hours. Okay, look Curtis, I might as well just tell you what happened. We had a really bad argument, and I asked her to leave."

"Did she do something?"

"She did, and while I love Alicia, I'm really upset with her right now."

"I'm sorry to hear that, Phillip. Is there something I can do?"

"No. This is just something Alicia and I need to work out with each other, so I hope you understand that."

"I do. I'm Alicia's father, but I would never get involved unless you asked me to. I just hate to see this happening while you're mourning the loss of your father. It's not good, Phillip, because if this was ever a time for the two of you to come together, this is certainly it."

"I know, and all I'll say is that Alicia tends to care about Alicia, and she doesn't always consider how her actions are going to affect other people. Specifically, how they're going to affect me."

"Are you sure you don't want me to talk to her?"

"No. I mean, you can talk to her if you want but I really doubt she's going to give you any details. If for some reason she does want to tell you, then that's fine but if not . . ."

"I'll respect your wishes, but I still hate this is going on right now."

"All I want to do is get through the next few days, make sure my mom is okay, and then try to get back to normal. Get back to whatever normal is now going to be for me."

"Well, I hope you'll call me if you want to talk or need me to do anything before the funeral."

"Well, I was hoping you'd say a few words at the service if you don't mind."

"I would be glad to, and it would be an honor."

"I think my mom and Alicia were working on the program earlier but we'd talked about it already, so I'm sure they have you listed."

"I look forward to it. And Phillip, I know this is probably the most difficult time in your life, but don't forget to keep your faith in God. Keep it strong and don't stop believing what He can do for you. Don't stop asking Him to give you the kind of strength and understanding you're going to need in the coming weeks."

"I won't."

"Well, I won't keep you, but tell your mom we're thinking about her."

"I will. And thanks, Curtis, for everything."

"Anytime."

Phillip hung up the phone and set it back down on the nightstand. Then he got up and went into the living room. His mom, Miss Thelma, and a few other men and women who were probably some of his parents' friends and church members were all sitting and standing around, laughing and talking.

"So you finally woke up," his mom said, walking over to him.

Phillip spoke to everyone, and then he and his mom went into the kitchen.

"Are you feeling better, son?"

"Not really."

"Well, you know I'm not one to pry in your business, but son, I just wish you'd try to get over this thing with Alicia. She made a mistake, but the two of you need to be together at a time like this."

"It's not that easy, Mom. Alicia has really crossed the line this time, and if I see her, it's only going to make me more upset than I already am."

"You're being stubborn."

"No. I just don't appreciate what she did."

"Nobody's perfect. And there's no such thing as a marriage without problems."

"I know that, but it wasn't even just the fact that she stopped at the mall when she knew how sick Dad was, it's more about the fact that she lied. She lied to me more than once and when people lie, they're letting you know right then and there that they can't be trusted."

"I hear what you're saying, and I'm not making any excuses for her, but the reason she probably lied is because she really does have a serious shopping problem. You and I just talked about that two days ago, remember?"

"Still. Problem or not, I should have been her priority. She should have been at that hospital, and she never should have lied to me. Because after this, how am I ever going to know when she's lying or when she's telling the truth? And now that I think about it, how do I know she hasn't been lying to me about one thing or another since the very beginning?"

His mother sighed and moved a couple of dirty glasses into the sink. "I hate this."

"I hate it, too, but it is what it is. I married a woman I really didn't know, and now I'm dealing with the consequences."

"That's not true. Because I can tell that Alicia really does love you, and I know you love her."

"Mom, that may be true, but that still doesn't dismiss her lying to me. And she did it on the day I lost my father. Of all the days for her to concoct some ridiculous story, she had to choose yesterday, and I'm just not happy about it."

"Are you hungry? Why don't you get something to eat and go sit down at the table for a while."

"Maybe later."

"You really need to eat at least something."

"I just don't want anything right now. But hey," he said, taking both his mother's hands. "I really want to apologize for bringing all this drama into your house, because you've got more than enough to worry about."

"It's hard, and I do miss your father so much. But we have to keep pressing on until we lay him to rest. And then, we'll have to keep pressing on even after that. I don't know what I'll do without him, but I'm just going to believe that I'll be fine. I just choose to believe that God is going to be there for me the same as always."

Phillip hugged his mother, and then she went back out to visit with her company.

He knew it was rude of him not to join them, too, but he wasn't feeling very social. He knew people meant well when they came by to see how you were doing or when they dropped by to bring over food, but all he really wanted was to be left alone. He wanted to spend time with himself so he could reminisce about his dad. He wanted to think about all the good times they'd shared with each other and try to remember as much about their relationship as possible. He needed to do this now because he was afraid he might forget something important.

The other thing he was wrestling with was the fact that for the first time in years, he was starting to question God and why He did the things He did. He believed in Him and trusted in Him the same way his mother was just saying she did, but he was having a hard time figuring out why God had taken his father from him. Phillip didn't understand because he had always tried to be a good person. He'd always been a good child, the kind that did exactly what the Bible said—honor thy father and mother—and he'd always tried to do the right thing as an adult. He also didn't understand because his dad had always been a good father and husband, and even better, he'd been a God-fearing man his entire life—so none of this made sense. Phillip knew death was something every living human being would someday have to experience, but he couldn't understand why his father's time to go had come so quickly. He'd only been fifty-five years old and ready to live the last half of his life or, at the least, live the next thirty years or so.

Phillip shook his head in distress and went back into the bedroom and closed the door. He turned on the television and then looked over at his phone and saw that he had another message. This time it was from Alicia.

He couldn't imagine that she had anything important to say, other than the same old tired "sorrys" that she'd already inundated him with before leaving, so he dialed into his message system and pressed Delete before she spoke the first word.

He did this and then wondered something else about God and the things He allowed to happen. He wondered why God had allowed him to meet, fall in love with, and then marry a woman like Alicia.

He wondered why in all his life, he'd never felt worse.

Chapter 17

*A*licia sighed exhaustedly and drove onto the street she
and Phillip lived on. It had been a long, stressful, and
very tiring day, and she was glad it was almost over. She still
wasn't happy about Phillip and his insisting that she leave his
mother's house, though, because whether he'd realized it or not,
he'd really hurt her feelings. She'd apologized and then apologized again, but he hadn't wanted to hear any of what she was
saying. He'd acted as if he hated her and like he never wanted
to see her again, and there was a part of her that was worried
that he might never get over what she'd done. But what else
could she do except beg his pardon and try to make things up to
him? She'd even called his cell phone not more than two hours
after she'd left him, but he hadn't answered or even bothered
calling her back, and it was that very thing that had forced her
to stop at Woodfield Mall.

She'd been on her way home, but as she drove, the more
depressed she'd become about Phillip and the way he was ignoring her, and she'd needed to do something fun. She'd needed to
do something nice for herself, so she'd gone into one of her favorite specialty stores and purchased a cute pair of Lucky jeans.
Then, she'd gone into Victoria's Secret and found two pretty

push-up bras, one in hot pink and the other in periwinkle, and she'd purchased the panties to go with them. After that, she'd gone down to Nordstrom and found the most professional-looking business suit she'd seen in weeks and couldn't wait to wear it on her first day of work, whenever that was going to be.

Alicia stopped at the mailbox and removed today's mail, and then saw four packages lying near the front door. At first, she wondered where they might have come from and what was inside them but then she remembered that she'd selected two-day delivery for the online purchases she'd made on Sunday night from Neiman's and Saks, and QVC had probably shipped her a few items as well. But regardless of what had arrived, she was excited to see all of it and couldn't wait to get inside the house.

As soon as she went in and turned off the alarm system, she walked around to the front door, opened it, and brought in everything that had been delivered. She was glad she'd selected two-day delivery on the Saks and Neiman items because with her ordering them on a Sunday night, she'd known the order wouldn't be confirmed and shipped until Monday. That way she could be sure they arrived on Wednesday like clockwork, which was normally the day Philip stayed at the church later because of Bible study, and this gave her a lot of leeway and time enough to receive the packages and bring them in before he got home.

Alicia took everything upstairs and then opened each package one by one. The Manolo Blahnik shoes were just as beautiful as they'd been online, and so was the Cole Haan purse. The suit she'd ordered from Saks wasn't as breathtaking as the one she'd bought tonight, but it was definitely a keeper.

She laid everything across the bed, because for once, she didn't have to hide her purchases or rush to get them into her closet. Phillip wasn't home and he wouldn't be home anytime tonight. She did miss him and was sorry for the way things were between them, but she liked this newfound sense of freedom. It was nice feeling free to do whatever she wanted in her own household and not having to feel as though someone was guarding her every move.

Alicia spent the next few minutes admiring her new possessions and then browsed through the stack of mail she'd also brought upstairs with her. She flipped through all of the bills and junk mail but then tossed them to the side when she saw an envelope addressed to Phillip—one that had the word "preapproved" printed just above his name—and she opened it. After doing so, she skimmed through the Platinum Visa offer letter and saw a statement at the bottom, which said the company had a website that customers could go to if they preferred doing their application online. Alicia went into her office and wasted no time typing in their Internet address.

Once there, she entered the code they'd given her for access and then entered Phillip's personal information, such as his Social Security number, *her* cell number, and the P.O. box address she'd finally gotten the day before Phillip's parents had come to town, and then she entered his income amount. Next, she entered her own information as a co-applicant and since she'd be starting her job at the church shortly, she entered what her salary was going to be. She decided it was okay to do this because the other letter had also stated that if you applied online, you'd receive an answer in minutes. So, she doubted very seriously that they'd be checking any of the information she was submitting, at least not tonight, anyway.

When she finished, she pressed Enter and it took less than sixty seconds for the screen to show that they'd been approved for a credit line of ten thousand dollars. Alicia was so excited but reread the message on the screen to make sure she hadn't made a mistake. However, it really did say ten G's. She was excited because this was double the amount that the Master-Card company had approved them for. She'd already started using that one, so now when this one arrived, it would serve as a safety net and she would only use it in emergency situations.

As Alicia sat finalizing the application process, the phone rang. When she looked and saw that it was her father, she debated whether she should pick it up. She'd been avoiding his calls because she hadn't wanted to tell him what was going on, but now that he was calling their home number, she wondered if Phillip had told him everything.

"Hello?"

"Alicia, where have you been?"

It was never a good sign when he called her Alicia versus his normal "baby girl," and she knew he was upset.

"When I left Mom Katherine's house, I stopped at the mall and then got something to eat."

"You know you had me worried, though, right?"

"I'm sorry, Daddy, but I've had a lot on my mind today."

"Well, I talked to Phillip earlier and he told me that he asked you to leave his mother's house and that you and he are having some problems. Do you want to talk about it?"

"No. I'd really rather not."

"You do know this isn't a good time for you and Phillip to be having petty differences, not with his father dying?"

"Yes. I do know."

"You should call him."

"I did call him, but he didn't answer and he still hasn't called me back."

"You should call him again."

Sometimes Alicia wondered if it would have been better if she'd married someone her father didn't like because he was so pro-Phillip all the time. "I will. I'll call him before I go to bed."

"Good. Phillip also told me that the funeral has been confirmed for Saturday."

"It has been. We took care of everything today but, Daddy, I'm really not looking forward to seeing Dad Phil lying in some casket. The whole thing is so disheartening and so morbid. Even the funeral home itself was morbid. I hate those places, and I didn't like having to see your mom lying in a casket, either. I was a lot younger then but for a long time, I remember thinking how cold Granny Pauline must have been with her having to be buried in the ground the way she was. And even after I got older and knew she couldn't feel a thing, I still hated thinking about her being six feet under."

"Death is never easy for any of us, and most of us go our entire lives not really understanding what death really means or how it will feel because there's just no way to know until you actually die. But the one thing you can be sure of is that if you live your life right and live it according to God's Word, your soul will be saved and that's what really counts. Right?"

"Yep. I remember the first time you told me that. I must have been maybe five years old, and I laughed at you for saying it because even though you told me everybody's soul could be saved if they wanted it to be, I still thought that the only people who had a chance at going to heaven were the Soul Train dancers and Don Cornelius. Because that's the only 'soul' I understood."

Curtis laughed. "Yeah, I remember that, and your mom and I used to laugh about that even years later."

"Daddy, can I ask you something?"

"Of course."

"You promise you won't get mad at me?"

"About you asking me a question? No."

"Is Charlotte near you?"

"No. Why?"

"Because I love Charlotte, and I would never want to hurt her feelings."

"What is it?"

"I just wondered if you ever regret what happened between you and Mom and if you wish that you and she were still together."

"Wow, that's definitely a question."

"You don't have to answer it if you don't want to."

"Well, let me just say this. The only reason your mom and I are divorced is that she wanted it. But don't get me wrong. I understand why she wanted it, because you know I had a lot of issues back then. I did some horrible things. But if she'd been able to put up with me, I'd still be with her."

"Oh."

"Does that still bother you?"

"Sometimes."

"I didn't realize that, and I hate that I put you through so many changes. I'll always be sorry for that."

"It was the past, though, Daddy, and I forgave you a long time ago. You know that."

"I do but that doesn't dismiss everything that happened."

"You're still my heart, though, no matter what."

"And of course, you're mine."

Alicia heard her cell ringing and saw that it was Melanie.

"Daddy, this is Mel, so I'll talk to you tomorrow, okay?"

"Have a good night, and I love you."

"I love you, too."

"Hey, Mel."

"Hey, girl, where are you?"

"Home."

"Oh, I was thinking you were staying in Chicago. Is Phillip there with you?"

"No."

"Did you drive over just to get some extra clothes or something?"

"No, Phillip and I had an argument, and he wanted me to leave."

"Come on. Really?"

"Yes."

"Well, what was the argument about?"

"Nothing major, but it's a long story."

Alicia wanted to tell Melanie but she knew Melanie would never understand, not with the way she already viewed Alicia's spending habits. She also didn't want Melanie finding out that when she'd talked to her while sitting in the car waiting for the tow truck she hadn't been completely honest with her, either, as far as where her car had broken down. She'd hadn't lied to her, but she hadn't told her that she was stranded in a mall parking lot.

"Well, I hope you guys work things out."

"We will."

"Oh, and I wanted to let you know that I switched my work schedule around so that I'll be off Friday and Saturday. That way Brad and I can come spend Friday evening with you and Phillip at his mother's house, and then just come back again on Saturday morning for the funeral."

"I really appreciate that, Mel, and it will be good having you there."

"No problem, and if you need anything before that, just let me know."

"I will."

"Well, I guess I should get going so I can get to bed. I have to be at work at six o'clock."

"My goodness, that's early. Too early for me."

"Yeah, sometimes it's hard, but a woman's gotta do what a woman's gotta do."

"I guess."

"But the good thing about it is that I have my evenings off, and once I work my four twelves, I'm off for three days."

"Yeah, when you don't pick up extra hours, which you know you always do."

"You're right. More hours mean more money."

"Let's not get started, because you know we could debate that subject for hours."

"That's for sure. But, hey girl, I love you, and I'll chat with you tomorrow."

"I love you, too. Bye."

Alicia pressed the End button and thought about how pleasant and down to earth Melanie always was, and Alicia was glad she was her best friend. Melanie was one of the few people Alicia would do anything for, anything at all, and she knew Melanie felt the same way about her. They had each other's backs in good times as well as when times weren't so happy.

Alicia decided she would go ahead and try Phillip's cell number again, but this time it went straight to voice mail, which meant he'd turned his phone off completely. So she tried his mother's number instead.

"Hello?"

"Hi, Mom Katherine. How are you?"

"I'm fine. What about you, sweetheart?"

"I'm okay."

"You make it home safely?"

"Yes, I got here a little while ago."

"I've been thinking about you and Phillip all evening, and I just wish I could talk some sense into him."

"Did he ever come out of the bedroom?"

"He did. But just for a short while. And mostly he stayed to himself."

"I really am sorry, Mom Katherine. I really, really am, but I can't change what I did."

"I know you can't and eventually Phillip will realize that. I know he will."

"I'm not so sure, because he was really upset today."

"Do you want to try to talk to him now?"

"That's fine."

"Phillip? Honey, pick up the phone. It's your wife calling."

Alicia thought she heard him say he didn't want to talk to her, but she wasn't sure.

"Did he say he didn't want to talk to me?"

"I'm truly sorry about this, Alicia."

"Please don't apologize, because this isn't your fault."

"I know, but I don't like seeing you kids like this. You're normally so happy with each other."

"I know, but I'll just try to call again tomorrow."

"You do that, okay?"

"I will. Sleep well."

"You, too."

Phillip's adamant refusal to speak to her was definitely painful, but at the same time, Alicia didn't see why she should have to keep begging her own husband. Whatever happened to all that forgiveness he'd talked about in his sermon just a few days ago? So, to her, if he wasn't planning to ever forgive her for what she'd done, he was nothing more than a hypocrite. He was nothing more than a man who gave great advice but didn't have the sense to take it. Who was he to criticize her about anything?

Chapter 18

The house was jam-packed. From Melanie and Brad to Curtis, Charlotte, and Matthew, to Tanya and James, to loads of people she didn't even know, everyone was piled into Phillip's parents' home. Even Elder Jamison and Elder Dixon, one of the oldest members of Deliverance Outreach, and one of Alicia's favorite people, had driven over from Mitchell to show their respect. They were all planning to come back for the funeral tomorrow as well, so Alicia thought it was nice of them to be there this evening. Which had turned out to be a real blessing to Mom Katherine because her spirits were way up. People were talking, laughing, eating every kind of food imaginable and just having a very good time, and Alicia could tell this was Mom Katherine's best day thus far.

Even Phillip seemed a lot less unhappy and was across the room, laughing with Brad, Curtis, and the two elders. He still wasn't really speaking to her, though, and while she was trying to be as understanding and as patient as she possibly could, she was starting to get a little fed up with his cold and very mean-spirited attitude toward her. All day yesterday and then again this morning, she'd been begging and pleading with him by phone, at first through voice mail and also when he'd finally decided, in his own precious time, that he was ready to answer her call. She'd told him how sorry she still was, that she was dead wrong, that there was no excuse for what she'd done and that she'd learned her lesson. She'd even told him how, even though she didn't see anything wrong with buying nice things, she was now more than willing to sit down with him to figure out a monthly budget, both for their general household expenses as well as for her personal spending—if that would make him happy.

She'd said everything she could in order to make things better between them, but it hadn't made any difference. He'd listened but then basically told her he had more important things to concern himself with right now and that *their* problems would simply have to wait. Alicia did understand to a certain extent because they were preparing to bury his father tomorrow and, yes, that was extremely important, but she hadn't seen where that gave him the right to shut her out in the meantime. Shut her out until he was good and ready to try and fix things. She was still his wife, and regardless of what issues they were at odds about, he owed her a certain amount of respect. Alicia had watched her father demand respect for as long as she could remember, and he'd also raised her to never accept anything less for herself, not under any circumstances. And she wouldn't. She'd give Phillip the time he needed to deal with his father's passing, but she wouldn't grovel or kiss his behind forever—not over something as small as her stopping at a mall for only a couple of hours. She wouldn't do that, and if Phillip didn't eventually come to his senses, well, she didn't want to think about any of that right now. All she knew was that she wouldn't keep pursuing someone who didn't want to be bothered.

Alicia grinned when she saw her brother walking toward her with a plate crammed with three different kinds of cake. "I know you're not going to eat all of that by yourself."

Matthew took a bite of the red velvet cake and spoke with his mouth full. "Watch me."

"You crack me up."

Alicia loved her little brother so much and was very proud of all of his accomplishments. He was a sophomore in high school, pretty much received all A's in his classes, and he was Mitchell Prep Academy's top football star.

"So, are you still planning to run track again this spring?"

"Yep. Coach doesn't want us becoming too idle or getting out of shape, and that's why he requires us to participate in at least one other sport besides football."

"That's good."

"Actually, I like track. I don't love it as much as I love playing football, but I really like the individual and sometimes one-on-one competitiveness that it offers."

"I could see that."

Matthew bit into the caramel cake and raised his eyebrows. "Wow. I gotta get some more of this before it's all gone. I'll be back."

Alicia shook her head at him, and Melanie made her way through the group of ladies who looked to be sampling some of the same cakes Matthew was filling up on. "It's really wonderful to see so many people dropping by to give Phillip and your mother-in-law so much support."

"It really is. I was just standing here thinking the same thing. How this is really good for Mom Katherine. She seems so uplifted."

"She does, and I just hope that even after tomorrow is over, people will still come by to see her."

"I do, too, but either way, Phillip and I are going to be here for her as much as we can, and Miss Thelma will definitely be here also."

"There's nothing like having family and close friends who care about you, and Miss Thelma is such a sweetheart. She seems like the kind of person who would do anything she could for Mrs. Sullivan."

"She's the best, and she's been with her every step of the way."

"I'm just sorry I had to work the last couple of days and couldn't be here every day myself."

"Girl, please don't give it another thought. You've called me I don't know how many times, and just hearing your voice has really helped me. And then you took off today and tomorrow from work. Which I *know* isn't something you would do for just anybody," Alicia teased.

"You're right about that. But no job is more important than you. Period."

"I know that, Mel, and I really appreciate it."

Alicia glanced over at Phillip who just so happened to be looking in her direction, but then he quickly turned away from her. He was still upset; however, Alicia simply shook her head and returned her attention to Melanie, who said, "So, you're spending the night here in Chicago, right?"

"Yeah. That's the plan, anyway."

Melanie lowered her voice just above a whisper. "Are you and Phillip doing okay?"

"Not really."

"I'm sorry to hear that. Why won't you tell me what this is about?"

"Because I don't want to burden you with our problems, and to be honest, I'm trying my hardest not to focus on it."

"Okay, but when you're ready to talk about it, I hope you'll call me."

"I will. I promise."

Alicia looked in Phillip's direction again, but then she saw

Brad smiling and winking at Melanie. Alicia smiled as well and remembered when there was a time Phillip would have shown the same sentiments toward her. He would have shown her the utmost kind of affection and would have never considered treating her in the heartless way he had over the last three days. He had always been such a gentleman, so loving and caring, and so concerned with her happiness and well-being. He hadn't seemed to concentrate on much else, and that made Alicia love him more every day. She'd been sure that there was no better man and that he was her soul mate. She'd been sure that they were meant to be together.

But it was amazing how quickly things tended to change and how, no matter how much one wanted to prevent change, a person rarely had control over it. People were who they were and that was just a fact. Phillip had begun complaining about the money she spent more and more, and while she'd had this same thought not long ago, she couldn't help thinking again how she'd shopped in the same exact manner before she'd met him and while they were dating. She hadn't tried to deceive him in any way, but maybe Phillip had somehow made himself believe that he would have no problem changing her once they were married. If that were true, then Phillip had deceived himself and he was the one who was wrong for trying to turn her into someone she wasn't. No one had the right to do that, and her husband was no exception.

Alicia's mother walked over and joined Alicia and Melanie. "Sweetie, do you need me to do anything before I go? I just asked Katherine the same thing, but she said everything was in order."

"No, Mom, I think we're fine. But thanks."

"I really like it when you wear your hair back in a bun," Melanie said to Alicia's mother.

"Well, thank you. But I have to tell you, I only wear it this way because I'm tired of curling hair and tired of rolling it. This is the lazy woman's hairdo."

The three of them laughed, and then Alicia said, "I get tired of curling hair, too, and that's why I sometimes wear mine pulled back as well."

Melanie agreed. "I do the same thing for the same reason, but it's just that it really, really becomes your mom," she said, now looking at Alicia's mother again. "You should wear it like that all the time."

"I appreciate the compliment and now when I feel lazy and want to wear it like this, I won't feel guilty. I'll just think about what you said."

"I'm glad to be of service," Mel said, and they all laughed again.

Her mother really did look nice, Alicia thought, but then it wasn't like this was something new because she always looked that way. She'd always been just as beautiful as she was today. That was one of the reasons Alicia had never fully understood why her mother hadn't been enough for her father. She was beautiful, kind, and decent, and she'd loved him completely, so Alicia didn't see why he'd always had to find comfort in another woman's bed. She grew up wondering about that all the time but basically had kept her questions to herself. But then he'd done the same thing to Mariah and the same thing to Charlotte, and both of them were noticeably attractive, too. Any man would have wanted either one of them and even now, as Alicia scanned the house and finally spotted Charlotte, the woman looked flawless. Her hair was in place, her makeup was perfect, and the fuchsia turtleneck and matching fuchsia leather jacket she wore screamed class and stylishness.

But that was neither here nor there and not something she

should be worrying about because she had her own marital problems to deal with. Plus, it wasn't like her mother was still dwelling on the past. She had James, a man who had treated her like a queen from day one and who unquestionably deserved some sort of an achievement award for best stepfather of the century because he'd always been wonderful to Alicia and still treated her like she was his biological daughter.

Alicia smiled when she saw him walking over to them.

"You okay?" he asked her.

"I'm fine, and thank you for being here."

"Where else would I be?"

"I guess you're right."

James placed one of his arms around Alicia and hugged her.

Her mother smiled at both of them and then said to James, "So, honey, are you about ready to get going?"

"I'm ready when you are."

"We should probably leave, but we'll be here in the morning, a couple of hours before it's time to line up for the funeral procession."

Alicia embraced her mother. "Okay, Mom, and thanks for everything."

Her mother hugged Melanie and then said good-bye to Mom Katherine and a few other people and then everyone else slowly started filing out. Melanie, Brad, and Miss Thelma had been the last ones to leave, and now Alicia and Mom Katherine were in the kitchen.

"Well, there's really not much else for us to do because Thelma has already put all the food away and cleaned up everything. She's such a doll, and I honestly don't know how I would have made it through this week without her."

"Melanie and I were talking about her earlier. She's such a good friend. Such a good person."

"And she's always been that way, too. We met about fifteen years ago when I was forty and she was fifty, and at our age, you don't expect to find best friends. One day, we struck up a conversation at the beauty salon, exchanged phone numbers, and we hit it off from there. Then she and her husband joined our church, and he and Phil became very close friends, too. But then her husband passed away about five years later, and that was about ten years ago."

"And she never thought about getting married again?"

"No. She doesn't even really see other men. There's a widower from the church that she sometimes goes to lunch with and maybe to a movie, but that's about it."

"Well, as long as she's happy."

"It's more about not being able to find another man you can love as much as you loved your husband. So, just a little companionship every now and then is about all you can expect. And then when you get past fifty, you're pretty set in your ways and you're not willing to change those ways for a new relationship."

"I guess not," Alicia said and thought about how she felt the same way at twenty-two.

"Why don't you go on in there with your husband? Because I'm fine. Really. I'm going to have me a piece of that German chocolate cake you brought, and then I'm going to take a shower and go to bed."

Alicia was glad she'd thought to pick up her mother-in-law's favorite cake for her before driving back over this afternoon.

"You're sure you're okay?"

"I'm fine. Now go."

Alicia hugged Mom Katherine and then walked through the house and into the bedroom. Phillip was already in bed, with the lights out, but it looked as though he was watching David Letterman.

"Phillip?"

"Yeah?"

"Oh. I was just checking to see if you were awake."

He didn't say anything else, so Alicia turned on one of the lamps and opened her bag. She pulled out her nightgown and then started toward the guest bathroom.

"Alicia?"

"Yeah?"

"I can't do this without you. I've tried, but now I know that there's no way I can continue harboring all this animosity and also deal with my father's funeral."

Alicia wasn't sure what to say, but she was glad he'd finally spoken a few pleasant words to her.

"Is that okay with you?"

"It's more than okay, Phillip, because I need you, too."

Phillip reached out his hand and Alicia sat down and then lay next to him.

"All I want to do is hold you, make it through tomorrow, and move on with our lives."

Alicia snuggled closer to him. "That's all I want, too."

"But there is one thing I have to say."

"What?"

"That what happened on Tuesday can never happen again. You have to make me as much of a priority as I always try to make you, and I don't think that's asking too much."

"It's not, and I will make you my priority. I promise that I'll consider how you feel a lot more than I have been."

She promised and hoped she could live up to every word she'd just said.

Chapter 19

It was the last Saturday in April, exactly two months since they'd buried Alicia's father-in-law, yet here she and Phillip were, going at it like enemies. They'd done pretty well, starting with the day of the funeral, but their cease-fire, truce, compromise, or whatever a person wanted to call it, hadn't lasted more than two weeks. For a while, Phillip had seemed content with her and their marriage, and they'd spent most of the time at his mother's house. However, when Mom Katherine had insisted that she was fine, that she thought it was time they got back to their own lives in Mitchell and that it would be good for Phillip to get back to what he loved, which was the ministry, they'd spent a lot more time at home. But the more time they spent together and the more they resumed their day-to-day activities, the more they began arguing again. They couldn't seem to agree on anything, and it was now to the point where Alicia wasn't even sure she loved Phillip anymore. She guessed she did love him—no, she knew she loved him—but she couldn't be sure if she was *in* love with him the way she had been months earlier.

A person could only take so much yelling, criticizing, and complaining and Alicia was getting tired of it. Especially since she'd gone out of her way to do what she knew would make him happy. She'd started working, and even though she was earning her own money, she'd still bypassed a number of things she'd really wanted to purchase. She hadn't even taken as many trips to the mall, in Mitchell or over in Chicago, and she hadn't ordered nearly as much from QVC or the Home Shopping Network as she could have. In fact, she'd seen a variety of items on both channels that she'd wanted pretty badly, but because of the promise she'd made to Phillip about making him the priority in her life, she'd resisted the urge to buy them.

However, the sad part about all of this was that the changes she'd worked very hard to make still weren't enough for Phillip, and now her patience with him was practically nonexistent. He just couldn't be satisfied, and Alicia was sick of trying to appease him. She was tired of trying because it wasn't doing a bit of good, anyway.

Phillip threw his hands into the air. "You're never going to change, are you?"

"Nope. And if that's what you're waiting on, then I'm sorry to tell you that you're wasting your time."

"Why is it that no matter how much I try to reason with you or how much I try to explain it, you just don't get it? Why is that?"

"Because you have your philosophy in terms of how we should live our lives, and I have mine. I've told you that time and time again, and that's just the way it is."

"But when you get married, Alicia, it can't be about two different philosophies. The Bible says that when you marry, you become one, and to me that means we should do whatever we have to do in order to stay in agreement. I'm not saying that we should never disagree because that's not being logical, but what I am saying is that for the most part, the majority of the time, we should be of one accord."

"I agree. But we've now been married for eight months and you still think this is just about you and that we should do things your way and only your way. And I'm not going for that."

"So, what are you saying?"

"I mean exactly what I just said—that I'm not going for it—and I'm not sure how much more I can simplify that particular statement."

"So that's it? You've basically decided that you're going to continue doing whatever you want, regardless of how I feel about it?"

Alicia shook her head and went over to the refrigerator and pulled out a bottle of Perrier.

"Oh, so now you don't have anything else to say, I guess."

"Phillip, the bottom line is this. Our marriage just isn't working."

Phillip folded his arms and then sighed. "So, what do you want to do about it?"

"I don't know, but I don't see how we can keep going on like this."

"Are you feeling as though things are so bad that there's no way of fixing them?"

"I don't know that, either. I just know I can't keep arguing with you like this every time you see something new in my closet or something new that I've bought for the house. I mean, because even like today, you came in here ranting and raving like some natural-born lunatic all because I decided it was time we upgraded our family room furniture. Which is just insane to me because buying furniture is what most wives do. It's normal, Phillip, and I would think that you'd be happy about the way I'm always trying to make sure our house looks its absolute best."

"But not when we can't afford it, Alicia, and that's why I'm so upset."

"But it's not like I used any of your money."

"But it still affects me and ultimately I will have to pay for it in one way or another, because whether you financed it through the furniture store or used a charge card, it only means more debt for both of us."

"No, it doesn't, because I'm the one who's going to be paying for it. I have a job now, remember?"

"You only work part-time, and I rather doubt that you'll be able to pay for a room full of Italian leather furniture anytime soon. And that means not only do you have the principal to worry about, but you'll be paying a ton of interest, too. You'll be paying forever."

"But that's my choice, Phillip, and I don't have a problem with that. Plus, it's not like I'm always going to be working part-time. Once I finish my book, which you know I've been working on for over a month now," she said, even though she knew it really wasn't the truth, "I'll be able to pay that furniture bill in full."

"You just don't see what I'm saying, do you? Because even if you do pay for it and I never have to spend one dime on it, that money could have been saved or used toward some of our household bills."

"My father never ever expected my mother to pay one bill around the house, and she only worked because she wanted to. His second wife didn't work at all, and the only reason Charlotte worked at the beginning of their marriage was that she and my dad had just moved here and started a new church with only a few members. But then once he started earning a lot more money, she quit and hasn't had to work since."

"Well, I don't make the kind of money your father does, and

you and I could definitely accomplish a whole lot more than what we have if we stopped all this your-money-my-money business. That's why a lot of married couples find themselves struggling financially, and it's all because they don't put their money together. They keep separate accounts, they pick and choose what they're going to pay for or not pay for, and it's my experience that when the right hand doesn't know what the left hand is doing, the result can only be one thing. A total disaster."

"I disagree."

"Well, it's the truth. When I was an associate minister over in Chicago, I counseled a number of married couples and hands down, the ones who were having the most serious financial problems were always the ones who kept their money separate. But the couples who deposited all their money into the same account never had those kinds of issues. They paid all their bills from one pot, regardless of who made the most money, and they were also able to save for their futures. They might have had other problems, but rarely did those kinds of couples have money trouble."

"Well, it's like you said, I only work part-time, so it's not like I make all that much."

Phillip laughed out loud. "So, when it's convenient, you don't make very much, but when you want to buy something, you make more than enough to pay for it."

"You know what? This really isn't getting us anywhere."

"No, I guess it's not, so like I said before, what is it that you want to do? Get a divorce?"

Alicia was shocked that he was actually suggesting this, but she couldn't deny that it had already crossed her mind, too. More than once.

"Is that what you want?"

"No, because when I married you, my goal was to be married until death. But things are pretty bad between us, and to me the only chance we might have is to go to counseling."

Alicia really wasn't all that interested in discussing her personal business in front of some stranger, especially with her being the daughter of a pastor, author, and speaker who was known nationwide as well as in other countries.

"I don't know. If we did, we'd have to be very careful of who we confided our situation to."

"I agree, and I'm willing to look for someone if you decide you want to go this route."

"Let me think about it."

"Actually, I'm sure your dad has to know someone who we can trust and someone who's good at what they do."

"That's fine, but, Phillip, I don't want you telling my dad any details. You can tell him that we're having problems and that we need a counselor we can trust, but that's it."

"Whatever you want. But if it's okay with you, I'd like to ask him right away."

"That's fine. Because it's like I said, I can't keep living like this."

"I agree, so let me call him now."

Phillip went into his study and called Curtis's home number and Charlotte answered.

"Hey, Charlotte, how's it going?"

"Good. How about you?"

"I'm okay."

"And I would ask about your mom but I just talked to her a little while ago. Thought I'd call just to chat with her for a while."

"That was nice of you."

"She's really doing well, Phillip."

"She is, and I'm glad because if she wasn't, that would really worry me."

"I can imagine. But let me not hold you up because I know you're probably calling for Curtis."

"I am."

"Here he is, and you take care."

"Hey," Curtis said when he got on the line.

"How are you?"

"Fine, what's up with you?"

"If you have a few minutes, I need to ask a favor."

"Go ahead. Anything."

"Well, as much as I was hoping we'd never have to go this route, Alicia and I have both decided that it's time we saw a counselor."

"Really? I knew you were having some problems around the time your dad died, but I thought things were a lot better and back to normal."

"They were for a while, but now it's pretty bad again."

"Well, you know I hate hearing that, but you're doing the right thing by getting some help."

"What I wondered was if you can recommend someone who is good but also someone we can trust because Alicia is worried about confidentiality."

"I understand, and actually I know the perfect person. Pastor John Abernathy. He's the pastor of Abundant Life Missionary Baptist Church over in Chicago, but he also has a master's in counseling and had a private practice when he was in his early thirties. You've heard me talk about him and, remember, I spoke there last summer."

"I think so. You just met him about a year and a half ago, right?"

"Yeah, but he's the one who really helped me come to terms

with that whole Tabitha scandal. He quickly became like a father figure to me, and he's very good. He's a great man of God, and he doesn't play any games. He's the real deal."

"Isn't his church the one where that woman who won the lottery goes to? The one who won that huge Mega Millions jackpot?"

"Yeah, it is."

"Well, if that's who you really think we should go with, then I'll run it by Alicia."

"He's definitely your man. Just let me know, and I'll call him right away."

"Thanks, Curtis, because we really do need to talk to someone soon."

"No problem, and while I know you don't feel comfortable sharing with me whatever is going on, I still want you to know that I'm always available. I also don't want you thinking you can't come to me just because you're married to my daughter. It takes two when it comes to any marriage, and I know my daughter can be a little self-absorbed sometimes. You mentioned something like that the last time we spoke about this, and it's true, so if you want me to talk to her, I will."

"No. But I appreciate the offer."

"Okay, well, let me know if you want me to contact Pastor Abernathy."

"I will. See you tomorrow."

Phillip hung up but wished he'd gone ahead and told Curtis everything. Especially now that Curtis had admitted that he knew his daughter had faults. But Phillip knew if he told Curtis anything, Alicia would be furious because she'd made it clear that she didn't want her father knowing any details about their situation.

Phillip opened the door to his study and then went down the hall to the kitchen.

"I talked to your dad, and he suggested Pastor Abernathy over in Chicago."

"Really? I guess that's fine. My dad talks about him a lot and I know he trusts him, so that's the most important thing."

"So, it's a go, then?"

"Yeah."

"Then I'll let your dad know," Phillip said and then noticed that Alicia had her purse on her shoulder. "You leaving?"

"Yeah, I'm meeting some women from the church for dinner."

"How long will you be gone?"

"Maybe a couple of hours or so. You don't have a problem with that, do you?"

"No, I was just asking."

"Okay, well, I guess I'll see you in a little while."

Alicia turned toward the door leading to the garage, but Phillip stopped her.

"So, you're not even going to kiss me good-bye?"

Alicia hesitated but then pecked him on the lips. "See ya."

"See you later."

Phillip watched her walk out the door, and then it came to him. Maybe it was time he did something special for her. Something that would let her know just how much he still loved her and how much he really wanted their marriage to work.

He decided he would surprise her in a way he never had before, and he couldn't wait to see her reaction.

Chapter 20

*A*licia had only been seeing Levi Cunningham for the last couple of weeks, but already she couldn't get enough of him. The man was just that amazing. He had every single thing she could ever want in a guy—money, power, and such extraordinary sexual skills—and she wasn't sure how she'd ever be able to wean herself off of him. And she couldn't deny that she'd gone looking for the affair she was having with him because she had. She'd tried her best to forget about him, ever since that day he had approached her at Macy's, but he'd always been in the back of her mind. She hadn't been able to stop thinking about how tall and handsome he was, or about the black LS series Lexus he drove, or about the amount of money everyone in the city knew he had. She'd known it wasn't right for her to fantasize about another man but the more she and Phillip argued, the more she'd thought about Levi, and it had only been a matter of time before she'd made it her business to find him.

So, one evening, after she and Phillip had found themselves in yet another tired screaming match and he'd slipped and said that she was a daddy's girl and needed to grow up, she'd left the house and driven to Levi's mother's restaurant. She'd seen his car parked right out in front but after twenty minutes of sitting, she still hadn't gotten out and walked inside. The reason: She'd been trying to talk herself out of following in her father's old footpath, committing the ungodly sin of adultery, and she'd tried to convince herself that she and Phillip were going to be just fine. She'd even gone ahead and turned her ignition back on, preparing to drive off, but it was at that moment that Levi walked out of the restaurant and saw her. Even then, she considered driving away, but with every step he'd taken in the direction of her vehicle, she'd felt just a little more drawn to him, a little more mesmerized and like she couldn't move. It was as if he'd been some sort of drug that had paralyzed her.

She remembered the way the entire evening had gone, no differently than if it had happened yesterday. He'd walked right up to the driver side of her car, and she'd rolled down her window.

Levi had flashed what she now called his signature smile. "Well, it's about time."

"And what is that supposed to mean?"

"That you've had me waiting for almost two months now."

"That's funny because I don't remember ever saying I was coming."

"No, but you didn't have to. I just knew when the time was right, you would be here."

Alicia had smiled and then looked away from him.

"So, what's up?"

"You tell me."

"Well, before we take this any further, there're three things I want you to know up front. I never lie, I don't play childish games, and if I say something, I always mean it. And on the flip side, I expect the same exact things back from you, no exceptions."

"You make it sound like we're about to enter some sort of business deal or something."

"No, but I use the same rules in my personal relationships that I use with business. That's the way I've always been, so I guess what you have to decide is if you're down for that or not."

Alicia hadn't been sure she'd liked how serious he had sounded because even if she did make the decision to sleep with him, it wasn't like they would ever have anything more than that. They couldn't. She was a married woman with a real-life husband at home and there was no pretending otherwise. Not to mention, her father would kill her if he ever found out she was even talking to Levi, let alone spending time with him.

"So, what happens if people lie to you, play games. or say something they don't mean?"

"When it's personal, I drop them from my life like a bad habit and I never have another thing to do with them. When it's business, well, that's when my reaction becomes a little more involved. But you don't need to worry about that because your relationship with me will always be personal and never about business."

"That's good to know."

"So, what's the verdict? You in?"

"I'm not sure, because deep down I know this is wrong."

"Because of your husband?"

Alicia looked at him.

"Is that it? Because if it is, I'm not going to sit here and tell you that it's not wrong when we both know it is. That's just a fact."

"Are you seeing anyone?"

"If I was, I wouldn't be standing here talking to you, and I certainly never would have approached you a couple of months ago. I don't operate like that. I'm a one-woman kind of man. I was in a relationship, but I ended it about four months ago."

"Why?"

"She lied straight to my face and never even stuttered. And that's all it took for me."

"How long had you been dating her?"

"Five years."

"And you dumped her just like that?"

"Just like that. I told you. Those three rules of mine apply to everyone."

"So, you expect me to sit here believing that you're going to see only me, even though I'll be going home to my husband whenever I leave from being with you?"

"Yeah, that's pretty much the size of it."

"Why?"

"Because from where I'm sitting, it looks to me like your marriage is only temporary. If it wasn't, you never would have come looking for me."

"But what if I'm not planning to ever leave him?"

"Then that'll be your call, and eventually you and I will have to come to an end."

Alicia had looked ahead through her front window and wondered if she was getting herself into something she would soon end up regretting. She'd wondered if Levi would actually allow her the kind of freedom to come and go as she pleased without any hassles or pressure like he'd been saying. It had all seemed too good to be true but her desire to be with him had been very strong, and her heart had told her it was okay to take a chance.

"Where do you live?"

"Just outside of the city limits. But I think it would be best if we find somewhere to leave your car and then you can just ride with me."

Alicia had debated her decision for a few minutes longer and then decided she didn't have anything to lose. She'd known that cheating on her husband wasn't something to take lightly, but she had finally settled on the idea that what Phillip didn't know wouldn't hurt him.

That was two weeks ago, and as of today, she was glad she'd taken that drive with Levi because now she was lying next to a man who made her feel like a real woman. He made her feel like she was the most important thing in his life and like she deserved everything the world had to offer and then some. Already, he'd opened up his home to her, explaining that it could all be hers, and two days ago, he'd given her a beautiful heart-shaped diamond necklace. Then, about a week ago, she'd talked about having to pay one of her credit card bills that had a balance of one thousand dollars, and he'd given her the cash so she could pay that off, too. But the only thing was, she needed a lot more than that because she'd already maxed out the five-thousand-dollar credit line on the MasterCard she'd signed Phillip's name to, maxed out another three-thousand-dollar line of credit that Phillip had received an offer for, and now that she'd spent nearly four thousand dollars on the new family-room furniture, she was already cutting into the ten-thousand-dollar line they'd been given on the Visa she'd applied for online. Then, there were her Neiman's and Saks accounts, which she'd maxed out as well, at five thousand dollars each, which of course never took long to do at either one of those stores, but she'd needed clothing for her new job at the church. She'd needed the accounts because there was no way she could walk around wearing just any old thing and embarrassing her father. Everyone knew she was Curtis Black's daughter, and she had no choice but to live up to that.

If only she made a lot more money and could pay off her

balances much more regularly and stop paying just the minimum payments, she was sure Neiman's and Saks would gladly raise her credit limits, the same as they'd done over the years when her father paid her bills. But in the meantime, she needed more cash and she would just have to figure out a way to ask Levi for it. She didn't want to request too much too soon because she didn't want him thinking that she was only trying to use him—which she wasn't—but she was going to have to ask him before the beginning of next month. She'd have to do so or resort to her only other option, asking her father, and she definitely didn't want to do that.

Levi repositioned his pillow and gazed into Alicia's eyes. "Are you happy?"

"With you?"

"Yes, but more importantly are you happy with the way I make love to you?"

"Can't you tell?"

"Maybe. But I wanna hear you say it."

"I'm happy with the way you make love to me."

"Am I better than him?"

Alicia thought it was interesting how Levi would never say Phillip's name. He would only say "he," "him," or "your husband," but maybe he did that because without using Phillip's name maybe that made Phillip seem less real.

Levi repeated his question. "Am I?"

"Yes."

"Good. Because otherwise it wouldn't be worth it for you."

"Not worth it how?"

"It wouldn't be worth you being here with me when you have something better at home."

"I guess not."

"I know not, and that's why I'm amazed when people have

affairs but don't get anything more than what they're already dissatisfied with."

Occasionally, Alicia had a hard time believing that Levi was a big-time drug dealer and mostly she tried not to even think about it at all. But he made a lot of profound statements, the kind most drug dealers wouldn't even think about, and that sort of surprised her.

Alicia drew invisible circles on Levi's chest. "Are *you* happy?"

"Very. I told you that I've wanted you for a very long time, and it feels good to finally have you. Well, partially have you, anyway."

"But I'm all yours when you and I are together."

"I know and I'm content with that for the time being. But I never forget what the reality is."

"This is a hard situation because I was never counting on caring about you as much as I do."

"You can't help who you have feelings for or who you have chemistry with. It's just not possible to do anything about that. Some people may never admit their attraction for another person, but everybody's eventually attracted to someone other than the person they're with, at some point in their relationship. Everyone."

"I don't know about that because had Phillip not started trying to tell me what I could and couldn't buy and hadn't started arguing with me all the time, I don't think I'd be here with you."

"Maybe not. But you still would've been attracted to me, even if you'd never done anything about it."

"I don't know if I agree with that."

"So, you're still trying to insinuate that you weren't attracted to me, even before you met your husband?"

"I think I'll just plead the fifth on this one."

Levi laughed. "That's what I thought. Because you know you'd be lying if you said you weren't, and you know how I feel about that."

Alicia playfully punched him, and he grabbed his chest like she'd done major damage to him. "What are you trying to do, kill me?"

"Yeah, right."

Levi rolled the front of his body to the side of hers. "You ready for round two?"

"I was ready as soon as round one was over with."

Levi grinned. "Then, let's get to it."

Alicia sped into the subdivision and hung the first corner faster than normal because she hadn't meant to stay at Levi's for seven whole hours. She'd gotten so caught up, the same as every other time she'd been with him, but she didn't want to make Phillip suspicious. She couldn't afford that, not when she'd just agreed they could get counseling and not after seeing the hopeful look he'd had on his face just before she'd walked out the back door. She didn't think counseling was going to do much good for them, but now that she'd betrayed their marital vows and was sneaking around with another man, she felt as though she at least owed him a chance at trying to work things out. Plus, she did still love him.

But she had to admit that the more she was with Levi, the more she wished she was married to him instead of Phillip, even though there was always that menacing reminder dangling in the background: the illegal business Levi operated and the danger it could bring to him and her if she wasn't careful. To this day, she'd never seen anyone come to his house, and she'd never heard him talking on the phone with any of the people who worked for him. But the way he lived spoke a multitude of words: the waterfall on the front lawn, the most glamorous chandelier she'd ever seen, five bedrooms, five bathrooms, an inground swimming pool, a spacious theater room, a workout room, and a sauna—the list went on and on. He had just about everything her father had in his house. The only difference was, her father was legit. Her father hadn't acquired any of his fortune by dealing drugs as Levi was doing.

Still, at thirty-two, the same age Phillip was, Levi had everything a woman could want or need and he was offering it to her. He was offering his heart, soul, and money to Alicia, and she was having a hard time passing on it.

She pulled into the driveway, opened the garage, and then drove inside it. Then, she turned off the radio, left her vehicle, and went into the house.

Phillip met her at the door. "Where were you?"

"Out. At dinner, and then I stopped at the mall."

"And you couldn't return my phone calls?"

Alicia realized how she hadn't even thought to check her cell. "I'm sorry."

"This is just crazy. Here I keep trying to hold on to what little bit of a marriage we have left, while you act as though you want out."

"That's not true. But, Phillip, you know how things have been between us lately, and then we had that argument today, and I just needed some space. I needed some time to myself."

"I thought you went to dinner with some ladies from the church?"

"I did, but then I went to the mall."

"It's always about shopping, isn't it?"

"No. But today, I just needed some time away from here. That's all."

"Well, I wish you had told me before I went out of my way, trying to make this a special night for you."

"What'd you do?"

"You know what, Alicia? It doesn't even matter."

Phillip grabbed his jacket and walked out of the house. Alicia heard him drive away and felt terrible. Then, once she'd gone upstairs, she felt worse.

Inside the dimly lit room were five dozen long-stemmed red roses, at least twenty glowing votive candles, and playing softly on the sound system was one of Luther Vandross's greatest hits CDs. A pure-white satin nightie and matching robe, neither of which she'd seen before, adorned the bed while matching slippers sat on the floor. Phillip had never done anything like this in the past, and the guilt she felt was tearing her apart. He was really trying and had obviously worked hard, putting such a wonderfully romantic scene together, but the sad thing was, the whole time he'd been doing it, she'd been making love to another man. Even sadder, Phillip's more than kind gesture still wasn't enough to stop her from seeing Levi. Right now, nothing was.

Chapter 21

It was official. Phillip felt like a complete fool. A naive child. A man who needed to wake up. But still, even now, he just couldn't help the way he felt about his wife. He loved her. He wished he didn't and that he could simply walk away from her, especially with the nonchalant attitude she was taking toward him and their marriage, but it just wasn't that easy for him. He'd even spent the last few weeks trying to imagine what life would be like without Alicia, but whenever he played those kinds of scenarios in his mind, all he did was cause himself more misery.

Which was crazy because she was only one woman, and he doubted he'd have any difficulty at all meeting someone else. He was sure there were dozens of decent women right there in Mitchell, let alone throughout the rest of the country—women who wanted a husband they could love and find happiness with. As a matter of fact, Shandra, his high school sweetheart, the one who had shown up at church a couple of months ago, had spent the last two weeks telling him exactly those same words. Phillip had known he had no business taking her phone number, but when he'd seen her and her best friend at a local gas station one Saturday afternoon, they'd chatted, he'd enjoyed it, and she'd asked him to call her. To be honest, he hadn't planned on doing so, not until that day he and Alicia had argued worse than ever before and he'd needed someone to talk to. Someone who had pleasant words to say to him and someone other than his mother.

He'd called Shandra that very night, and they'd been talking on and off ever since. They talked, they laughed, and they enjoyed each other's company, even if it wasn't in person, and it was the reason he was dialing her number now.

Phillip pressed on the brake, brought his vehicle to a complete stop, and waited for the light to change. Shandra's phone had rung three times, but just as he prepared to hang up, she answered.

"Hey, you."

"How's it going?"

"I'm good now that you're calling. I hadn't heard from you in a couple of days, and I was starting to think you no longer wanted to talk to me."

"No. Nothing like that. Just been a little occupied is all."

"You're still trying to make things work with her, aren't you?"

"Well, yeah. I am. I'm doing what any man would do. That is, if he loves his wife."

"But you see, that's what I don't understand because, based on everything you've told me, it's pretty clear that your wife couldn't possibly love you back. If she did, she'd be doing everything she could to make you happy. She would treat you like the wonderful man you are, and she'd do whatever she had to in order to make things right with you."

Phillip didn't say anything because he felt a little guilty about some of the things he'd confided to Shandra. He hadn't told her every detail regarding his marital problems, but he had told her about the day his father had died and how Alicia hadn't been there for him. He'd explained that instead of coming straight to the hospital, Alicia had gone shopping and he'd also told Shandra about Alicia's outrageous spending habits.

"If you were my husband, you wouldn't have all these issues."

"But I'm not, Shandra. I'm Alicia's husband."

"I realize that, but, Phillip, you deserve so much better than what she's dishing out. You're a truly good man, and you deserve having a real woman in your life."

"No marriage is perfect."

"Maybe not, but you shouldn't be having these kinds of problems so soon. I mean, you've only been married eight months."

"Yes, and that's why I don't want to simply give up without doing everything I can to save our relationship."

"But is that what she wants? Because if that's not what she wants, then you can try all you want and it won't do a bit of good. You'll have wasted a ton of precious time for nothing."

"That could be, but I have an obligation to Alicia, and I'm going to see it through."

"For how long?"

"I don't know."

"Well, tell me this. What happened tonight? Because you only call me this late when things are really bad between the two of you."

"It's not even worth going into."

"Well, whatever it is, it's obviously got you pretty upset, so why don't you drive over here?"

"No. It's bad enough that I'm having these phone conversations with you, so coming to your house is out of the question."

"You're only an hour and a half away and with it being almost eleven on a Saturday night, you could probably get here a little sooner."

"Shandra, you know I'm married and that I can't do that."

"Why? Because it's not like we have to do anything except talk."

"We're doing that now."

"I know, but it's not the same as if we were doing it in person. It would be so much more personal, and I really think you'd enjoy being here with me. It would be like old times."

Phillip chuckled. "Yeah, and that's exactly what I'm afraid of. Because you and I both know what old times used to be like for us."

"It was good. We were good *together*, Phillip. And I've never forgotten how good you always made me feel. We were so in love, and when our feelings for each other started to drift during college, it practically killed me. I was so hurt."

"So was I. But being three thousand miles away from each other took a serious toll on us. I was in Virginia and you were in California and we were young."

"I remember that whole first year away, all I thought about was giving up my volleyball scholarship so I could enroll at Virginia Tech."

"But now that you have that UCLA degree, aren't you glad you didn't?"

"I guess. But I still hate that you and I aren't together. I hate that you're married to someone else. A woman who doesn't treat you nearly as well as I would."

"Sometimes things don't always turn out the way we want them to."

"That's true, but just the fact that we've reconnected after all these years means we still have a chance at having what we wanted."

Phillip turned into Brad's driveway and turned off his ignition. "Maybe if this were a different time, but not now. I took vows before God and it's like I said to you earlier, I have an obligation to my wife."

"I understand that, but at the same time, I refuse to believe that God wants any of us to be miserable."

"He doesn't want us going against His Word, either."

"All you'd have to do is file for a divorce and then we wouldn't have to commit any sins at all. If you did that, then you and I could get married and move on with our lives. I mean, why keep being so unhappy when you don't have to be?"

"Shandra, I can't do that."

"But I could make you so happy, Phillip. I could be the woman of your dreams and offer you every ounce of who I am as a person. I would love you with every inch of my soul and make you my top priority for the rest of my life. I would be everything you could ever possibly want in a woman."

Phillip leaned his head against the backrest and took a deep breath. Shandra was making things very difficult for him, and the more he listened to her, the harder it was becoming for him to deny her invitations. He didn't want to start seeing another woman behind Alicia's back, but as he sat there weighing all the arguments, animosity, and resentment that now fueled his and Alicia's marriage against the peaceful and compassionate talks he shared with Shandra, well, his talks with Shandra won out every time. He was so much more content when he spoke with Shandra, and just hearing her voice tended to calm his nerves whenever Alicia had upset him.

But he knew his thinking was wrong. *Thoughts, ideas, and suggestions.* He knew if he acted upon any of the three, he'd find himself in a lot of trouble and that God would be very disappointed in him.

"Look, Shandra, I'm really sorry but I need to hang up now."

"Why? Where are you?"

"I'm at Brad's."

"Why so late?"

"I just needed to get out of the house is all, so I called him before I left home and told him I was coming by."

"Are you delivering the message in the morning?"

"Just at the early service only."

"Do you want me to drive over to hear you?"

"No. And to be honest, I don't think it's a good idea for you to visit Deliverance again."

"Why? Because you're worried about what might happen between us? Are you worried that you might not be able to resist being with me?"

Exactly, Phillip thought, but he would never admit that to her. "I just don't think it's right."

"Well, if I hadn't taken it upon myself to visit a couple of months ago, we wouldn't even be having this conversation, and I never would have realized just how much I still cared for you and how much I wanted you back."

"And you think it was right, coming to visit a church when the only real reason you came was because you wanted to see me? All the while knowing I was a married man?"

"I never said what I did was right. But when Donna told me that you were the assistant pastor, I couldn't stop thinking about you or what we once had together. I thought about it for months, and then finally I made up my mind to drive over and come to church with her."

"You're too much. But hey, I'm going to head inside Brad's, okay?"

"That's fine, but, Phillip, I'm not giving up on you. And you should also know that I'm the kind of woman that tries very hard to get whatever it is she wants."

"Good-bye, Shandra."

"Talk to you later."

Phillip got out of his truck and looked around the neighborhood as he strolled toward the front door. He had always loved Brad's subdivision. Each house was unique and sat on no less than a one-and-a-half-acre lot, and all the houses were less than three years old. The only thing, though, was that they were way too pricey for his and Alicia's budget, so it would be a long time before they'd be able to afford something like this, if ever. Alicia, of course, hadn't talked about much else the night she'd left Brad's house for the first time and couldn't understand why they couldn't build a house in the same area. But what she didn't seem to get was the fact that Brad earned well over two hundred thousand dollars annually from his law firm and because of this huge wrongful death case he'd been working on for months now, this year his income would be even higher.

Brad opened the exquisitely designed oak wood door. "Hey, man. Come on in."

Phillip stepped inside and kicked off his shoes. "I hope I'm not keeping you up."

"No, not at all. You know I stay up late, anyway. But what's up with you? You're never out this time of night, so I was surprised to get your call."

"I'm not even sure where to begin."

Brad led the way down to the lower level and sat down on the navy blue leather sofa, which looked very similar to what Alicia had just purchased for their family room. "Have a seat. And can I get you anything?"

"No, I'm good."

Phillip sat in the oversize chair.

"So, man, what's up? Is everything okay with your mom?"

"She's fine."

"And Alicia?"

"She's okay in general, but our marriage is falling completely apart."

"What? Since when?"

"Since for a while now. We were even having problems when my dad died, but I just couldn't tell you."

"Why not?"

"I was too embarrassed, I guess."

"And we've been best friends for how long?"

"I know, but man, I'm really ashamed."

"Well, you shouldn't be. Marriages fail all the time."

"Still, I wasn't counting on things being like this between Alicia and me."

"Is there something specific that happened?"

"Yeah, but pretty much every incident has to do with all the money she spends. She shops like we're millionaires, and no matter how I try to talk to her about it, she continues doing whatever she wants."

"Wow. Does she do it all the time?"

"Every chance she gets. Man, I even found a sixteen-hundred-dollar suit in her closet."

"You've got to be kidding? You have to be."

"No, I kid you not. Sixteen hundred dollars."

"Well, it's not like she has some high-paying job, so where is she getting all this money from?"

"She had a quite a bit left over from the wedding budget that Curtis gave her, and she also uses credit cards. But by now, I know all that wedding money is gone, and it's only a matter of time before she maxes out her cards."

"Maybe she needs counseling."

"She does, and this afternoon, we had at least agreed to see a marriage counselor, but now I'm not even sure that's going to happen."

"Why not?"

"It's a long story, but for the most part, Alicia is basically acting as though she doesn't want us to get help."

"Man, I'm really sorry to hear that."

"What I was thinking was if I could talk her into seeing a marriage counselor, then I could eventually get her to see someone about her shopping addiction."

"Maybe Melanie could talk to her. You know how close they are and now that I think about it, Melanie has mentioned some of Alicia's shopping sprees to me in the past, but I really didn't think much of it."

"I don't know. Maybe. But if you want to know the truth, I'm not even sure Alicia will listen to her, either."

"So, what are you planning to do?"

"I really don't know."

"You and Alicia seemed so perfect for each other. Right from the beginning. So, this is really flippin' me out."

"You? I'm shocked every day by the way things have turned out. We argue and fuss about everything all the time, and it's wearing me down."

"Well, as much as I hate to say it, that's why I'm having second thoughts about asking Melanie to marry me. Because from what I can tell, marriage is a total crapshoot, and you never know if it's going to end up good or bad until after you've signed on the dotted line. And by then, it's too late to change your mind."

"True. But there is a such thing as a good marriage. There are a lot of bad marriages out there, but there are definitely good ones. There are some people who truly do love and honor each other, and they're really happy together."

"Yeah, but how many people do you actually know who fall into that category?"

"A few."

"Like who? Your mom and dad?"

Phillip laughed. "You're terrible."

"I'm serious, man, because most people are only together

because of children or because they've gotten comfortable with the person they're married to."

"But that's only because most people aren't willing to work on their marriages. They're not willing to communicate with each other the way they should, make time for each other, or make their spouse their main priority. All of which are very necessary, if you want success in your relationship."

"Well, it's like I said, I'm having second thoughts. I mean, don't get me wrong, I love Melanie but I'm just not sure I can settle down with one woman. You know yourself, that this is the longest I've ever been with one woman at a time, anyway."

"Ain't that the truth."

"It is, and sadly, I don't know how much longer I can keep it up."

"But, man, Melanie is a really good woman. She's beautiful, sensible, hardworking, and responsible, and if Alicia had ten percent of those particular qualities, you wouldn't hear me complaining about anything. Don't get me wrong, Alicia is clearly beautiful, but she's seriously lacking in the other three areas."

"You're right. Melanie is a good woman. Actually, she's a great woman and the kind of woman who is very hard to come by, but the idea of being tied to one person with no freedom for the rest of my life seems not only suffocating but downright terrifying."

Phillip laughed again and so did Brad.

"It's the truth, man. I'm scared to death of what that will feel like."

"I hear you, but you should definitely think long and hard before you do something you'll end up regretting," Phillip said and thought about his own situation with Shandra and how he needed to take the same advice.

Brad's phone rang and he looked over at the caller ID screen. "Well, what do you know. This is my girl calling now."

Phillip relaxed further into the chair and turned his attention toward the television. *SportsCenter* was on, but Phillip couldn't concentrate on much of anything except Alicia and Shandra. He thought about Alicia and the same old thing—how no matter how bad things were between them, he still loved her. But he also thought about Shandra and how right she'd been about their teenage love affair because they really had loved each other so deeply. Then, he thought about everything she was promising him today, as a grown woman, and it was hard for him to simply ignore it. It was hard to resist the obvious temptation she was causing him and hard not to fantasize about being with her sexually. It was hard not thinking about how great it might be, lying in her arms and feeling loved the way a man ought to feel loved. *Thoughts, ideas, and suggestions.* Thank God for Dr. Price's sermon because if it wasn't for those three words, Phillip would be in his car and on his way to Chicago. He'd drive as fast as he could to Shandra's house, so he could experience the kind of satisfaction she was offering him.

Brad told Melanie that he loved her and that he would see her tomorrow.

"Sorry about that, man."

"Please. No problem at all."

"I talked to her earlier but she got called into work and just got off."

"See, that's what I'm talking about. You should feel proud to have a woman like her. A woman who wants to have something in life and one who also cares about her future. A woman who's nothing like my wife."

Brad walked over to the glass and steel-framed bar. "Can I get you a drink, Rev?"

"Yeah, right," Phillip said and they both laughed.

"But back to Melanie. I do hear you, and I know you're on

key. But I just want to be sure I can handle being married for life. That's all I'm saying."

"That's fair."

"So, does Alicia know where you are?"

"No, and actually, if you don't mind, I think I'll just crash over here tonight."

"Of course, and you know you're welcome anytime."

Phillip stood up. "I packed a garment bag, so I guess I should run out to the car to get it."

"I take it your girl wasn't home when you did that?"

"No, I put it in the truck before she came back, so all she saw me leave with were my keys."

Brad drank some of whatever he'd just mixed together. "Things'll get better."

"I hope."

Phillip went outside, and for some reason, he thought about tomorrow morning when he'd be speaking at the early service. He was glad Curtis was doing the main service because this meant he wouldn't have to put on a smiling face and pretend he was happy in front of two different groups of people. It would be difficult enough, doing it in front of one, and he also hoped Alicia wasn't planning to be there. He was a lot calmer now than he had been a few hours ago, thanks to both Shandra and Brad, but if Alicia showed up at church, there was a chance that much of his pain and anger just might resurface, and he couldn't guarantee what he might say in front of the congregation. He remembered what had happened the last time Alicia had upset him, the time his parents had been visiting, and he'd directed his entire pastoral observations toward her. But he didn't want to do that again. So, yes, it was best if Alicia stayed home. Best for her, him, and the members of Deliverance Outreach.

Chapter 22

Thankfully, on Sunday, things had gone Phillip's way. Not only had Alicia not shown up for the early service, but she hadn't attended the second one, either. He wasn't sure why she'd missed both, but he was glad just the same because her absence was the reason he'd been able to enjoy his morning in peace. He'd been able to worship God, pray, and preach his sermon without any distractions and he felt good about that. Curtis had wanted to know why Alicia wasn't there, but Phillip had talked around the subject and certainly hadn't told Curtis that he'd spent the night at Brad's. Having problems was one thing, but sleeping in separate households was something different, and Phillip wasn't proud of it.

He also wasn't proud of the fact that, even though he'd slept at home Sunday night, Monday night, and last night, he hadn't slept in bed with Alicia. He'd debated whether he should try to talk to her, but then he'd decided that maybe it was better for him to keep his distance. He knew it was sort of silly, but he was hoping that just maybe if he completely ignored her, she'd feel a lot differently about him. He was hoping that that old cliché, the one he'd been hearing for years, actually had some truth to it—that a person really didn't miss their water until their well ran dry. He wasn't sure this new approach at getting Alicia's attention was going to work or backfire, but he didn't see where he had a lot to lose. Of course, she had tried talking to him yesterday and again this morning, but he'd only responded with one-word answers and she'd finally left him alone. He could tell how irritated she was, and he had to admit that there were a couple of times when he'd wanted to grab her into his arms and tell her how much he loved her, but he hadn't.

About another hour passed and Phillip heard a knock at his door. The Kings were right on time for their appointment.

"Please come in and have a seat."

Mr. King looked beaten down emotionally. "Thank you, Pastor."

"Yes, thank you for seeing us again," Mrs. King added and sat down.

"So, how have things been going over the last week?"

"Exactly the same, and if anything, the situation is worse," Mrs. King spoke matter-of-factly.

"I'm sorry to hear that, but is there a reason why you feel that way?"

"I can't stop thinking about what Harold did to me. I mean, no matter how I try to figure it, I don't understand how he could be so low-down and stupid. How he could be so naive and ignorant."

Mr. King turned to his wife. "But, puddin', I keep telling you how sorry I am, and I don't know what else I can do."

"That's just it, there's nothing you can do. Not a thing."

"But if you'll just give me a chance, I'll do what I can to make things up to you."

"How?"

"I don't know, but I'm willing to do whatever you want."

"Hmmph. What you should have done was kept that little,

ol', shriveled-up . . . excuse me, Pastor. I won't say what I want to say out of respect for you and the church, and I apologize. But anyway, Harold, you should have kept that thing of yours tucked inside your pants. That's what *you* should have done."

Phillip didn't move or speak.

"I know that now, puddin', and I'm sorry."

Mrs. King squinted her eyes. "Didn't I tell you to stop calling me that? I mean, I don't even know how you could fix your lips to call me a pet name when you've been sleeping with that whore niece of mine all this time."

"But I'm not sleeping with her now and I haven't been for months."

"And what? Is that supposed to make everything okay?"

Mr. King gave up trying to reason with her, the same as he did each of the other four times they'd met with Phillip. Actually, Phillip had tried to meet with them more times than that, at least once per week, but Mrs. King had called and canceled on several occasions.

"Mrs. King, if you don't mind me asking, did you think any more about what Mr. King said to you during our last session?"

"What? About that time I had an affair on him? Please. That was thirty-some-odd years ago when I was in my late twenties."

"Yes, I know. But, remember Mr. King talked about how he'd never gotten over it?"

"So, you're saying because I made a mistake almost forty years ago that this gave him the right to sleep around on me now?"

"No. Not at all. But what I am saying is that Mr. King was really hurt by what happened and that for all these years, he's kept all that pain inside him."

Mrs. King seemed uncomfortable and ashamed, and she dismissed the whole notion. "That's just crazy. Plus, Harold knew

The Best of Everything

I was a little on the wild side when he married me. Right, Harold? You were thirty, but I was only twenty. I was young and dumb back then. Then, when I had that affair, I was still young and couldn't have been more than twenty-eight at the most. But I didn't go looking for it. I told you I was out partying with some friends, I had a little too much to drink, and it just happened. The man I slept with didn't mean a thing to me and that's why I told Harold, right after it happened."

Mr. King nodded in agreement.

"You know, Pastor, these sessions really aren't doing much for us at all."

"Well, we have brought out some things that neither you nor Mr. King has talked about in years, so that's a very good start."

"But it's not enough, because every day when I wake up, all I think about is him lying in bed with my niece and how they now have a baby together."

"It's going to take some time to deal with all of this, but I really wish you and Mr. King would continue coming here to talk. Especially since the one thing you've said more than once is that you do love Mr. King, and that means a lot."

"I do, but that's why I don't think I can stay with him," Mrs. King said and stood up. "It hurts way too much, and I'm tired of feeling this way. But I want to thank you for everything you tried to do for us."

"Well, would you consider maybe seeing someone else? Because there's a chance someone else might be able to better help you."

"No, Pastor. I know you've suggested that for weeks now, but I have no interest in sharing our business with anyone else, and you're as far as I'm willing to go. But again, I want to thank you because you really are a kind and caring man. Your wife is very blessed to have you, and I hope she knows it."

"I hope so, too."

Mr. King reached his hand across Phillip's desk. "Thank you so much, Pastor."

"You're quite welcome. And Mrs. King, are you sure I can't recommend someone else for you and Mr. King to speak to?"

"No, I think it's time I did what I should have done from the very beginning."

"I really hate to see you file for a divorce without at least trying for a little while longer."

"I just can't keep fighting such a losing battle. I've tried, but it's just not possible."

The Kings said their good-byes, and Phillip wished he could have done more to help them. Either that or he wished he could have convinced Mrs. King to see another professional who specialized in marriage counseling. But she'd been so dead set against it, and it wasn't like he could make her do anything she didn't want to.

Still, he wished he'd been able to help them save their marriage because somehow divorce seemed a lot sadder when it involved a sixty-year-old woman and a seventy-year-old man, which was exactly how old the Kings were. It seemed a lot more dismal than if they'd been somewhat younger. The more he sat thinking, though, he realized that a divorce was a divorce and that it would be just as heartbreaking for a man in his thirties and a woman in her twenties—a man and woman like him and Alicia.

If Alicia had known she'd end up reporting to some straight-by-the-book, dot-every-*i*-cross-every-*t* PR manager, there was no way she would have ever told her father that she wanted this lowly position, the one he'd practically begged her to take. Initially, the elder board had decided that hiring Alicia on to work as a part-time PR specialist would be enough, at least until they moved forward with breaking ground for the new church, but as of two weeks ago, they, along with her father, had decided that what they also needed was a full-time person. Someone with a few years of marketing and public relations experience, they'd said. Alicia had known immediately, as soon as she'd met Carmen Lake, that she didn't care for her and that it would only be a matter of time before Alicia gave her two weeks' notice.

If she could, she would quit right now, but the truth of the matter was, she needed the money. She needed it a lot more than she'd been counting on because pretty much every time she turned around, it seemed that there was some credit card statement stuffed inside her P.O. box, waiting to be paid—not to mention, she was already two months behind on most of them. She hadn't thought it would be so bad, not as long as she paid the minimum amounts due, but by the time the church took out federal and state taxes on the first and fifteenth of every month, her monthly take-home pay was barely sixteen hundred dollars. Actually, it was just under that, so what this meant was that each of her checks was barely seven hundred-plus and certainly not enough to pay bills, fill up her tank, sometimes a couple of times a week, depending on how often she drove over to Chicago, and certainly not enough to take herself to lunch and dinner, pay for her weekly hair and manicure appointments, cover her biweekly pedicures, monthly hot-stone massage and deep-cleansing facial, none of which she could or should have to go without.

So, sadly, things had definitely gotten tight. Cash was limited, and she'd had no choice but to use every dime of that credit line that Phillip still didn't know about or tap into that newest

Visa to pay for all of her necessities. She'd been thinking that she would only charge the furniture on the Visa, but now that she was sitting there looking over the bill, she saw that she already had a fifty-one-hundred-dollar balance. Although, it was all for good reason, because by using this card, it meant she hadn't had to use her Macy's whenever she shopped there and now she was happy to say that she only had a hundred-dollar balance and still had forty-nine hundred dollars left open to make purchases with.

This was also the reason she'd been trying to ignore the promotional piece sitting on her desk, the one she'd received in the mail, announcing Macy's big sale—the kind of sale where as long as you used your Macy's card, just about everything, including top brand-name items that were rarely reduced, would be 20 percent off—starting today and through the weekend. It was the kind of deal she really didn't want to miss. At the same time, however, she didn't want to start racking up charges on the last department store account she had in just her name, especially since the only other credit she had besides Macy's was the less-than-five-thousand-dollar balance left on the Visa. Of course, she did have joint accounts with Phillip at Nordstrom and Lord & Taylor, and her name was also on a couple of other major credit cards he'd gotten before they'd met but had added her name to once they were married, but she didn't dare use those. Not when she knew how stingy Phillip was with them and how he'd probably go into cardiac arrest if she did use them—which was crazy, if you asked her, because it was a husband's duty to make sure his wife was happy and well taken care of. But instead, all he talked about was how he had to pay a two-thousand-dollar mortgage for a house that *she* just had to have, pay his truck note, pay utilities and insurances, and save for old age. If she had a cookie for every time he'd said those words to her, she'd be wealthier than Mrs. Fields and every other cookie conglomerate. Complain, complain, complain was all he did and she was sick of it.

Still, maybe it wasn't a good idea to go to Macy's, after all; maybe it was best to wait until another time. Maybe it was best she went straight home and tried to do some more writing. If she did, she'd be that much closer to getting a book deal and able to pay off the ton of money she now owed.

About an hour later, Alicia pushed one of the preliminary marketing plans to the side, the one her "boss" had asked her to type in the corrections for, and started toward Phillip's office. She'd been trying to keep her mind focused on work, but this whole silent-treatment business Phillip had been dishing for four days now was beginning to unnerve her. Partly because she didn't think it was right for him to carry a grudge for so long, but mostly because she still felt guilty for being with Levi all the while Phillip had planned the night of a lifetime for the two of them.

Alicia knocked three times.

"Yes."

"Do you have a minute?" she asked, closing his office door.

Phillip never looked up. "Not really."

"Why?"

"Because there's nothing to say."

"Phillip, why are you doing this?"

"Doing what?"

"This. Ignoring me and acting as though I'm your worst enemy."

Phillip wrote a few words on a legal pad but didn't say anything.

"Did you call Pastor Abernathy to schedule our counseling appointment?" she asked, but wasn't sure why because she really doubted anyone could help fix their problems. She doubted it because there were just so many of them.

"No."

"Why not?"

Phillip finally looked up. "Why should I, Alicia? Why should I do anything else to try to save our marriage after the way you disappointed me on Saturday night? Do you know how much trouble I went to? Do you realize how bad I felt when hours started to pass and you still weren't home yet?"

How many more times was she going to have to say she was sorry?

"I know, and I'm sorry. I'm really sorry, and I had no idea you were planning a surprise for me."

"Regardless. You should have come straight home after your dinner or at least called to say you were going to be late. And not only that, you wouldn't even answer your phone?"

"I forgot to turn it back on when I left the restaurant."

"Yeah, right. And by the way, who are these ladies you went to dinner with, anyway?"

"I don't think you even know them. They're just a group of women my age who came up to me before service one Sunday, asking if they could take me to dinner."

"But even if that's true, and you went to the mall right afterward, why was it after ten when you got home? Because the mall closes at nine."

"And that's exactly what time I left. After that I stopped at the drugstore and also at Baskin-Robbins to get some ice cream."

Phillip stared at her but didn't respond, so Alicia couldn't tell whether he believed her story or not. But finally, he said, "I really need to get back to work."

"So, you're kicking me out? Just like that?"

"No, but I have things I need to do, and I'm sure you need to get back to what you do best, anyway."

"Meaning what?"

"Shopping. What else?"

"Excuse me?"

Phillip shook his head and then picked up some document and began reading it.

"So, now you're going to act as though I'm not even standing here?"

Alicia stood waiting with her arms folded, but Phillip flipped his document to the next page and never looked at her again.

So Alicia left his office. She hated that smug look on his face and wondered just how self-righteous he'd continue to be if he knew about Levi. She was sure he wouldn't act nearly as uninterested in her as he was trying to act today. But Alicia wasn't going to waste any more time trying to figure Phillip out, one way or the other, because all it was doing was upsetting her, which was totally unnecessary when there were clearly much more satisfying things she could be doing—things such as shopping or lying in bed with Levi. It was simply a matter of choosing one of the two, but then she thought, why choose either over the other when she could easily do both before the night was over.

Chapter 23

It was already four o'clock, but since Macy's was staying open an hour later until ten, Alicia still had six hours before closing time. She would have had a bit longer, but traffic had started to pick up a bit once she'd gotten on the Kennedy Expressway. She was here now, though, and glad she'd made the decision to drive downtown. She'd known she wouldn't have been able to find the kind of brands she was interested in at the Macy's in Mitchell, and probably not a whole lot more at the Macy's at Woodfield, so that had left only Oakbrook Center or Water Tower. But since she'd always had great luck and had never left the Macy's at Water Tower Place without finding something she loved, she'd settled on that location. The State Street Macy's would have been the best of all, but with some of the designers they carried, Alicia would have easily maxed out her card with just a couple of outfits. Water Tower was certainly a better bet, at least today, anyway.

She walked inside, looked around at all the customers scattered throughout the first floor, and felt excited. The atmosphere was noisy and flooded with loads of conversation, and Alicia loved being a part of this kind of an environment. During the entire drive down to Michigan Avenue, she'd felt downright miserable about her situation with Phillip, but now she felt wonderful. She felt happy and like she was riding on a natural high.

She eased through the cosmetics section, all while turning down a couple of ladies offering the opportunity to test new colognes and then made her way toward the back of the store and over to the sunglass department. She hadn't purchased a new pair of sunglasses in five to six months, but she really needed a different style for the summer.

She browsed the case for a few minutes and then saw something she liked. "Can I please see those?"

The petite, caramel-colored woman pointed inside the glass case. "These? The Versaces?"

"Yes."

The woman held the glasses by their brown, tortoise-shelled frame and passed them over to Alicia.

She quickly slipped them on and gazed into the mirror sitting on the counter. "I really like these." She pulled her hair back with her hand, checking to see how they'd look with her hair away from her face. "I really do like these."

"They look very nice on you."

"I'll take them. And also, can I see the black Gucci pair right there?"

"Sure." The woman pulled them out and gave them to her.

Alicia tried them on, looked in the mirror, and pulled her hair back again.

"I really like these, too."

"Then get them both."

"That's what I'm thinking. Are they on sale?"

"No, unfortunately, not these."

"Hmmm." Alicia debated her purchase.

But not for long. "I need a black pair and a brown pair, so I'll just take both."

"Sounds good. Can I show you anything else?"

"No, I think that'll be it."

The woman rang up both items. "Your total comes to five hundred twenty-three dollars and eight-four cents. Will this be on your Macy's?"

"Yes." Alicia swiped her card, signed her name, and pressed Enter.

She watched the woman pull out two cases, one Versace and one Gucci, place the glasses inside them, and then wrap both in white tissue paper and slip them inside a plastic bag. "We really appreciate your business, so thank you."

"You're welcome."

Next, Alicia took the elevator up to the seventh floor to intimates, and as soon as she laid eyes on the first item, she knew she didn't have to look any further. The low-cut, black satin negligee displayed right in front of her was perfect. It was so her and something she knew Levi would love. They even had one in royal blue, and it was one of the most beautiful shades of royal blue she'd seen in a while. It was if they'd been made specifically for her and she didn't even need to try them on because she could already tell they would fit. At eighty dollars each, they were a little pricey, but they were well worth the look she knew Levi would have on his face once he saw her in them.

She went over to the checkout counter and paid for them. She then browsed through a couple of bra and pantie sets but since nothing really stood out, she headed down to the Michael Kors clothing section. This particular line was a less expensive version of Michael's original signature line, but still, it always had a lot of cute casual items to choose from.

She smiled at a woman who was looking at a spring sweater and then moved closer to a rack of skinny jeans. She thumbed through them until she found her size in both black and in a dark blue. She laid them over her forearm and then moved on to a row of sleeveless cotton blouses that had an attached cotton belt tied around the waist. There was no question that she was getting a white one, but she was also loving the emerald green one, too, so she pushed her shoulder bag closer to her neck, switched her sunglass bag to her other hand and then grabbed the hangers the two blouses hung on.

"Can I start you a room?" a young woman asked.

"Yes. Please."

Alicia handed her everything she'd collected thus far. "Thank you."

"No problem. And just let me know if I can help you find something."

Alicia scanned the department and checked out a few other items, and by the time she was ready to go into the dressing room, she'd given the sales clerk two pairs of dress pants; a couple of three-quarter, ribbed, button-up sweaters; and a cute little summer dress that draped down to her ankles.

Inside the fitting room, she removed her clothing and first tried on the black jeans and white cotton blouse. She loved anything sleeveless and she also loved how small the belt made her waist look. Not that her waist wasn't small on its own, but she still liked the fact that this blouse made it look even smaller. She liked the entire look and even pulled out her Gucci sunglasses and put them on just to try them out. They were just what she needed for this particular outfit and she pulled her hair up in a bun to see how it would look from that perspective as well. She liked that style even better.

She gave herself another once-over, gazing between both mirrors, and then took everything off. There was no need to try on the blue pair of jeans or the other sleeveless blouse because the sizes were the same as the items she'd just gotten out of. She tried on the rest of the clothing, one piece after another, and was thrilled to see that it all fit nicely.

Then, once Alicia was dressed, she gathered all that she'd tried on and started out toward the checkout terminal. But she stopped when she saw a table full of T-shirts that had Michael's first and last name embroidered across the front in rhinestones. So, she snatched up a black and a white one in small and added them to the pile she was now passing over to the salesgirl.

"You sure did well today."

"Yes, I certainly did."

"And it doesn't hurt that everything you chose is on sale."

"I know. It's rare when certain regular-priced items are twenty percent off, so this is really great."

"Definitely."

The woman rang up everything Alicia had selected and announced that her total was seven hundred thirty dollars and seventeen cents. Alicia hadn't planned on spending more than fifteen hundred dollars, which, including this purchase, was about the amount she'd spent already, but the thing was, she hadn't found any dresses or suits for church yet. Although, the more she calculated, even if she did end up spending another thousand, she'd still have nearly twenty-five hundred left open on her credit card, which was fine.

She finished the transaction, thanked the woman who'd helped her, and found her way over to the Ellen Tracy, Anne Klein, and Dana Buchman section. "Oh my God. This is too cute."

She was basically talking to herself but this red skirt suit had the most chic stand-up collar and not only did the material look rich, it felt rich. She smiled when she thought about Charlotte and how Charlotte would be beside herself if she saw it. Alicia had a mind to pull out her phone and call her because she knew

Charlotte always got just as excited as she did when it came to must-have suits or dresses. She'd certainly want one for herself, but since they attended the same church, they'd agreed a long time ago not to buy the same of anything that could be worn to Deliverance Outreach. They did buy some of the same sportier items, though, but that was pretty much it.

Alicia rushed into the dressing room and slipped on the fire-red suit that fit her like a glove, and then she tried on another one that she'd brought in with her, which was white and beautifully trimmed in black. This one looked tailor-made, too, something she was thrilled about because for a long while now, she'd been thinking about having a suit designed with her exact measurements and this was proof that it was well worth checking into.

Alicia took one last look at the white-and-black suit before taking it off and realized that it would be perfect to wear on Mother's Day. It was only a couple of weeks away, but as always, she was planning to spend it with her mother and attend her church that Sunday.

After paying for the suits, Alicia went down a few escalators and then stopped so she could get a better grip of the two large shopping bags she was struggling with, along with the garment bag of suits she was carrying. But when she turned to the side, she spied the shoe department. Of course, she wanted to check them out, see what they had new, but she stood there debating. Actually, though, the two suits had only come to eight hundred dollars together, so she still had two hundred more dollars to go before she arrived at the twenty-five hundred dollar limit she'd set for herself anyway.

She debated a bit longer and before she knew it, she'd gone all the way downstairs, out to the parking garage, and placed her bags inside the trunk of her car. She'd decided this was best because with everything locked up, she wouldn't have to wrestle with any of what she'd already purchased, and she'd be able to look for and try on as many shoes as she wanted in peace.

Now, she was glad she had because she'd found a sharp pair of red three-and-a-half-inch heels to match her red suit and also a pair of cute metallic sandals to match the summer dress she'd bought earlier. But those were pretty much the only pairs she'd really wanted, and she was finally ready to leave the store. That is, until she made it back to the main floor. She was now officially just over her personal limit for the evening, but didn't see where it would hurt to simply take a look in the fine jewelry section. So she walked over and for the most part only skimmed a number of glass cases. But then she did a double take and leaned closer when she saw a pair of princess-cut diamond earrings. They weren't nearly as large as the pair that had been stolen from her by that thug who'd followed her from the mall that day, but they had great clarity and would be cute whenever she wanted to dress very casual. They'd even be nice to wear when she was working out at the health club or maybe when she was volunteering at the church's clothing bank the way she did from time to time.

Alicia leaned much closer than she had before and saw the price tag, which was normally turned down on all jewelry pieces, but maybe the salesperson had mistakenly left it right-side up. Actually, they weren't bad at all, not when the fine jewelry department was offering 50 percent off plus an additional 15 percent for the next few days, so this would mean the final price would only be around nineteen hundred; that was great because Alicia still had nearly twenty-three hundred dollars left open on her Macy's charge card.

She sighed and then a woman with grayish-white hair asked if she could show her anything.

"Right now, I'm just looking."

"Well, just let me know."

Alicia did want to see the earrings but she wasn't sure about buying them because if she did, her Macy's would be almost maxed out. On the other hand, the earrings were much too good a deal to pass up.

"Okay, yes. Can I see the princess cuts right there?"

The woman slid open the door to the case. "All right."

When she gave them to Alicia, Alicia held them up to her ear.

"Do you want to try them?"

"That's fine. Yes."

When she placed both of them in her ears, she glanced inside the mirror and then pulled her hair all the way around to her left shoulder. She liked them with this hairstyle even better. So, she told the woman to ring them up, and then she signed her name for the sixth time tonight and prepared to leave the store for good. Which she would have done had she not spotted one of her favorite colognes. She loved Angel by Thierry Mugler and went ahead and purchased a new bottle of it and also the shower gel, body lotion, and deodorant.

But that was finally it—this time, really—Alicia thought, now down in the parking garage, walking to her car. Unlike the last time, though, when she'd purchased expensive jewelry, this evening she was a lot more cautious of her surroundings, and thankfully, no one seemed to be following her.

It was now nearly ten o'clock and the only thing she regretted about having driven so far away from Mitchell was that by the time she got home, it would be almost eleven thirty and much too late to go see Levi. She'd called him while she'd been on her way to Chicago and of course he would be happy to see her, regardless of how late she showed up, but just the same, she didn't want to push her luck with Phillip. This afternoon, Phillip had made it clear that he hadn't wanted to be bothered with her, and to be honest, she really didn't want to be bothered with him, either. Nonetheless, as a married woman, who did still care about her husband, she didn't feel comfortable staying out after midnight or well into the wee hours of the morning. So, like it or not, she would just have to see Levi sometime tomorrow.

Chapter 24

Hey, can you call me back in about fifteen minutes?" Shandra asked. "My mom is on the other line."

"Of course. Talk to you then."

Phillip pressed the End button on his phone and sat it down on the desk in his home office. Bible study had let out two hours ago, and he'd come straight home to relax. From his meeting with the Kings to the strained conversation he'd had earlier with Alicia to all of the other work responsibilities he'd taken care of today, it had all exhausted him completely.

Now, he'd been chatting with Shandra and though he would rather not admit it, talking to her had already begun helping him wind down. She made him feel special, and he couldn't deny that the more he conversed with her, the more he was tempted to go see her. He felt comfortable with her and even though he'd told himself that he wouldn't do it, he'd been sharing more and more details about his and Alicia's problems. He'd tried his best to avoid doing this, but Alicia was slowly but surely pushing him to do things he didn't want to do. He knew, especially as a Christian man, that his actions were very wrong, but no matter how diligently he tried to move forward and forget about his and Alicia's past disagreements, Alicia always did something worse. It was bad enough that she'd purchased that furniture without discussing it with him, but this afternoon, he'd taken it upon himself to call the customer service numbers at Neiman's and Saks and he'd learned that she'd charged right up to the maximums on both accounts. Needless to say, when he'd listened to each automated response, he'd barely been able to contain himself and had become more incensed than he had been earlier in the day.

He'd also noticed that none of her bills were coming to their house any longer, but little did she know, he'd written down her account numbers and her Social Security number a few months back, making sure he'd have the ability to check her balances anytime he wanted. He was starting to wonder just how much further she was willing to go and just how long it was going to take before she became desperate and did something crazy like trying to sign his name to loan and credit card applications he didn't know about. He didn't want to believe that she would ever stoop to such levels, but based on what he'd already seen her do in the past, he knew he couldn't deny the possibility.

The only reason he wasn't too worried right now was because he'd also checked her Macy's account and learned that, strangely enough, her balance was barely over a hundred dollars and she still had nearly five thousand dollars open. But he would definitely continue monitoring this account on a regular basis, too, because if she ever did max out the limit, he knew she'd then have no other choice but to figure out a lot more creative ways to support her habit.

After a few more minutes passed, Phillip picked up the phone and called Shandra back.

"Are you still on with your mom?"

"No, I just hung up."

"You haven't told her about us talking, have you?"

"No. But the only reason I haven't is because she would never be okay with the fact that you're a married man."

"And she shouldn't be okay with it, because it's like I keep telling you, what we're doing is wrong."

"Then, if it's so wrong, why do you keep calling me?"

"I've asked myself that question a number of times, and I don't know why."

"I think you do."

"Why do you say that?"

"Because I know exactly why you keep calling. And if I know, then you know, too."

"I guess I call because we've always been able to talk and because I do feel a connection with you that I haven't felt with my wife for a while."

"Exactly. Also, where are you now?"

"Home."

"And she's not there? This late?"

Phillip hated answering her questions because the fact that Alicia and he were now coming and going whenever they felt like it and were no longer bothering to give each other any details regarding their whereabouts, well, that really bothered him.

"Let's not talk about my wife."

"Okay, then, let's talk about us."

Phillip chuckled. "No, let's talk about you. Like, for example, why aren't you dating someone? Or are you?"

"No, I'm not. I was a few months ago, but because it wasn't working out, we ended it. And then I already told you, I was once married but then got divorced."

"But you've never told me what happened."

"That's because I don't like to talk about it. But if you really want to know, it's as simple as this. My husband was very abusive and very controlling and after five years of living in hell, I finally got out."

"No woman should ever have to go through that, and I'm sorry to hear about what happened to you."

"We've been divorced for two years now, and thankfully, he's never contacted me since."

"That's good."

"So I'm as free as can be and ready to settle down with someone decent. Someone I can love and who will genuinely love me back. I'm ready to settle down with someone like you, Phillip."

"I really wish you wouldn't talk that way because you know that's not possible."

"Why do you keep saying that? Because anything is possible if you want it to be."

Phillip switched the phone from one ear to the other, and Shandra continued.

"Look, I know it's wrong for me to come after you like this, but I can't help the way I feel. I knew I still had feelings for you, but the more I talk to you, the more I feel it growing into something a lot deeper."

Phillip was feeling the same way, but he knew it would be a mistake to admit it to her.

"If you'll just give me a chance. Because if you do, I promise you won't be sorry."

"This is wrong, Shandra."

"Okay, so it's wrong. We both agree on that particular fact, but I can't give up on the idea that we were meant to be together. I mean, think about it. We were head over heels in love in high school, and I really don't think it was a coincidence that I decided to attend service at your church at the same time you and your wife are having problems. Everything is for a reason, and you and I both know that."

Phillip closed his eyes and tried to imagine what the inside of her house looked like. If she was already making him feel this at ease by phone, he could only imagine how wonderful she'd probably make him feel in person. He fantasized about the layout of the rest of her house, but when he pictured her bedroom and also with him and her lying together inside of it, he snapped back to reality. *Thoughts, ideas, and suggestions.*

"I'm sorry, Shandra, but I think it's time we hung up."

"Why?"

"Because I don't want to do something I'll end up regretting. Something that I'll have to pay for years down the road, if not sooner, and pay serious consequences for."

"So, you'd rather be miserable with your wife even though I'm offering you complete happiness?"

"No, but I'm not going to let desire and temptation cause me to do something I won't be able to take back."

"You're making a big mistake."

"Maybe. But right now, at this very moment, I know I can't do this anymore."

"You do know that she'll never change, right?"

"Well, if she doesn't, then that'll be on her, but I do love her and that's the one thing I've never denied even to you. And because I love her, I'm going to give our marriage my all before simply giving up."

"Well, when she starts treating you worse than she already is—and she will—then I'll be right here waiting."

"You take care of yourself, Shandra."

"You, too."

Phillip searched through his contact list but just as he prepared to click on Alicia's number, his phone rang. At first, he thought it might be Shandra; however, he was relieved when he saw that it was Mrs. King instead.

Phillip pushed the Answer button. "Hello?"

"Pastor Sullivan, I'm really sorry to bother you this late, but you've always said I could call you any time, day or night, if I needed to."

"Yes, and I meant that. Is everything okay?"

"No, it isn't. I've tried to find peace with this thing my husband has gone and done behind my back, but no matter how hard I try, I just can't get over it." Mrs. King paused and then burst into tears. "I . . . feel . . . like . . . I'm having . . . a nervous breakdown," she said, sniffling. "I feel like I'm going to lose my mind, and I really need to talk to someone."

She sounded very troubled and the whole thought of what she and Mr. King were going through truly saddened Phillip. "You don't have to say another word. I'm on my way."

"Thank you, Pastor."

"I'll be there soon."

Chapter 25

Phillip had only been sitting in front of the Kings' residence for five minutes at the most, and Curtis was now pulling up behind him. Phillip knew Mrs. King hadn't wanted Curtis to be involved but with her sounding so distraught on the phone, Phillip had decided it was time Curtis intervened. Plus, even though Mrs. King totally disagreed with him, he really thought they needed someone more experienced to help them with their problem.

Phillip and Curtis walked up the sidewalk and up three stairs to the front door and Phillip rang the doorbell. He looked over at Curtis who was dressed in all black. Black pullover shirt, black pants, and a black leather jacket. The reason Phillip noticed it was that he was basically dressed the same way. As a matter of fact, they had on so much black that he hoped their attire wouldn't make Mrs. King feel uncomfortable or like they were detectives coming to interrogate her.

Phillip rang the doorbell again but just as he did, Mrs. King finally opened the door. At first, she only stood there, gazing back and forth at them, and it was obvious that she wasn't too pleased to see Curtis. But she didn't say anything, and a few seconds later, she opened the screen door and invited them in.

"Please have a seat."

Phillip sat down first. "Thank you."

Curtis sat at the opposite end of the sofa. "Yes, thank you, Mrs. King."

"Can I get either of you something to drink?"

"No, ma'am," Curtis answered.

"No, thank you. We're fine."

Phillip watched her take a seat in a chair that she must have brought in from her dining room. She sat right in front of them, and there was another chair just like it sitting not far from her. Phillip watched how calmly she acted and was glad she'd settled down a great deal since she'd called him. One thing sort of concerned him, though, and that was the crooked way her wig was pulled onto her head. Mrs. King wore wigs all the time, but this was the first time Phillip had seen one of them looking as though she'd slapped it on, fast and in a hurry.

Phillip looked down the hallway. "Where's Mr. King?"

"He's in the bedroom. He'll be out in a minute."

"Are you having second thoughts about filing for a divorce?"

"No. But I've been on edge for hours now, and that's why I finally decided it was best that I call you."

"I'm glad you did, and we're willing to stay for as long as you need us to. We'll do whatever we can to try to help you."

Just then Mr. King moseyed out, shook both Phillip's and Curtis's hands, and then sat in the chair near Mrs. King. As soon as he did, Mrs. King no longer seemed calm and appeared a lot more agitated.

"Pastor, I just don't know what to do," she said to Phillip. "I've been having all sorts of crazy thoughts, and it all started when I left the grocery store this afternoon."

"What kind of thoughts?"

Mrs. King tossed her husband a nasty look and then reached

down inside what looked like her purse. Phillip watched as she pulled something out, and he gasped when he saw what it was. He swallowed hard when he saw Mrs. King pointing a .38 at the man she'd been married to for forty years.

Phillip could tell Curtis was just as shocked as he was, and poor Mr. King was terrified.

"You see, it's like this, Pastor. No matter how many ways I tried to weigh this whole crazy mess, I finally realized that *this* is the only way to pay Harold back for what he's done to me."

Curtis spoke in an immediate tone but also with compassion. "Mrs. King, with all due respect, I know you're upset, but this isn't the way to go about handling things."

Mrs. King looked at Curtis without any emotion. "Why? Because this isn't the way your wife handled things when you went out and got that illegitimate baby of yours?"

Phillip interrupted. "Mrs. King, I think what Pastor is trying to say is that violence isn't going to solve anything. It won't change what happened, and we don't want you doing something you'll regret. There's no doubt that you have every reason to be upset with your husband, but just the fact that you still love him is enough for you to think twice about what you're doing."

"You're right. I do love him, and that's why I'll never be able to get past this. I've tried but now I know that it's just not possible."

Curtis and Phillip looked at each other, and Phillip wished Alicia had answered her phone when he'd tried reaching her from the car thirty minutes ago. If this went on for hours, maybe Alicia would try calling him back, get worried when he didn't answer, and then dial the police. Although, at least he had left her a message, so maybe if too much time passed by, she would think to contact one of the church secretaries to find out where the Kings lived. He wondered if maybe Charlotte would do the same if it ended up that Curtis was gone a lot longer than he should be—because this entire situation was looking worse by the second.

"Pastor Black?" Mrs. King said.

"Yes?"

"Was it really that good to you? Because if it was *that* good to you, then maybe it was just that good to ol' Harold here, too."

"I'm not sure I know what you mean."

"Of course you do. You know exactly what I'm talking about."

Curtis readjusted his position on the sofa. "I'm sorry, but I really don't."

Phillip could see that Mrs. King was becoming impatient. "You *do* know what I'm talking about. I'm talking about that thing between that whore's legs. That thing you obviously couldn't get enough of and that's how you ended up with that bastard child of yours."

Phillip was mortified and while he didn't dare look away from Mrs. King, he wondered just how Curtis was planning to respond to her.

"Mrs. King, what I did was wrong. Way wrong. And I'll never stop trying to make up to my wife for what I did. But by the grace of God, Charlotte has finally found it in her heart to forgive me. It took a lot of time, but we're closer now than we've ever been, and I believe the same thing can happen for you and Mr. King."

"See, that's where you're wrong, Pastor. Harold and I can never be a happy couple again. The pain he's caused me runs far too deep, and the only consolation I can see myself ever getting is by taking him out of here."

Phillip eased toward the edge of the couch. "Mrs. King, please. You're a good person. A good Christian woman, so I know you really don't want to do this. You're just hurt is all. You're hurt, and this has been a very difficult time for you."

"I just don't see why men do this. I know I did the same thing to him back in the day, but I would never do something like this after all these years of being married. I would have given my life for this man if I had to, but now . . . today . . . I'm going to have to take his," she yelled and then held the gun with both hands.

"Puddin', please don't do this. I'm so, so sorry. I'm so sorry that I don't know what to do. Please don't take my life over this. What about our children?"

"What about them?"

"They'll be so hurt over this. They'll be hurt about everything."

"You should've thought about that before you went out and laid up with that tramp. If you cared about them, you never would have done that," Mrs. King said and then closed her eyes and shook her head frantically, almost as if she was trying to shake something out of it. She then pressed both sides of her temples, one with her hand and one with the gun. Then, she opened her eyes, stood up, and looked over at Curtis. "Harold, what are you doing over there? How did you slip away without me seeing you? Get back over here," she demanded and pointed the gun at Curtis. "I said get over here!"

At first Curtis hesitated but when she yelled again, he stood and walked over to where Mr. King was sitting.

This was crazy. Phillip had not seen this coming before this evening, but Mrs. King had clearly lost her mind and now all their lives were in danger because of it.

"Mrs. King. I'm not your husband. I'm Pastor Black."

"Shut up!" she demanded and then looked over at Mr. King. "Who are you, and what are you doing in our house?"

It was clear that Mr. King didn't know what to say or do, so he did and said nothing.

"Well, whoever you are, I want you to get over there, sit down, and keep quiet. And you'd better not trade places with my husband again, you hear me?"

Mr. King took a seat at the end of the sofa where Curtis had been sitting.

Mrs. King sat back down and smiled at Curtis. "Remember, Harold, when we first met? Remember how beautiful you thought I was and how you said you'd never seen a woman more beautiful in your whole life? Remember that? Remember how we used to ride in your sixty-eight Mercury? You'd pick me up and take me to the park, push me in the swing, and then we'd have a picnic on the grass and laugh and talk until sundown. Remember how special those times were? Remember how in love we were with each other? And then remember how happy we were when Harold Jr. was born and then we had him a little sister. That boy loved little Elena so much, he acted more like her father than he did her brother."

Mrs. King reminisced for another twenty minutes but neither Phillip, Curtis, nor Mr. King moved an inch, nor did they breathe one word. Phillip listened and hoped all the happy times she was speaking about would be enough to draw her back to reality.

But they weren't; instead, things turned ugly again.

"Life was good, Harold. Real good until you went out and slept with that whore-niece of mine. Then, today, I went to the grocery store, minding my own business, but no sooner than when I went into the produce section, I saw her and that baby. I saw your child, your own flesh and blood, Harold, and it slit my heart in two. Just tore me to pieces."

Now Phillip understood. Seeing the baby for the first time

was what had set Mrs. King off and the reason she'd slipped into this disturbed mental state.

"And that's why I decided, right then and there, that only one thing would make me feel better about all of this: blowing you to hope field."

Phillip took a deep breath and prayed that Mrs. King would come to her senses. But she didn't. Instead, she pointed the pistol straight at Curtis and cocked it like a professional gunman. "I'm sorry, Harold, but it's time."

Mrs. King slowly stood up but as soon as she did, Phillip charged toward her and wrestled her to the floor. Mrs. King fired the gun at the wall and Phillip tried his best to take the gun from her. He tried but Mrs. King scuffled against his strength and fired the .38 again.

Phillip yelled and grabbed his thigh with both hands, but in a split second, he managed to overpower Mrs. King and shake the gun away from her. Curtis immediately grabbed it.

Mrs. King burst into tears. "I'm so sorry, Daddy," she said to Phillip. "I didn't mean it. I didn't mean to hurt anybody, so please don't put me on punishment. I'll be good from now on, Daddy. I promise."

Crying like a baby, Mrs. King lay her head against Phillip's chest.

Curtis pulled out his cell phone and bent down to Phillip. "Are you okay? Let me see your leg."

With all the commotion over the last few minutes and even though he was in excruciating pain, Phillip hadn't thought much about the gunshot wound. "I don't think it's that bad. It's bleeding and it hurts like crazy, but I don't think it's serious."

Curtis took a look for himself. "Still, we need to get you to a hospital right away."

Phillip watched Curtis dialing 911 and then glanced over at

Mr. King, who acted as though he was afraid to move or speak a word to anyone. He sat quietly and to be honest, Phillip didn't know what to say to him, either. So, instead, Phillip rubbed Mrs. King's back, trying to comfort her, and waited for the ambulance and police officers to arrive on the scene. He waited and hoped he would never have to experience anything close to this ever again.

Chapter 26

Alicia had decided for sure that she wasn't going to drive over to see Levi tonight, but when she'd listened to Phillip's message, saying he was heading over to the Kings' house, she'd changed her mind, called Levi, and the next thing she knew, she was in her car and on her way over to see him. She knew that she should have followed her first thought and stayed home the way she'd planned, but the more she'd conversed with Levi, the more she'd longed to be with him. She also knew that if Phillip arrived back home before she did, she'd have a lot of explaining to do—which was why she already had her lie prepared and ready. She would tell him that one of the ladies from the church that she'd gone to dinner with on Saturday was having some problems with her husband and had asked if they could meet at an all-night restaurant to discuss it. Alicia knew no such woman existed and that she'd never gone to dinner with anyone, but she would tell him that this mysterious woman had really needed to talk to her, the same as Mrs. King had needed to talk to him. She'd also tell him that because the woman had made her promise not to reveal her name, she couldn't tell him who she was.

Alicia wasn't sure if Phillip would buy her story or not but, he would have no choice but to accept what she told him. He would accept it or she'd bring up the fact that he'd just spent the night away from home himself on Saturday night and that she actually had no proof at all that he truly had stayed at Brad's. She did believe that he had, but she would pretend that she didn't and use it as ammunition if he challenged her about this evening.

Now, once again, she was lying next to Levi, face-to-face, feeling as satisfied as any woman could hope for when it came to lovemaking. It was true that she did feel an underlying sense of guilt, but when she thought about the terrible way Phillip had been treating her, her guilt waned considerably.

Levi stroked Alicia's hair. "You know, you really are the woman of my dreams."

Alicia smiled.

"You're the woman of my dreams, and I can no longer deny that I've fallen in love with you."

Alicia's smile slowly faded.

"I've pretty much known it the entire time we've been seeing each other, but I hadn't wanted to admit it to you or to myself because legally you belong to someone else."

Alicia was shocked and had no words to say, because even though she did enjoy Levi's company, she was far from being in love with him. She loved the way he made her feel sexually, but that was basically where her love for him ended.

"So, sweetheart, how do you feel about that?"

"I don't know."

"Well, my feelings for you are very real, and what I want now is to be with you on a full-time basis. When we first started this, I was sure that being with you every now and then would be fine, but it just isn't. It's not enough for me anymore."

"But, Levi, you know what my situation is."

"Yeah, I do, but you can fix that anytime you get ready, right?"

Alicia looked away from him.

"And there's something else I need to tell you as well. I'm thinking about leaving Mitchell for good and moving to another state."

Now, she looked at him again. "Why?"

"There are a couple of reasons, but I really think it's best that I don't give you any details or involve you in any of my business matters."

Alicia wanted desperately to ask him straight out what his line of work actually was because, even though she already knew, they'd never openly discussed it. The subject hadn't come up, and now Alicia wondered if things were spinning out of control and that maybe he was worried about being busted.

"Levi, I really do want to know why you're planning to leave the area."

"It's not worth going into right now, and the most I can say is that moving will be a good thing and that I'll be able to give you an even better life somewhere else. All you have to do is say you'll go with me and that you'll marry me."

"How can I do that when I'm already married to Phillip?"

"You can do it just as soon as you divorce him."

Alicia looked away again and wondered how she was ever going to tell him that she would never be able to do that. She wondered how she would tell him that even if the day did come when she and Phillip found themselves splitting up, she would never be able to move away with or marry a criminal. She liked Levi a lot, but she could never settle down with someone who might be killed or arrested on a moment's notice. As it was, she knew that every time she visited him, she was placing her life in at least a slight amount of danger, but she could never be his wife. She could never live with him on a permanent basis the way he was suggesting.

Levi turned her face back toward him. "Hey, I'm really serious about what I'm saying. I mean, I now love you so much that it scares me. To be honest, the whole idea that I fell in love with you so quickly makes me feel weak, and feeling weak is not something I've experienced in my adult life. Alicia, you are the only woman who has ever made me want to end the business I'm in and start a completely brand-new life. You're the first woman I ever actually wanted to live with for the rest of my days and have children with."

Alicia waited a few seconds and then said, "I'm sorry, but I just can't up and ask Phillip for a divorce. I just can't."

"I know this won't be easy, but I promise you, I'll make it worth your while in the end. I'll be everything a husband should be to his wife emotionally, and I've got enough money to give you pretty much anything you could ever want. All I need is the chance to prove it to you."

Alicia sat up on the side of the bed and gazed back at him. "Levi, I'm sorry. Maybe things will be different at some point, but I can't do this right now."

"So, that's your final decision?"

"Unfortunately, I guess it is."

Levi swung his legs over the side of the bed and stood up. "Then, as much as it hurts me to say this, you and I are over."

"Why?"

"Because I can't allow myself to continue being this vulnerable. My guard has been let down more over the last few weeks than it has been in years, and I can't live like this. I can't keep making love to you and baring my soul to you when I know you're going home to your husband. I thought I could deal with that, but now I resent it. I resent it, and I don't like feeling this way."

Alicia strolled over to him and wrapped her arms around his waist. "Please don't end things between us. Because I really don't want that, and I know you don't want that, either."

Levi gently pushed her body away from his. "Sweetheart, my mind is made up."

Alicia didn't know what else to say, and Levi pulled on his plush robe and left the bedroom.

She took a quick shower, got dressed, and went to look for him. She checked the living room, then the kitchen and finally found him sitting in the theater room.

"So, this is it? You really don't want to see me anymore?"

Levi left his chair, walked over to where Alicia was standing, and kissed her without delay. He kissed her so passionately that she was sure he'd rethought his position and was now having a change of heart.

But then, Levi slightly pulled his lips away from hers and held both sides of her face. "I really wish things could have been different, but I also want you to know that there are no hard feelings. None at all, because I always knew you had a husband. I was never in the dark about that, so this isn't your fault. I also want you to know that I wish only the best for you in the future."

Alicia opened her mouth, preparing to speak, but Levi stopped her. "Let's just leave well enough alone and move on with our lives. Let's move on before I end up more hurt than I already am."

Levi kissed her again and then left to go get dressed. Alicia sat down and decided that maybe his decision was all for the best. Of course, she wasn't happy about giving up the good thing she had going with Levi, but at the same time, she knew she wasn't in love with him and that she wasn't willing to do any of what he was asking. She knew it, and there was no sense leading him to believe anything different.

As soon as Levi pulled into the parking lot of the strip mall, Alicia leaned over and kissed him one last time. Then, she got out of the car, unlocked the door of her own vehicle, opened it, and got inside. After she started it up, she watched Levi drive away, and she drove in the opposite direction.

She headed down the dark and deserted rural road and after a few minutes, she reached inside her tote and grabbed her cell phone. She'd purposely turned it off as soon as she'd left to go see Levi, but now she hoped Phillip hadn't tried calling her again. Unfortunately, the moment her phone registered its tower signal, she saw that she had three messages.

No doubt they were all from Phillip and she could only imagine how angry he was. She even considered not listening to them at all but then figured she probably should listen, just in case one or two of them were from someone else. Although, since it was almost 2:00 A.M., she didn't know who else would be calling her.

She dialed into the system and played the first message.

"Baby girl, hey, it's your dad. We're at Mitchell Memorial with Phillip, so please call me or get here as soon as you can. I love you."

Alicia frowned and wondered what that was all about. Then, she skipped to the next message.

"Baby girl, where are you? Honey, I didn't want to tell you this until you got here, but Phillip has been shot. The doctor says he should be fine, but they're taking him into surgery to remove the bullet and you really need to get here."

The next one was from her stepmother. "Alicia, this is Charlotte, and I hope you're okay because we've been trying to get in touch with you for the last couple of hours. I was hoping that maybe you went to see your mom but she said she hadn't talked to you since yesterday. So, honey, please call us because Phillip really needs you."

Alicia was sure her heart had missed a few beats, and she tried recollecting the last time she'd been this afraid. But she knew exactly when it was. She knew it was the day she'd been raped.

Alicia thought about a lot of things, including the affair she'd been having with Levi, and then stepped on the accelerator. She drove as fast as she could and prayed all the way. She prayed because she'd never forgive herself if Phillip was worse off than her father had told her. She'd never forgive herself for not being there for him—once again—the same way she hadn't been there when his father had died.

Chapter 27

Alicia glanced up at the clock on the wall, saw that it was three in the morning, and looked back over at Phillip. The surgeon had successfully removed the bullet and stitched Phillip back up. Thankfully, it hadn't done nearly as much damage as it could have. The doctor had explained to them that he'd found the bullet lodged just beneath the skin and that it was basically a miracle, what with Mrs. King being at such close range when she'd shot him. Of course, Phillip, even through his grogginess, had smiled at the doctor and told him that this was all a result of prayer and God's mercy.

Now, he was resting in the room he'd been assigned to and Alicia's father, Charlotte, Melanie, and Brad were preparing to leave. Alicia had thought her father was simply going to kiss her good-bye, the same as the others, but instead he asked her to go out into the hallway with them.

"You're staying the night, aren't you?" he asked.

"Yes."

"Good. But why don't you walk out with us."

Alicia wondered why and hoped he wasn't going to question her about where she was when he'd been trying to call her.

At the elevators, Charlotte reached over to hug Alicia. "Hey,

I'm going to let you and your dad talk, but I'll see you tomorrow, okay?"

"Thanks, Charlotte. Thank you for being here."

"Of course."

Melanie hugged her next. "I love you, girl, and I'll call you as soon as I get a few hours of sleep. My shift was supposed to start at six, but I think I'll just come in sometime around noon and work into this evening."

"Thanks, Mel."

"Let us know if you need anything at all," Brad said, embracing her.

"I will."

The door opened and they all went outside, but when the door shut, her father started right in. "Baby girl, is everything okay?"

"I'm fine, Daddy. Really."

"Well, what took you so long to get here, and where were you when I first started calling you? I called your house several times and then I called your cell."

Alicia hated lying to her father, but he was leaving her no choice except telling him the story she'd originally concocted for Phillip.

"There's a woman from church who's having problems with her husband and she asked me if I would meet with her. She really needed to talk to someone, so I told her we could meet at a restaurant. We went to the one that never closes not too far from our house."

Her father stared at her without the slightest blink, and Alicia looked over at the waiting area.

"Alicia, I know you're an adult and that you have the right to live your life any way you want to, but I'm telling you now, you'd better end whatever it is you've gotten yourself into and you'd better end it right now. I'm begging you not to do the terrible things I once did. I'm begging you before it's too late."

"Daddy, what are you talking about?"

"Don't, Alicia. Don't lie to me because I know you're doing something that you shouldn't be and that if you don't stop, it's going to cause you and Phillip a whole lot of heartache. It'll generate a ton of problems, the kind you won't be able to make up for."

Alicia wanted to insist how wrong he was, but she could already tell by the look in his eyes that he knew exactly what she was up to. He knew, without a doubt, that his "baby girl" was sleeping with another man, so she said nothing.

"I promise you, it's not worth it. Whoever he is, Alicia, he's not worth it."

Tears streamed from Alicia's eyes and her father embraced her tightly.

"Everything is going to be fine, but you can't keep doing what you're doing. You have to forget about this person and start focusing on your husband. Phillip is a good man who really, really loves you, and it's time you realized that."

Alicia held on to her father and wished she never had to let him go. She wished he could stay there with her forever.

"Hey, you'd better get back down to Phillip's room, and I need to catch up with Charlotte. But you remember what I said, okay?"

"I will, Daddy. And I'm so sorry."

"You're young and you're human, and while that doesn't excuse any of your actions, God always forgives. He forgave me, and now what you have to do is be the best wife you can be to Phillip."

"Thanks for not hating me, Daddy."

"Baby girl, I could never hate you. I'll love you until the day

I take my last breath, and even after that, I'll always be in your heart."

"I'll call you tomorrow, and tell Charlotte I said thanks again."

Curtis pressed the down button for the elevator and it opened immediately. "I love you."

"I love you, too."

Alicia went into the restroom to wash her face with cold water, dried it off, and went back down to Phillip's room. As she walked in, he looked over at her and smiled.

"What are you doing awake?"

"I guess I was looking for you."

Alicia leaned down and kissed him and then grabbed one of his hands.

"I was so scared when my dad called me."

"It really wasn't that bad. But why weren't you answering the phone when your dad was calling you from the ambulance?"

Alicia asked God to forgive her for the lie she was about to tell and then rattled off the same alibi she'd just given her father.

Phillip took it all in but then asked, "Who is she?"

"She asked me not to reveal her name, and I assured her that I wouldn't. So, I hope you can understand that."

"I do understand but only if you're really telling me the truth."

Alicia wasn't sure what had come over her, but suddenly she felt as though she wanted to come clean. For some strange reason, she wanted to tell Phillip everything and just get it over with. But she couldn't. She wanted to be straight with him from now on, but she just didn't see where confessing her affair was going to benefit either one of them.

"I am telling you the truth."

"Then, I'm fine with it, and I'm just glad you're here now."

"You should try to go back to sleep."

"In a little while."

"And another thing. You do know that your mother is going to be livid once she finds out that you didn't call her right away."

"I know, but I just didn't want to worry her or have her driving over here so late at night. I'll call her as soon as we get home tomorrow."

"Whatever you say, but I'm not taking the blame for it. If she asks me why we didn't call, I'm telling her it's because you told us not to."

Phillip chuckled. "I'm sure you will."

"I also hope you're planning to do exactly what the doctor has instructed."

"Which is what?"

"Staying off your leg and taking it easy for a few days."

"Please. I'm fine."

"That might be so, but you're not doing anything at least until Monday."

"Monday? Isn't today Thursday?"

"It is now."

"You think I'm going to lie up in bed for four full days?"

"I don't *think* anything. I know that's what you're going to do."

Phillip smiled and then fluttered his eyelids, clearly trying to stay awake.

Alicia kissed him again and sat down in the recliner next to the bed and leaned back. She moved around until she was comfortable and then glanced over at her husband who was now fast asleep. She watched him slumbering peacefully, but then the reality of the last few hours hit her like an out-of-control semi. Phillip actually could have been killed. He could have died, and the idea that she was probably having sex with Levi at the same time he'd been shot was unsettling. It was outrageous and just plain disgraceful. What she'd been doing behind Phillip's back was not only dishonorable, it was downright shameful, and she wished she could erase every moment she'd spent committing adultery.

But the brutal truth was that she couldn't. She couldn't remove her sins of the past, and all she could do now was move forward. All she could do was love her husband with all her heart and do whatever she could to make him happy—because now she knew that she would never want to live without him. What she could do was stop being the selfish person she'd been ever since the day they'd gotten married.

Alicia closed her eyes and realized that Levi's ending their relationship had turned out to be a blessing in disguise, and she vowed to never go outside of her union with Phillip again.

Chapter 28

It was the first Friday in June, an entire month after the shooting incident, and Phillip couldn't be happier. When he was growing up, his mother had always told him that from everything bad, something good came out of it and now he knew she'd been right. He knew, because his getting shot had turned out to be the best thing that could have happened for his and Alicia's marriage. Ever since the night he'd been admitted into the emergency room, her whole attitude had changed, and she'd started giving him her undivided attention. He had immediately seen the worry in her eyes and even after a few days, when he was basically able to do things on his own again without problems, she had still continued to wait on him. She'd taken care of him the way any man would hope to be taken care of by his wife, and they were now extremely content with each other.

The other thing was that Alicia hadn't spent a lot of time away from him over the last month, either, meaning she wasn't sneaking out to go shopping and that life for them now reminded him of the first couple of months they were married. So much so that he no longer felt they needed marital counseling after all. His mom had come and stayed with them for the first three days he was home—days when Alicia surely could have gone wherever she wanted—but Alicia had still made it a point to do everything she could for him on her own.

Phillip buttoned up his perfectly starched, snow-white shirt, and, without warning, he thought about Mrs. King. Because she still remained in a catatonic state, there hadn't been any real court proceedings, other than a hearing, and she would probably stay on at the mental institution until she was better. Phillip, Alicia, Curtis, and Charlotte as well as other members of the church had gone to see her, but there was never any change in her condition. Phillip also thought about Mr. King and how the man had seemed to age twenty years, just in the last month. Mr. King had told Phillip that all of what had happened to his wife was his own fault and that even though he'd asked God to forgive him, he didn't think he could ever forgive himself for what he'd done. Phillip had responded by saying that Mr. King had a duty to forgive himself the same as God had and that he was going to have to find a way to go on with his life. Phillip hadn't been sure his words had resonated with Mr. King, but what he hoped and prayed was that Mr. King would feel better with time.

After arranging his tie, Phillip went downstairs to the kitchen, draped his suit jacket across the back of a chair, and then walked over and kissed his wife.

"You look beautiful."

"Why, thank you, sir."

"Of course. Anytime."

They both laughed and then Phillip sat down at the table. Alicia put a plate of pancakes in front of him and next to it, a small dish of sausage links. When she'd poured their orange juice, she took her seat as well and Phillip said grace.

When he finished, he forked a couple of flapjacks onto his plate. "So, what have you got planned for today?"

"I'm really going to try to buckle down and get back to writing."

"Good. But you do know that I wish you had given the job at the church a few more weeks."

"I'm sorry, but I just couldn't. I tried to hang in there but what Carmen needs is someone who doesn't aspire to do anything more than a few clerical duties and that wasn't working for me. I realize that I've only been out of school for a year, but I also didn't spend four years in college just so I could end up in that kind of a position. Plus, I really didn't care all that much for Carmen, anyway, and I don't think she liked me, either."

"Well, the thing is, Carmen really did come highly recommended and that's why everyone was so in favor of hiring her."

"That's all well and good, but I wasn't planning on being someone's little assistant or secretary."

Phillip wasn't sure what to say, because the last thing he wanted to do was start a fight with Alicia, especially since they hadn't argued once in four weeks.

"Plus, it wasn't like I could go to a job and take care of you at the same time," she said teasingly.

"Yeah, right."

"I'm serious."

"I was only down for a few days, so that wasn't nearly reason enough for you to quit working."

Alicia smiled, but Phillip thought about how Alicia had taken off the whole first week after he'd been shot and then after that she'd called Carmen to tell her that she was resigning. Of course, Curtis hadn't been happy about Alicia's decision in the least and he hadn't hesitated telling her she was making a huge mistake. He'd told her that she needed the experience and that he wanted her doing something that would help the church.

Nonetheless, though, Curtis's feelings hadn't seemed to affect Alicia one way or the other.

"I know you were disappointed and so was my dad, but writing is what I really want to do."

"And you know I support that one hundred percent but I just hope you take it a lot more seriously and that you go ahead and finish a full manuscript."

"I will, and actually, I'm going to try to be finished with the first draft in a couple of months."

Phillip raised his eyebrows in awe. "Really?"

"Yeah. I mean, up until now, I've been dragging my feet and I can't deny that all the other times I told you I was writing, I really wasn't. I always planned to, but I always seemed to get distracted and then I never got anything done. But now I'm really going to do this. I was also thinking that at some point, it would be good for me to purchase a notebook computer. My desktop version is fine but if I had a notebook, I could take it outside or take it anywhere that inspires me to write."

"If you finally get going and stick with it, I'll see what I can do about that."

Alicia beamed. "You really mean that?"

"I do. Especially, if you're claiming you're going to have a full draft within the next two months. That is what you said, right?"

"Something like that."

"Well, I'm impressed. And I think it goes without saying that I can't wait to read it."

"I'm a little self-conscious about my work, but I'll let you read some of it as soon as I feel it's ready."

When they finished eating, Phillip got up and slipped on his jacket. "I won't be home until after nine or so because I'm staying for the men's ministry fellowship."

"Oh, that's right. You told me that."

Phillip picked up his briefcase and then went over to the sink and kissed her good-bye. "I love you, baby, and I'll see you tonight."

"I love you, too."

Alicia had tried her best to forget about Levi but now here she was lying in his bed—again. She'd tried and had succeeded for all of four weeks but then, a couple of days ago, she'd picked up the phone and called him. She'd told him how she missed him and that she really needed to see him. Of course, she hadn't been sure how Levi was going to respond, but he'd told her how much he missed her, too, and that he wanted her to come right over. He wanted her to come right away—but only if she'd made the decision to leave Phillip and file for a divorce. He'd gone on to say that while he respected her attempt at trying to make her marriage work, it was finally time she realized the inevitable: that she and he and not she and her husband were meant to be together.

Alicia had gotten in her car and driven to the usual spot, and Levi had picked her up the same as always. She remembered how for the first time since their connecting with each other, they hadn't cared about it being broad daylight and had kissed fiercely. Alicia remembered how she hadn't been able to wait for them to drive out to his house, go inside, and make love to each other.

But the only thing was, even as good as Levi had made her feel, she hadn't come there for the sex. No, she'd come because she hadn't been able to stop thinking about all the money she knew he had and how he was the only person who could help her out of the terrible mess she'd gotten herself into. She'd only missed paying bills three months in a row, but already credit card companies were blowing up her cell phone and sending multiple notices to her P.O. box. She hadn't paid anything this month because she no longer had a job, but she could kick herself for not paying any of them the two months before because if she had, at least she'd only be thirty days behind, and it would be a lot easier for her to catch up. But worse than that, the total balance for all of her debts combined was so astronomical that she still had a hard time believing it was correct. It was difficult for her to fathom it, because for the most part, Alicia barely remembered all that she'd purchased on the credit cards or used the credit lines for in the first place.

But currently, that was beside the point because what she had to focus on now was making sure that Phillip never found out how deeply in debt they were. She had to make sure he never found out about her forging his name every chance she'd gotten. She had to do whatever it was she had to do, regardless of how morally right or wrong it was.

It was true that she hated using Levi, but she didn't see where she had any other choice because she still couldn't bring herself to ask her parents or Melanie for help. She wished she could, but no matter how she'd tried to weigh things, she knew they would never understand and that they would forever remind her how they'd told her this was eventually going to happen if she didn't stop spending so much money.

Levi had dozed off for a few minutes but now his eyes were open. He blinked a few times, looked at her, and sensed something was wrong. "Sweetheart, what's the matter?"

"Nothing."

"Come on now. You're not looking all down and out for no reason. Right?"

Alicia wasn't sure if this was the proper time to tell him or not, especially since she'd just started seeing him again two days ago, but she went for it.

"I've really gotten myself into a major bind with my bills and now that I'm not working, I don't know what I'm going to do. I have no clue how to see my way out of this awful situation."

"How much exactly do you owe?"

"You mean every month?"

"No, I mean total."

Alicia didn't know how he was going to react but went ahead and answered.

"Thirty-five thousand dollars."

Levi's eyes widened and Alicia looked away.

"Sweetheart, that's a lot of money."

Alicia was too embarrassed to comment.

"Are these bills in just your name, or are they joint accounts with your husband?"

"Both."

"Does he know about any of this?"

"No."

Levi fluffed two pillows and sat up straighter in the bed. "Okay, look, this is the deal. I'll pay off everything that you owe, but only if you tell your husband tonight that you want a divorce from him and you hire an attorney first thing on Monday to handle it."

Alicia's stomach churned because while she knew she wasn't going to do anything of the kind, she had no choice but to agree with whatever Levi wanted because she really needed that money.

"Fine. I'll tell him as soon as I get home, and I'll also call a lawyer."

"I hope you really mean that because I'm very serious about you filing for a divorce. As a matter of fact, I've never been more serious about anything. So, please don't play games with me. Don't tell me you're going to do this if you're not."

"I wouldn't do that."

"Good, because remember I told you right from the start that I don't take kindly to people who lie to me."

"I'm really going to tell him when I get home. I promise."

"And?"

"And I'm calling an attorney on Monday."

Levi smiled. "That's my girl. And, hey, I know this isn't going to be easy for you, but just know that you really are doing the right thing."

Alicia hated this. She hated lying to him and lying to Phillip, and she hated admitting the worst thing of all: that sadly, she was her father's daughter. She hated the fact that after only being married for nine months, she was already lying and sleeping around, the same as her father had done for so many years.

Levi drew her into his arms. "I also have one other condition."

"What?"

"I need you to tell me that you love me."

Alicia felt like dying but then reluctantly spoke as convincingly as she could, "I love you."

"You're sure?"

"Yes. I'm positive."

"Then, from this day forward, I'll do whatever it takes to make you happy. I'll do anything for you."

Alicia wished she could break and run from this place, but she knew she couldn't think about doing anything of the sort until Levi gave her some money. Plus, she needed to know just how much he was planning on giving her today.

"Are you really going to pay off the entire thirty-five thousand?"

"Eventually. But for now, I'm going to give you five, so you can catch everything up and also so you can pay the retainer to whatever attorney you decide to go with. Although, actually, now that I'm thinking about it, it might just be easier if I pay my own attorney to take care of this. I'm not sure if he does divorces but even if he doesn't, he can easily assign it to another attorney at his firm."

Alicia didn't like what he was saying because if Levi paid his own attorney, she'd have no choice but to really file for a divorce. There would be no way to delay it as she was planning.

"I disagree because I just think it would be best if I find my own representation."

"But that's not necessary, because not only will my guy take care of everything, he'll do it as quickly as possible. Not to mention, I've dealt with him for years and I trust him completely. The other thing is that he'll probably start the process without any up-front payment because I already pay him a monthly retainer for other services. As a matter of fact, knowing him, he probably won't charge anything for this at all, but let me just check to make sure."

When Alicia saw Levi reaching for the phone on his nightstand, her heart sunk. *Oh no, what is he doing?*

"Hi, Shelley, this is Levi Cunningham. Is he in?"

Alicia prayed and prayed that he wasn't.

"No problem. Just tell him that I called and that I have a personal matter that I need to discuss with him."

Alicia couldn't hear what the woman was saying to him but she guessed that with today being Friday, the attorney wouldn't be returning Levi's call until Monday.

"You have a great weekend," he said and hung up. "He's away with his family up at their cottage in Wisconsin, but I'll chat with him first thing next week."

At this point, Alicia saw no way out. She decided it was just best to go along with the program, get as much money from Levi as she possibly could, and then simply tell him that she'd changed her mind about leaving Phillip. He'd be upset about the way she'd lied to him and led him on, but it wasn't like he was going to do any harm to her because she still remembered how on the first night they'd slept together, he'd told her that when a person lied to him and it wasn't business related, all he basically did was drop them from his life and never had another thing to do with them. She was sorry she was going to have to deceive him in such a cold and uncaring way, but there just weren't any other options. She was sorry, and all she could hope was that he'd one day be able to forgive her. But even if he didn't, the good news was that she'd only have to sleep with Levi maybe a couple of more times at the most. By then she would have more than enough money to pay the minimum payments for each of her bills over the next few months. Even better, Phillip would never have to find out about anything—not about Levi or about the number of times she'd falsified Phillip's name on credit applications.

When they finished getting dressed, Levi gave her a stack of hundreds, which she forced into her leather shoulder bag, and they went outside to the garage. Once they were in the car, Levi backed out and headed down the long, winding driveway. There was an iron gate at the end, and as they approached it, Levi pressed a button and the gate slowly moved to the left.

While they waited for it to open completely, Alicia admired the flawlessly maintained, rich-looking, bright-green lawn and the exquisite water fountain positioned right in the center of it. Levi truly was living the good life, and regardless of how he made his money, Alicia had to give credit where credit was due.

Levi drove through the gate, closed it, and then a few feet

into the street, slammed on his brakes. They screeched loudly, and Alicia's heart plummeted as she watched, in what seemed like slow motion, a massive number of detective vehicles and squad cars closing in on them, one after another.

"Take that money out of your purse." Levi said.

"What?"

"I said take it out now! Drop it anywhere!"

Alicia frantically did what she was told and watched countless officers of the law jumping out of their cars, drawing their weapons and holding their positions.

She watched and knew there was no chance of escaping.

Chapter 29

Over the last hour, Alicia had cried a bucket of tears, and she could feel how swollen her eyes were. Now, though, two of the arresting detectives were holding her in a small room with a table and two chairs, and the situation wasn't pretty. The thirtysomething officer had been standing the entire time and was seemingly treating her pretty nicely, but the fiftysomething gentleman, sitting adjacent to her, had a very nasty attitude. He'd questioned her over and over about one thing or another and was furious because she wouldn't say anything. She'd kept her mouth shut because after watching enough *Law & Order*, *Law & Order: SVU*, and *Law & Order: Criminal Intent* episodes to last a lifetime, she knew how to protect herself.

"Look, we know you're the girlfriend and that you've been helping Levi push a ton of drugs through this city," the mean detective said. "So, why don't you just make things a lot easier on yourself and tell us everything?"

Alicia looked at him. "For the hundredth time, I'd like to make my phone call now."

"Just as soon as you tell us what we need to know."

"I know my rights, so like I said, I want to make my phone call."

The elder detective laughed out loud. "For what? So you can lawyer up? So you can buy some time and work on getting your lies together? So you can run home and try to hide some of that dope and the thousands of dollars you've been making off it? Well, if so, little lady, I hate to be the one to tell you, but at this very moment we're getting warrants so we can search your vehicle and your house."

Alicia wasn't worried about them finding anything because she knew she was innocent but when she thought about Phillip, and how hurt he was going to be, she burst into tears. She hadn't thought she had any more tears left to shed, but here they were showering down her face again.

The nice cop unfolded his arms and walked closer to her. "Okay, fine, one phone call."

Alicia wiped her face with both hands, slid her chair back, stood up, and walked outside the room. The officer directed her to an empty cubicle and stood a few feet away.

Alicia picked up the phone and dialed her father's cell.

"Daddy, it's me."

"Hey, baby girl. What's up?"

Alicia tried to contain herself, but she couldn't.

"Baby girl, what's wrong?"

"I'm . . . at . . . the . . . police . . . station . . . and . . ."

"You're what?"

"Daddy, they arrested me, and I need you to come down here."

"Oh my God. Arrested you for what?"

This was the one question Alicia didn't want to answer, and she was glad when she heard someone calling her name. When she turned to see who it was, she realized it was Brad.

"Daddy, Brad is here, but please hurry."

"I'm on my way."

Alicia hung up the phone and then hugged Brad like he was her blood brother. She was so happy and relieved to see him. Happy because she knew he was the one person who would be able to help her.

Brad embraced her as well. "I thought that was you, but what are you here for?"

"They arrested me."

"For what?"

Alicia saw the detective who'd escorted her to the phone talking to one of his colleagues, and she was glad to have this moment alone with Brad. "It's a long story but I really need you to represent me."

"Very rarely do I even come to the police station but it just so happens that, today, one of my business clients got picked up for something bogus. Anyway, let's find somewhere to talk."

The good cop came toward them. "Brad, long time, no see."

"John. Hey, man, how are you?"

The detective shook Brad's hand. "Good. And you?"

"Well, I was fine until I just learned that you're holding a close friend of mine."

"Man, we've been trying to get Levi Cunningham for a very long time, and everybody around here knows it."

Brad frowned. "Levi Cunningham? The drug dealer Levi?"

"That's the one."

"Now I'm completely lost, but if you don't mind, can I talk with my client alone?"

"Of course." The officer led them back to the interrogation room and closed the door. Alicia was glad the mean cop had gone elsewhere.

Alicia and Brad sat down and Brad laid his black leather Tumi briefcase on the table. Alicia could spot Tumi anywhere, but right now name brands of any kind were the least of her worries.

"What does them busting Levi have to do with you?"

Alicia's hands shook, so she removed them from the table. "I was in the car with him when they picked him up."

"Why?"

"Brad, this is all just a really big mistake, and I really need you to help me out of it."

"That's fine, Alicia, but what I need to know is the absolute truth. I need to know everything or otherwise I can't help you to the best of my ability."

"We're friends."

"Who? You and Levi?"

The high pitch in his voice told her that the idea of her being anything to Levi was basically ridiculous and impossible.

"Yes. We're friends."

"Okay, wait. Either you're not telling me something or I'm not understanding, but either way, I don't get what you're saying."

"I told you, this is just a huge mistake. I'm friends with him and that's all."

"What kind of friends?"

"Just friends."

"Well if that's true, does Phillip know about this so-called friendship?"

At that very moment, Alicia knew Brad was turning on her. It was as if he'd had a revelation and was no longer buying her story.

"No, he doesn't. But I've known Levi for a long time, so that's why he's a friend of mine."

"Wait a minute. Were you cheating on my boy, Phillip, with that criminal?"

"Brad, please. I really, really need your help."

"Unbelievable," he said, standing. "Un-freakin'-believable.

You've been sleeping behind my best friend's back and now you have the audacity to think I'm going to help you?"

Alicia swallowed the lump in her throat.

Brad snatched his briefcase from the table and went over to the door. "You're a real piece of work, Alicia, and if Phillip knows what's good for him, he'll dump your little skank behind before the sun goes down."

Alicia sniffled and covered her forehead, and the younger officer came back in again. This time he didn't stand over her but instead took a seat.

"Look, the sooner you tell us something about Levi, the sooner we can work on getting you out of here."

She debated whether she should respond, but for some reason she no longer saw any harm in telling the officer the truth— or at least most of it, because she wasn't about to reveal how, just recently, Levi had said that he was thinking about leaving Mitchell for good and that it was best he didn't tell her why.

"I don't know anything. I never heard anything or saw anything that had to do with drugs. Never."

"Well, if that's so, it's really too bad that you got yourself mixed up with the likes of Levi. And it's even worse, considering how prominent your family is in this city."

Alicia closed her eyes and prayed that they weren't going to release her name to the media. Until now, she hadn't even thought about any of that, and she couldn't believe how careless she'd been over the last few months.

"I'll leave you to yourself until your father gets here. But remember what I said. The sooner you talk, the sooner you'll be out of here."

When he closed the door behind him, Alicia anchored her elbows on the table and then rested her face inside the palms of her hands. This was one of the worst days of her life, and she had no clue as to how she was going to get out of it. She couldn't tell if they were trying to figure out some way to pin something on her or if all they really wanted was the statement they kept asking for. But it wasn't like it mattered, one way or the other, because the only thing she knew about Levi was that he had a lot of money, he had a fabulous house, and he treated her like a queen. She did know about all the rumors, the same ones everyone else in the area knew about, but she'd never seen him do anything illegal. Of course, with him giving her a large sum of cash on two different occasions—cash that he hadn't had to withdraw from a bank—she couldn't deny that this was usually a sign that something unlawful was going on, but again, she'd never witnessed anything with her own eyes.

To be honest, he'd only actually given her money one time because the police had now confiscated the five thousand dollars Levi had demanded that she take from her purse and toss away. She'd sort of been upset about him making her do that because that same five thousand dollars was going to take care of a lot of her money problems. But now that she'd had time to think about it, she knew he'd only done it to protect her, and she would always be thankful to him.

Alicia was so tired and couldn't wait to get out of there, but she smiled when she heard the door open and saw her dad walking in.

"Daddy," she said, rushing toward him.

"Hi, baby girl."

"Daddy, I'm so glad to see you."

"Let's sit down. And where is Brad?"

"He left."

"Why?"

"He's really mad at me, Daddy."

"Okay, it's time you tell me what this is all about so I can get my attorney over here. And tell me the truth, Alicia."

He was calling her by her first name again, and she knew he wasn't playing games with her. "I was arrested with Levi Cunningham and . . . he's the man I've been having an affair with."

"Levi Cunningham?! Have you lost your mind?"

Tears streamed all over again. "I know, Daddy. I'm sorry."

"I can't believe you would do something like this. It was bad enough that you were sleeping around on Phillip but with a known drug dealer? The same drug dealer I cut ties with and told you not to even talk to when you were younger?"

"I'm sorry," she repeated.

"Dear God. This is a mess. And it's going to kill your mother, Alicia. It's going to hurt a whole lot of people, and if the police release your name it's going to mean yet another scandal for our family and for the church."

"I know" was all she could think to say.

"Why couldn't you just leave him alone when I had that talk with you at the hospital? You promised me that you were going to end whatever relationship you'd gotten yourself caught up in and that was over a month ago. So, what happened?"

"I made a mistake, Daddy. A really big mistake."

"This is bad. And I hate even seeing the look on Phillip's face once he finds out about it."

"But you're not going to tell him anything, are you?"

"He wasn't in the office when you called me, but I left him a voice message telling him that you'd been arrested and that I wanted him to meet me here."

"Daddy, why did you do that?"

"Why? Because he's your husband. That's why."

"But you could have at least given me a chance to figure out how I'm going to explain this to him."

"What is there to figure out? Except the truth?"

Alicia knew it wasn't worth debating this with him, because the damage was already done. She'd slept with Levi, her father had told Phillip about her being arrested, and it was only a matter of time before he stormed in there, saying only God knew what.

But at least Phillip still didn't know about the credit card and loan payments she was behind on, so not all was completely lost. She had to do something and do it fast, and while she'd vowed not to ask her father to help her with her debt issues, he was now her only hope. But she wouldn't ask him today, not with him being so furious with her about this Levi fiasco. However, she would ask him before the weekend was over.

She'd have to do it because if she could keep the debt situation undercover, she had a feeling she'd be able to smooth over this problem with Levi. She and Phillip had been having so many marital problems over the last few months, she was sure he'd understand how easy it had been for her to slip into the arms of another man. She was sure he'd think about the commitment he'd made to her on their wedding day and how God really did expect him to stay with her for better or worse. He'd think about all of this, and in the end, she knew Phillip would do the right thing. He was a good man and that made her feel better already.

Chapter 30

Once Alicia's father had phoned his attorney, it had taken the attorney nearly an hour to arrive at the station but thankfully, through connections of his own and those of her father's, four hours later the police department had allowed her to leave on her own recognizance. Originally, they'd been talking at least a ten-thousand-dollar bond, which meant her father would have had to pay 10 percent of that, but they'd decided against it once they'd finished questioning her. The other blessing was that they'd never locked her in a cell, and, with the exception of the ride to the police station, they hadn't handcuffed her.

Still, though, the entire ordeal had been a nightmare and she hoped she'd be able to put this disgraceful episode behind her as soon as possible. She still hadn't told the detectives anything that she'd thought would make any difference to them, but for some reason they did seem a lot more satisfied when she'd told them about her relationship with Levi, beginning with the day she'd first seen him at the mall and how he had approached her before she'd gone inside the store. She hadn't wanted to tell the rest of the details in front of her father, specifically when and how many times she'd slept with Levi, but her attorney had advised her to not leave out one iota of information. He'd told her it was best to give them all that they were asking for because if she did, they'd feel more assured about her claim of being innocent.

She'd even told them about the five thousand dollars cash and how Levi had just given it to her this afternoon but then had instructed her to take it out of her shoulder bag once they were surrounded. She'd even confessed about his giving her another thousand dollars right around the time she'd first started seeing him, as well as the heart-shaped diamond necklace. They'd then wanted to know why he'd given her the money in the first place, and while she hadn't wanted to reveal her money problems, she'd been afraid not to tell the truth. So she'd told them that the reason he'd given her the money was so she could pay some of her bills.

Her father hung up the phone with the attorney and stopped at a red light. They were maybe ten minutes away from her subdivision, and Alicia wasn't looking forward to seeing Phillip face-to-face. Surprisingly, he hadn't come to the station, but she knew by now that Brad had told Phillip about their conversation.

"It sounds like you're going to walk away from this without any charges. Randall thinks that the police already knew you were just an innocent bystander but simply had to make sure of it. He also said that when they didn't find anything incriminating in your car or at your house, that certainly helped as well."

"Thank God."

"But it's still not over, because there's a chance the prosecution is going to call you as a witness during the trial and that's why Randall wants to meet with us sometime next week."

Alicia's phone rang and while normally she'd be happy to hear from her mother, she wasn't looking forward to it right now because she knew her father had already called her mother and told her everything.

"Hi, Mom."

"Alicia, what in the world were you thinking?"

"I don't know, Mom. I made a mistake."

"I'll say."

Alicia sighed in a not so cordial manner. "Mom, can I call you back?"

"No. Because aren't you in the car with your dad?"

"Yes."

"Well, once you get home, you don't need to call me or anyone else. What you need to do is talk to Phillip and as far as I'm concerned, he's the only person you need to talk to for the rest of the evening. You need to plead, beg, explain, and do whatever you have to do to keep that man from leaving you."

"He'll be fine. I mean, he'll be upset and it'll probably take a while before he gets over this, but Phillip would never leave me over one mistake."

"Don't be so sure. And even if he doesn't, you should spend the rest of your life making all of this up to him."

"Mom, please, can I call you back? I'm sorry but my head is killing me, and I just want to relax my mind before I get home."

"I'm really disappointed in you, Alicia. I love you more than anything, but this has got to be the worst thing you've ever done, and you've hurt a lot of people in the process."

"I realize that, and I'm sorry. I'm sorry about the crazy decisions I made, but, Mom, you have my word that I'll never do anything like this again."

"I truly hope not because, Alicia, this is bad."

"I'll call you later or tomorrow, okay?"

"You take care of yourself, and again, sweetheart, I love you."

"I love you, too, Mom."

Curtis drove past the health club where Alicia sometimes went to work out and adjusted his rearview mirror. "Your mom is really upset."

Alicia leaned her head back against the headrest and pretended she hadn't heard what her father had just said. But unfortunately, that didn't stop him.

"Can you imagine how your little brother is going to feel when he finds out about this?"

"Matthew knows that I love him, and that I'm not perfect."

"That he does, but I don't think he's going to be expecting to hear that you were hanging out with some drug dealer. Plus, once this hits the paper tomorrow, all of his friends are going to know about it, and I think you remember how embarrassed he was when that Tabitha scandal broke. He was so ashamed and so worried about what his schoolmates were going to say that he even wanted to change schools."

Alicia would have loved nothing more than to tell her dad that it wasn't her fault that Matthew was already a victim of family scandal, it was *his* fault. Every incident had been her father's fault and while he obviously wasn't thinking about it at the moment, he had caused her more pain and humiliation when she was Matthew's age than she cared to think about. Yes, it was true that she'd made the mistake of sleeping with Levi, but her father had slept with so many women over the years, he probably didn't even remember them all. Yes, it was true that she hadn't made the best of choices when it came to her overall spending habits, but it was her father who had taught her to buy only the top brands and the very best that money could buy. He'd taught her this from the time she was five years old, and she'd never known any other way to live.

But she didn't dare say any of these things to him because

she didn't want to give him even one reason to say no when she asked him for the money she needed.

Just as Alicia started to feel a bit calmer, her phone rang again. This time it was Melanie, and for some reason she didn't care what Melanie was going to say, good or bad, she just really needed to hear her voice.

"Hey, Mel."

"Girl, Brad called me earlier and I just don't know what to say."

"To be honest, neither do I. I really messed up."

"But of all people, Levi?"

"I know."

"Where are you now?"

"I didn't feel like getting my car out tonight, so I'm riding with my dad. They searched it, and for some reason, they impounded it and now I have to pay to get it out. But once they released me, I just didn't feel like doing anything except going home."

"I'm sure. Do you want me to come over?"

"Actually, I do, but I really need to talk to Phillip tonight, so I'll just call you when I get some time alone."

"Are you going to be okay?"

"I'll be fine."

"You're like a sister to me, Alicia, so of course I'm hurt and disappointed, but I still love you and I'm here for you."

"Thanks, Mel. I love you, too, and I'll call you tomorrow."

Alicia dropped her phone inside her purse as her father drove into her subdivision, curved around a couple of streets, and pulled into their driveway.

"You want me to go in with you?"

"Maybe just for a few minutes. Because maybe if Phillip sees you, he won't be so angry."

"Let's go."

They left the vehicle and went up to the front door; Alicia unlocked it and they went inside. She could already feel her nerves racing, so she took a couple of deep breaths.

But before she could gather her composure completely, Phillip walked down the stairs.

"So, is it true? I mean, with the police coming in here, turning our house upside down, I guess I already know, but I just want to hear you say it."

He seemed awfully calm but maybe it was like she'd thought, he'd see her mistake as nothing more than human error and after a while they'd be able to move on like this never happened.

Alicia started toward the kitchen. "Phillip, let's just go sit at the island, and I'll answer any questions that you have."

"Phillip," Curtis said, "if you don't want me to stay, then I totally understand."

Phillip turned to him. "No, Curtis, actually, I do want you to stay. I want you to stay so you can hear everything."

Alicia sat down. "Daddy has already heard everything, Phillip."

"Nonetheless, I still want him here."

Her father took a seat next to Alicia, but Phillip stood in front of them, leaning against the sink. "So, like I said, is it true? Was Brad telling me the truth when he said you've been sleeping with Levi Cunningham?"

"I never told Brad anything like that. What I told him was that we were friends."

Phillip folded his arms and squinted his eyes. "Really?"

Alicia didn't know why she was lying to him, what with the blow-by-blow statement she'd given to the police, but she just couldn't bring herself to admit the obvious to her husband.

"Can I at least try to explain some of this to you?"

"No, because I don't think there's much more you can tell me than I already know. For example, one of Brad's sources told him that the narcotics division has been following you for weeks, that they have a record of you leaving your car at some strip mall parking lot, as well as a record of Levi picking you up and taking you to his house. They even have a record of you being there the night I was shot, Alicia, and I think that hurt me the most. I mean, the fact that you were low enough and rotten enough to sleep with another man behind my back is painful enough, but to know you were doing it the night I could have been killed, well, it doesn't get any lower than that."

Alicia was stunned. She'd told the police all that Phillip had just spoken about, but now she knew she hadn't told them anything they hadn't already known.

"They were watching your every move, and the reason they started following you was so they'd have some sort of idea about when Levi was going to leave his house. They knew that every time he picked you up from that parking lot, he'd be bringing you back there for a few hours, so they finally chose today as the day they wanted to take Levi down. They followed you the same as always and then waited for the two of you to leave his driveway."

"Baby, I'm so, so sorry."

Alicia had said she was sorry so many times to so many people that her own words were beginning to sicken her. They didn't even sound genuine anymore, so she could only imagine how Phillip was taking them.

"You know, even with all the money you've blown and all the problems we've had, I still never thought you would turn out to be this dirty and underhanded. Selfish, yeah, because that's what you've always been since the day I met you, but sneaky, devious, and dishonest—I wasn't counting on that."

"Baby, I know this is the worst and that what I did was beyond stupid, but I really am sorry and I'll do whatever you want me to do. I'll do anything you ask."

"Okay, then why don't you answer one question for me?"

"Of course."

"Why is it that when I applied for a credit line at one of the electronic stores this afternoon, I was denied?"

Alicia's body went numb. She felt paralyzed, and now she knew why Phillip had wanted her father to stay there with them.

"Can you tell me that?"

Alicia wanted to say something but she couldn't think of anything.

"I mean, here I was in the store, thinking how excited you were going to be when you came home and saw the notebook computer that you'd talked about this morning. I was so looking forward to surprising you, but when they processed my application for no-interest financing, they told me I wasn't approved. So, silly me, I just figured it was some sort of a mistake, that is, until I found out that the reason they'd denied me was that I had opened too many new accounts in the last six months. Now, imagine my amazement and the shame I felt. Imagine how dumb I felt when I knew full well I hadn't opened any new accounts since you and I were married, yet my credit report was showing something far different."

Alicia knew her whole world was collapsing and that there was no way to stop it from happening. She even glanced over at her father with pleading eyes, hoping he would say something on her behalf, but the look he tossed back at her declared that he was just as livid as Phillip.

"So, tell me, Alicia. How can that be?"

"Phillip, if you'll just give me a chance, we can fix this."

"Fix this how?" he yelled. "Because I'd love to know how we can possibly fix my credit status when you've forged my name with three different companies and haven't made one payment over the last three months. How do we simply fix twenty thousand dollars of debt, not to mention all of your department store cards that are maxed solid? And if you're wondering how I know, I guess I can't deny that I was a little sneaky just like you were because I went into every one of your accounts online. And I also know that you've been having everything sent to some P.O. box."

Curtis turned to his daughter. "Alicia, is all of this true? You actually signed Phillip's name on credit applications without him knowing about it? And you're thousands of dollars in debt?"

"Daddy, I was going to tell you, but I didn't know how."

Her father shook his head. "Alicia, you've got a problem. You need some serious help, and I'm just sorry I didn't pay more attention to your spending habits while you were in college. I knew they were bad, but nothing like this. And then all of these lies."

That was it. Alicia had finally had enough of her father and the way he was condemning her, and it was time she set him straight.

"Daddy, how in the world are you going to sit there criticizing me when you've done ten times worse, pretty much your entire adult life? How can you say anything to me at all when I learned everything I know from you? I mean, you did it all. You slept around with I don't know how many women in the church, you lusted over money, and you stepped on whomever you had to in order to get whatever it was you wanted. And you did this all the way up until maybe two years ago when you finally started reaping so many consequences for all the horrible sins you'd committed that you didn't have a choice but to change.

Which is fine but it doesn't erase the very bad example you've always set for me since I was in kindergarten."

When Alicia saw tears forming in his eyes, she regretted how harshly she'd just spoken to him.

"Baby girl, you're right. You're right about everything you just said, so, Phillip, I guess you can blame me for a lot of this as well."

"Maybe. But, Curtis, Alicia is a grown woman and she knows right from wrong."

"But still, just the same, I'm truly sorry. Baby girl, I'm sorry that I wasn't a better father to you for so many years, and, Phillip, I'm sorry that you're also now feeling the backlash of my terrible transgressions."

"Well, it's not like any of this matters, one way or the other, because I'm through."

"Phillip, baby, you don't mean that," Alicia said.

"Alicia, I've tried to love you in every possible way I could, but it was never enough. I was never a good enough man, I could never provide for you the way you wanted me to . . . and I give up. I'm hurt, I'm tired, and I just don't have the energy to go on with you."

Alicia left her seat, walked around the island, and locked hands with her husband. "Baby, I know this is a difficult time, but I do love you. More than anything. And I still want to spend the rest of my life with you. So please don't walk out on me. Please don't throw away our marriage."

Phillip gazed into her eyes, and a lone tear fell down his cheek. "You know what the saddest part about all of this is? I love you, too. And I have a feeling that I always will. But that's also the reason I can't do this anymore. You've betrayed me in so many different ways that I'll never be able to trust you again, and I can't live like that."

"But what about our vows? What about for better or worse? What about what God wants? What about forgiveness?"

"Oh, I will eventually forgive you, but that's where it ends. And then as far as the vows we took, I know divorce is not what God wants, but, Alicia, we haven't even been married one full year, yet you've already slept with another man. And I'm sad to say, I just can't accept that."

"But, baby, you know we've been having a really rough time, and while I know this doesn't justify my actions, I felt so unwanted and so confused."

"Alicia, I felt the same way, but I still knew it was wrong to go out and sleep with someone else. And don't think I didn't have the opportunity because I did. I even went as far as having phone conversations with my ex from high school, but when I realized how important my marriage to you was, I ended them."

"And, baby, our marriage is still important. Even more so now, so let's just do whatever we have to so we can fix this."

Phillip eased his hands away from hers. "I'm sorry, but my mind is made up. And Curtis, I wanted to let you know that I'll be turning in my resignation first thing on Monday."

"I really wish you wouldn't."

"Actually, I doubted that you'd want me to stay on, once Alicia and I are divorced."

"That's not true. You're a wonderful minister and a wonderful man, and my plans for you at the church haven't changed."

"I really appreciate that. It means a lot, but I've decided that in order for me to move on with my life, it's best that I move back to the Chicago area and closer to my mother."

"Maybe you should take a little more time to think about this?"

"No, I really think that leaving is the right thing for me to do, and I just want to thank you for all the opportunities you've given me and for being the best father-in-law."

"You're quite welcome."

Alicia watched Phillip walk out of the kitchen and then cried a new river of tears. Her father tried consoling her, but there was nothing he could say to make her feel better. There was nothing he could do to save her marriage—nothing, because she'd already said and done more than enough and would regret all of it for the rest of her life.

Epilogue

Six Months Later

Even after Phillip had told her on the night of her arrest that their marriage was over, Alicia still hadn't fully believed him. She'd heard him say it with very strong conviction but still, she'd been sure he'd think long and hard about the love they had for each other and would eventually change his mind. But he hadn't. What he'd done was give his two weeks' notice just as he'd said he would, and once that period of time had passed, he'd said his good-byes to everyone at the church, told her again how much he loved her, and moved to Chicago. Alicia had wondered which pieces of furniture he might want and had even suggested he take whatever he needed, but he'd told her that all he was going to leave with was his clothing. He'd said that he wanted to start fresh in Chicago and hadn't wanted to take anything that would remind him of his life in Mitchell because it was much too painful. Alicia had listened to him but then had fallen to her knees, begging him not to leave her. She'd begged him to give her just one more chance, but he'd told her he couldn't. He'd told her that their marriage had meant everything to him, that he'd cherished what he'd considered to be a very sacred bond, but in the end, he'd finally realized that in some cases, love just wasn't enough. Alicia had then called her mother-in-law, trying to get her to talk to Phillip, too, but she'd told Alicia that although she loved her, she was very disappointed in her and that she wasn't going to interfere with whatever decision Phillip had decided to make.

So, now, six months later, her divorce from Phillip was already final and she'd never felt more alone in her life. She'd moved in with her father, Charlotte, and Matthew, but on most days, all she did was write. It was amazing how Phillip's leaving her had been the one thing that had ultimately inspired her to sit at her computer every single day. Her writing had even proved to be therapeutic, and this was probably the reason she was now composing a story that was loosely based on her marriage.

Of course, her father was thrilled that she was working so diligently on her manuscript and so were her mother and Charlotte, and they all believed she was definitely going to be published. She knew there were no guarantees that she would be, but like them, she did hope and believe that it would eventually happen.

Not to mention, she needed to start earning a living. She'd thought about going back to the church, that is, if they would have her, but strangely enough, her father had told her that if she took her writing seriously, he would give her a thousand-dollar monthly allowance for one full year but after that, she'd be on her own as far as money was concerned and that she would have to find employment. Alicia had known that his offer was more than fair, and she wasn't planning to let him down. She also couldn't thank her father enough for paying off the twenty thousand dollars she'd accumulated in Phillip's name because it wasn't like any of that had been his responsibility. But he'd done it because he truly loved and respected Phillip and he hadn't thought Phillip should have to pay for something he hadn't even known about. However, when it came to her balances with Neiman's, Saks, Macy's, and each of her other accounts, he'd caught them up to date but had made it clear that *she* was going to make the monthly payments from the money he was giving her every month.

Alicia hadn't liked this part of the deal at all because this had meant she wouldn't have much money left to shop with, but it wasn't as if she'd been in any position to debate with her father about anything. Actually, she had tried arguing her case, but for the first time in her life, he'd told her to take it or leave it. He'd told her that it was either his way or no way at all and that he would be fine with whatever option she went with. Needless to say, Alicia had relented and had agreed to do what she was told.

Thankfully, though, Charlotte did take her shopping every now and then, so she was glad about that. It wasn't the same as if she had her own income and could buy whatever she wanted when she wanted, but it was definitely better than nothing. Alicia knew everyone thought she had a problem—but she didn't—and was sure that once she got back on her feet, was earning a very good salary, and was living on her own again, she'd be fine. She'd pay her bills on time, add a little money to a savings account, and shop a lot more sensibly. She couldn't say that she would no longer buy the top brands of clothing and shoes she'd always purchased in the past, because if she did she'd be lying, but she would certainly spend her money in a much more controlled manner.

Alicia rolled the mouse across the rubber pad and signed on to AOL, but then she thought about Levi. At her attorney's suggestion, she hadn't had any contact with him since the day the two of them had been arrested, but she knew he was still downtown awaiting his trial and that it was taking place three months from now. She still couldn't believe she'd gotten involved with someone like him, but she would never forget how caring he'd been toward her. Of course, none of his compassionate ways were going to make a bit of difference once he was inside the courtroom, but she still thought about the good way he had always treated her.

Sadly, though, just like her father had thought, the local media had covered the story, and it hadn't been long before the national media had publicized it as well. It had seemed that none of them could wait to spread breaking news about the daughter of the world-renowned Reverend Curtis Black and how she'd gotten caught having an affair with a "drug kingpin," as some had called Levi. They'd talked about her being arrested and most importantly, how this was yet another scandalous saga for the "good reverend" and his family. The one consolation, however, was that they hadn't covered it for more than a couple of days, and now it was basically never mentioned at all, not even at church. There had been a few heads turning and a number of people whispering whenever Alicia had entered the sanctuary for service, but even that had died down after the first month or so.

Still, she knew that once the trial began, the media would start scrambling in a frenzy all over again because the evidence that the prosecution would be presenting would prove, without a doubt, that Levi was the head of a huge drug empire. Alicia had always wondered how he'd gotten busted and how much money he'd actually made over the years but now she knew, thanks to Brad and the information one of his sources had given him. Brad still wasn't speaking to Alicia, but he'd told a lot to Melanie and Melanie had relayed all that she'd learned. Melanie had told her that she could never mention any of what she was telling her, not to another living soul, but that she thought Alicia should know as much as possible before she took the witness stand.

Alicia still wasn't looking forward to giving open testimony and had no idea what she could possibly contribute, now that they had everything they needed to send Levi away for a very long time. Because as it had turned out, one of the narcotics officers whom Levi had been paying off for a number of years had been found out by some of his peers, and they'd told him that his only chance at any leniency was if he named names from the top down. Which he had. He'd named four other detectives in the division, the higher-up dealers who sold directly to hundreds of other dealers at all levels throughout the entire states of Illinois, Indiana, and Ohio, and most of all, he'd given up the manufacturing and processing location, which was in a farm community outside of Indiana. On top of that, the prosecuting attorney had offered a deal to Levi's attorney—the one Levi had told her he trusted completely—and he'd given up the locations and documentation for each of Levi's local accounts, none of which were in Levi's name, as well as the accounts his attorney had set up offshore—accounts that totaled more than ten million dollars.

So, without question, Levi was finished, and Alicia was glad she hadn't gotten more involved with him than she had because the outcome for her could have been a lot different. Right now, she could be sitting in jail, awaiting trial and eventually preparing to serve a prison sentence. But through God's favor, she was okay. She was actually a lot better than okay, because even though she had disgraced herself and her family and lost the love of her life, she was safe. God had protected her, even though she'd made a mountain of foolish mistakes, and He had allowed her the chance at turning her life around and doing the right thing. He'd stood by her and loved her unconditionally and remained true to His Word, the same as her father had always preached about in his sermons, and Alicia couldn't be more grateful.

She'd learned some very valuable lessons, and unlike her father, she wouldn't sin, ask for forgiveness over and over, and then go back to committing the same sins again. She wouldn't live her life that way and then, like her father, end up sorry for it. No, what Alicia would do is walk the straight and narrow and choose a much wealthier husband this next time around. She would marry extremely well and would finally be able to do what she'd originally set out to do with Phillip—live happily ever after with the man of her dreams.

She'd finally be happy, and she couldn't wait to meet him.

Reading Group Guide

1. Were you shocked to see that Alicia's personality was very similar to her father's in a great number of ways? If so, please explain why.

2. In the prologue, Alicia is having second thoughts about getting married. Do you know someone or have you yourself ever been in the same situation? Why do you think people sometimes get married, even when they aren't completely sure it's the right thing for them?

3. Do you know a real-life shopping addict—specifically a close friend or family member? If so, what is the most expensive thing you've ever seen them purchase? Also, what did you say to them afterward?

4. Can a spending addiction be as serious as an alcohol, drug, or gambling addiction? How might it affect family members and friends?

5. Why do you believe so many women and men in this country tend to spend well beyond their means?

6. With the exception of Alicia's excessive spending habits, do you believe she was a good wife to Phillip? If so, please explain why.

7. What did you think of Phillip? Was he the kind of man

any woman should have been happy to have as a husband? If so, why? Or why not?

8. Were you surprised to learn that Alicia was having an affair with Levi? What did you think of Levi overall? It is true that he was a known drug dealer, but was he the kind of bad boy that even the most decent woman might find herself attracted to, even if they could never admit it to another living soul?

9. Do you think Alicia started seeing Levi because she really liked him or because she needed money and a lot of it?

10. Do you believe Phillip made the right decision at the end of the book? If not, why? Do you think he'd taken as much as anyone should have to take from a spouse?

11. Do you think Curtis was shocked to hear Alicia blamed him for her terrible ways? Was she right in feeling that way? If so, how was she justified?

12. Now that Alicia has lost a man who loved her so unconditionally, do you believe she learned any valuable lessons? Do you think she now realizes that money isn't everything and that love and commitment are the most important aspects of any successful marriage? If not, what do you believe her next move will be?

13. After reading *The Best of Everything*, do you think you might have a shopping problem and/or need to become a lot more responsible with your spending habits?

Turn the page for a sneak peek into the enchanting
sequel to *The Best of Everything*

Be Careful What You Pray For

Coming soon in hardcover from William Morrow

Prologue

He was almost too good to be true, what with his at least six-foot-two body frame, flawlessly smooth skin, coal-black wavy hair, and pearly white teeth. He somehow didn't seem real, but Alicia knew he *was* real because at this very moment, she was sitting directly across the table from him at one of the most upscale restaurants in downtown Chicago. He was by far one of the finest-looking men she'd ever laid eyes on, and there wasn't a woman she could think of who would disagree with her findings. The man looked that good, and as if that wasn't enough, he also conveyed exceptional charisma and an alluring smile, and was the founder of New Life Christian Center, a five-year-old church that already had more than five thousand members.

Yes, Pastor JT Valentine was the kind of man Alicia had been hoping and praying for, particularly ever since her marriage to her first husband, Phillip, had ended just a few months ago, and she could barely contain herself. But since her father, stepmother, and a couple of Pastor Valentine's deacons and their wives were also dining right along with them, she took a deep breath, drank a sip of water, and coolly leaned back in her chair.

"Pastor Black," Pastor Valentine said, and Alicia couldn't

help noticing the very elegant and obviously tailor-made suit he was wearing. "I just want to thank you again for agreeing to come speak at our church this morning. Your words were even more powerful than the last time I heard you deliver a sermon, and I hope you'll consider blessing us with your presence again sometime in the future."

"I would be happy to, and I'm glad you were satisfied with what I had to share today."

Pastor Valentine chuckled. " 'Satisfied' isn't even the word. You have been the one man I've truly looked up to for a while now, even before I accepted my call into the ministry, so having you accept my invitation has been the highlight of my year."

"Well, I'm glad and it was an honor."

"And I also want to thank you, Mrs. Black," he said to Charlotte, "for taking time to make the trip here as well. I know you live only about an hour and a half away, but I do still remember what it was like for my wife, God rest her soul, and how demanding a first lady's schedule can really be."

"This is true, but unless our son, Matthew, needs me to be home to attend one of his football games or something else school related, I pretty much travel with my husband to most of his out-of-town speaking engagements. Which actually works out fine because Matthew loves staying with my aunt when we're gone, and Curtis doesn't travel nearly as much as he used to anyway."

Curtis lifted a forkful of Caesar salad from his plate. "No, these days, I tend to turn down far more opportunities than I take on, but after traveling around the country for so many years, I eventually decided that I wanted to spend as much time as possible with my family."

"Totally understandable," Pastor Valentine said, and then looked at Alicia. "So, Miss Alicia, and I guess I'm sort of changing the subject a bit, but your father tells me that you've written the next worldwide bestseller."

Alicia smiled. "Well, I don't know about all that, but I did just finish writing my first novel."

"That's really impressive. It takes a lot of patience and diligence to write a book, fiction or nonfiction, so I'm very proud of you."

"Thanks," Alicia said, smiling at him again, her stomach fluttering.

"She worked on it just about every single day over the last six months, and it's great," her father added. "She definitely poured her heart into it and that makes all the difference, regardless of what anyone is writing."

"It really is wonderful," Charlotte said. "I read it in one sitting, the same as I do with all the other books I read by well-known authors."

Pastor Valentine raised his eyebrows. "Wow, then maybe I should read it, too. That is, if you don't mind sharing it with me."

"No, I don't mind at all, and actually, I would love to have someone else's opinion. Someone who doesn't love me so unconditionally that they would tell me anything as long as it doesn't hurt my feelings."

Everyone laughed and then her father said, "You're right. I do love you, but at the same time, I would never tell you something was good if it really wasn't."

Pastor Valentine turned his attention to Alicia again. "So, you'll send me a copy next week?"

"Yes, I'll mail it tomorrow," she said, and it was all she could do not to blush like some teenage schoolgirl. She was pleased to know how interested he seemed to be in her work but what she was most thrilled about was how interested he was in her—

something she could tell more and more as they continued making eye contact. The chemistry between them was discreetly intense, and it was the reason Alicia suddenly realized something. JT wasn't just some man she was attracted to. It was true that she'd known him for only a few hours, but at this very moment she knew he was the man of her dreams. She knew it with all her heart.

She knew she was going to be the next Mrs. JT Valentine. No doubt about it.

Chapter 1

Seven Months Later

It was a fine and very warm first Sunday in May, and Alicia sat in the front row of the church, admiring her wonderful husband. He was actually sitting right next to her but was only minutes from heading into the pulpit to deliver his sermon. Alicia and JT had been happily married for one full month now but she was still in awe of his entire being, the same as she'd been the first day she'd met him. It was still so hard to conceive of how truly blessed she was to have found him—the perfect spouse, who, ironically, was ten years her senior, just like her first husband had been—not to mention how soon it all had happened. She'd sent him her manuscript as planned, he'd called her two days after receiving it, saying he'd read it and loved it, and the next thing Alicia had known, they'd found themselves on the phone for two hours. They'd talked about everything imaginable, and one thing had led to another. He'd driven over to Mitchell the next day to take her to dinner, and just one month later, JT had presented her with a three-carat, princess-cut, solitaire diamond ring. He had slipped the huge rock onto her finger and had asked her to marry him. For a few seconds, however, and only a few seconds, Alicia had been speechless and in tears, but then she had quickly told him yes three different times. She could still remember how happy she'd been, happier than she'd ever been in her life, and how even though they'd been together only for six short months, she felt as if she'd known this man for years.

There was one unfortunate aspect, however, that she couldn't push out of her mind: Her father didn't approve of JT and still hadn't accepted the idea that she'd gotten married to him. She'd tried her best to forget her father's words and all the reasons he'd given in terms of why she needed to end things with JT— reasons he'd given her for the umpteenth time the night before the wedding. But she couldn't.

"Baby girl, I really wish you'd think long and hard about what you're getting ready to do tomorrow," her father said. "Because all JT Valentine cares about is money, power, and women, and he'll never do right by you."

"Daddy, why can't you just be happy for me? I mean, why can't you just support my decision the same way you did when I married Phillip?"

"Because JT is nothing like your first husband. Yes, he's a minister like Phillip and he's thirty-three like Phillip, but that's where their similarities pretty much end. JT is all about JT, and when it's all said and done, all he's going to do is cause you a mountain of pain."

Alicia pleaded with her father to understand. "He loves me, Daddy. He really does, so I'm begging you. Please, just give us your blessing."

"I can't do that. I can't be happy about any man who I know is going to hurt you in the end."

"Daddy, the only person who's going out of their way to hurt me right now is you."

Be Careful What You Pray For

"I'm sorry for any harm this may be causing you, but I can't help the way I feel. I can't help the fact that I'm able to see straight through this man you're so desperately in love with. Or should I say who you *think* you're in love with, because I'm not sure if you actually love him for him, or if what you're really in love with is the amount of money he earns."

"I really resent that, Daddy. I resent it, and I'm shocked that you would have the audacity to say something like that to me. I love, trust, and believe in JT with all my heart, and regardless of what you or anyone else thinks about him, JT is the one."

Alicia sighed at her last thought and remembered how her father hadn't said another word and how he'd eventually walked out of her bedroom. Then, that afternoon, he'd pleaded with her one last time to reconsider, but when he'd finally realized she'd made up her mind to go through with the ceremony, with or without him, he had reluctantly escorted her down the church aisle and given her away.

JT peered at the crowd in front of him and Alicia gave him her undivided attention, the same as everyone else in the sanctuary. "It is so good to finally be back in the house of the Lord," he said. "Although I must say, while I really did miss seeing all of you, I definitely enjoyed having an entire month off to spend with my beautiful new bride," he said, and a vast number of "Amen's" could be heard throughout the congregation. "Most of you know how hard it was on me when Satan robbed me of my first wife two years ago and how I never thought I'd find true happiness again. But I'm here to tell you today that through God's grace, not only did I find true happiness, I also found the kind of genuine love every man ought to experience at least once in his lifetime."

"Glory to God," one woman said.

"Praise His holy name," another added.

JT glanced down at his wife. "Sweetheart, stand up and say hello to everyone."

Alicia smiled, stood, faced the parishioners, and waved. Many of them smiled back at her, chuckled, and chattered approvingly among themselves, and Alicia felt like a celebrity. In the beginning, she hadn't known how receptive the members of New Life Christian Center would actually be toward her. Especially since they'd clearly been very fond of their former first lady and also because JT hadn't known Alicia very long before popping the big question. So, she was very relieved to see how pleased they were to have her there.

She continued waving in a number of directions and then took her seat.

JT grinned and said, "And just for the record, don't think that the only thing my wife has are her noticeably good looks, because she's also a very talented writer. She's written a novel and once she finishes up a few revisions, it'll only be a matter of time before multiple publishers begin making offers for it."

The congregation applauded, and Alicia appreciated their kindness and obvious support of her endeavors.

"Most of you know, too," JT continued, "that I have lots of new goals for NLCC and a vision of how quickly I want to see our ministry grow, so I thank God for giving me a woman who loves me the way Alicia does and for all of you, the people who make all that I'm trying to do here so possible."

Alicia listened as JT spoke more about his future plans for the ministry, but she couldn't stop thinking about her new husband and how attentive and generous he'd been over the last seven months. He'd given her dozens and dozens of roses, spent every minute of his free time with her, and had surprised her with the kinds of gifts most women could only dream about. Alicia had wondered if she would ever find a man who loved her the way Phillip had but at the same time earned a salary that was well into six figures, and she was happy to say she'd found every bit of that and so much more.

Over the years, she'd heard a number of people insisting that it simply wasn't possible for any one person to have everything all at the same time, specifically lots of wealth and a perfect marriage. But Alicia was pleased to know that she and JT had proved every single one of them wrong. JT was such a loyal and honest man of God—the kind of man who had made it clear from the start that even though he was dying to make love to her, he wanted them to do the right thing and not have sex until after they'd taken their vows. He'd talked a lot about how he didn't want them doing anything that would defy God's Word or something that might diminish their very strong moral values and how he was more than willing to wait. Needless to say, Alicia couldn't thank God enough for bringing such a decent and wholesome man into her life. She was thankful that the fairy tale she'd prayed for actually wasn't a fairy tale at all. She was elated to know that the fabulous life she and JT were so happily living was clear-cut reality.

Chapter 2

O h, that's it!" Diana Redding screamed at the top of her lungs, and JT felt like he was going to pass out. His heart beat violently, he panted uncontrollably, and it was all he could do to try to catch a few breaths of air. In all honesty, he felt like he was going to die . . . but it was a chance he was always willing to take when it came to this wildcat who was old enough to be his mother.

JT rolled to the side of her. "You have got to be the most amazing woman I've ever met."

"Oh yeah?" she said. "Well, let me tell you . . . that's nothing compared to all the other tricks I plan on showing you before you leave here tonight. That is, if your little young behind can handle all of them."

Diana was incredible, to say the least, and strangely enough, JT had known from the first day he'd laid eyes on her, one year ago, that he had to have her. He'd known she had to be at least in her early to middle fifties, especially since she had a daughter who looked to be the same age as him, but she looked not a day past forty. She was lively and vivacious and her perfectly shaped body, youthful skin, and erotic smile had lit a raging fire right under him—the kind of fire that simply had to be put out. And he'd let her *put* it out five nights later at this very same condo out in Oak Brook, which was one of the many properties Diana and her real estate tycoon husband owned in the Midwest. They were multimillionaires in their own right and by far the wealthiest members of his congregation.

JT had originally seen Diana, her daughter, and her husband one Sunday at church and had spent days trying to figure out how he might be able to connect with her. He'd known he couldn't just simply walk up to her during one of their services, but as luck would have it, he had run into her at an Italian restaurant not far from where he lived. He'd been dining with his two assistant pastors and a couple of other church officers, but then he'd seen Diana, dressed to the hilt in some vogue-style, cream-colored suit and looking over at him. Shortly after, he'd spotted her heading toward the restroom, so he had quickly excused himself from his table and followed her. It had only taken him seconds to catch up with her and when he had, she'd smiled seductively and handed him a small piece of folded paper with an address and what time to meet her but never said one word. She'd then walked away, and less than twenty-four hours later, JT had found himself in bed with a fifty-five-year-old cougar who could run wide circles around just about any woman he'd been with.

Diana propped herself onto her elbow and caressed JT's chest. "You really gave a wonderful message this morning. I mean, you always give great sermons, but this one was another winner for sure."

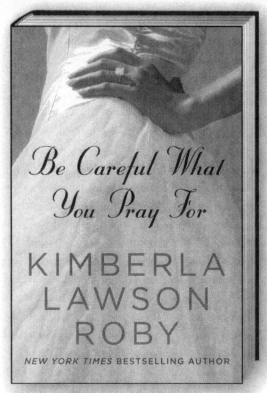

WORKS BY
KIMBERLA LAWSON ROBY

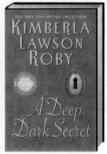

A DEEP DARK SECRET

978-0-06-144309-1 (hardcover)

"Powerful....An intense gem in an authentic voice."
—*Publishers Weekly*

THE BEST
OF EVERYTHING

978-0-06-144307-7 (trade paperback)

Meet Alicia, all grown up and just like her father—the
Reverend Curtis Black.

ONE IN A MILLION

978-0-06-144296-4 (trade paperback)

"Roby really knows how to cook up treats for her readers....
You're going to devour her first novella, *One in a Million*."
—*Essence*

SIN NO MORE

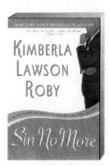

978-0-06-089252-4 (trade paperback)
The Reverend Curtis Black is turning over a new leaf...
or is he?

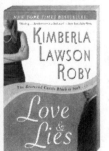

LOVE & LIES

978-0-06-089251-7 (trade paperback)

"Keeps the scandals coming...plenty of action."

CHANGING FACES

978-0-06-078080-7 (trade paperback)

"Roby dishes up enough drama, heartbreak, violence and redemption to keep the pages turning."
—*Washington Post*

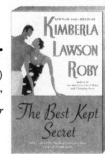

THE BEST-KEPT SECRET

978-0-06-073444-2 (trade paperback)

"Roby pulls you in until you're hooked."
—*Indianapolis Recorder*

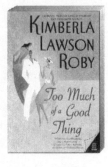

TOO MUCH OF A GOOD THING

978-0-06-056850-4 (trade paperback)

"Roby leaves her fans eager to know more about the next chapter in Curtis Black's ministry." —*Booklist*

BEHIND CLOSED DOORS

978-0-06-059365-0 (trade paperback)

"An uplifting account of struggles and adjustments."
—*Midwest Book Review*

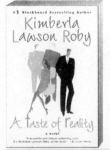

A TASTE OF REALITY

978-0-06-050567-7 (trade paperback)

"*A Taste of Reality* is a powerful and deeply satisfying read. It's Kimberla Lawson Roby at her best." —E. Lynn Harris

CPSIA information can be obtained
at www.ICGtesting.com
Printed in the USA
LVOW07s1758310317
529200LV00015B/142/P